PRAISE FOR SUSAN WALTER

Lie by the Pool

"The most fun I've had reading a thriller in a long time! *Lie by the Pool* is a delicious page-turner you will finish in one sitting. Full of juicy twists, a wildly original plot, and nerve-shredding tension, *Lie by the Pool* catapults Susan Walter into the top echelon of thriller writers."
 —David Ellis, *New York Times* bestselling author of *Look Closer*

"A thriller that thrills, crime fiction that is criminally good and feels like the real thing. A rich ensemble of characters, and protagonists that you hope don't wind up dead . . . because danger lurks around every twisty corner."
 —Ken Pisani, *Los Angeles Times* bestselling author of *AMP'D*

"Susan Walter has a knack for writing thoroughly entertaining stories that keep you flipping pages. Fun and fast and full of surprising revelations. What a pleasure to read!"
 —W. Bruce Cameron, #1 *New York Times* bestselling author of *A Dog's Purpose* and *Love, Clancy*

"Wow. What a terrific read! Walter's third novel is a vivid suspense thriller that's filled with surprises. An involving character study with a touching love story at its center. Great work, extremely enjoyable!"
 —Gary Goldstein, award-winning author of *The Last Birthday Party* and *The Mother I Never Had*

Over Her Dead Body

"Susan Walter is a master storyteller with an insider's view of the film business, and her novel glints with danger and brilliant insight into the hopes and dreams of an aspiring actress. I read it in one sitting, guessing the whole way through, stunned by the conclusion."
—Luanne Rice, *New York Times* bestselling author of *The Shadow Box* and *Last Day*

"A devilishly fun romp, full of eccentric characters and unexpected twists, *Over Her Dead Body* will keep you turning pages, as it pulls back the curtains on Hollywood from the point of view of a struggling actress caught up in a mystery laced with darkly comedic beats. Thoroughly enjoyable!"
—Ben Mezrich, *New York Times* bestselling author of *Bringing Down the House*, *The Accidental Billionaires*, and *The Midnight Ride*

"Susan Walter swerves the reader back and forth and around blind corners in a page-turning domestic psychodrama that will twist your sympathies and drop your jaw. An A-list Hollywood thrill ride, right through to the breathtaking end!"
—Judy Melinek and T.J. Mitchell, *New York Times* bestselling authors of the Dr. Jessie Teska Mysteries and *Working Stiff*

"With its eccentric ensemble cast and all the family drama of *Knives Out*, *Over Her Dead Body* is darkly funny and highly entertaining, with more twists than a bus tour through the Hollywood Hills. Fans of Janet Evanovich and Elle Cosimano will be delighted."
—Tessa Wegert, author of *Death in the Family*

"*Over Her Dead Body* is a whodunit with more twists and turns than a boardwalk roller coaster, where secrets abound and nothing is what it seems. If you're looking for a book that will keep you turning pages deep into the night, Susan Walter has absolutely written one."

—Barbara Davis, bestselling author of *The Keeper of Happy Endings*

"What a clever, fun, twisty, juicy ride! *Over Her Dead Body* will keep you guessing over and over with its kaleidoscope of conflicted characters, crisscrossed allegiances, and masterful point-of-view shifts. *Knives Out* has nothing on this quintessential LA story of ambition, greed, and good intentions gone wrong. You've never read a mystery quite like it."

—Gary Goldstein, author of *The Last Birthday Party*

Good as Dead

"Susan Walter's debut novel is so full of surprises it should come with a warning label. From the daringly original premise to the shocking climax, you'll never see the plot twists coming until you turn the page. I cannot wait for her next book!"

—W. Bruce Cameron, #1 *New York Times* bestselling author of *A Dog's Purpose* and *A Dog's Courage*

"Susan Walter's *Good as Dead* had me holding my breath through every thrilling twist and turn until the downright explosive ending. Fearlessly tackling themes of love, wealth, personal responsibility, and life and death, it was pure pleasure to read, and a brilliant debut."

—Alethea Black, author of *You've Been So Lucky Already* and *I Knew You'd Be Lovely*

RUNNING COLD

OTHER TITLES BY SUSAN WALTER

Good as Dead

Over Her Dead Body

Lie by the Pool

RUNNING COLD

A NOVEL

SUSAN WALTER

LAKE UNION
PUBLISHING

Text copyright © 2024 by Susan Walter

Published by Lake Union Publishing, Seattle

www.apub.com

Amazon, the Amazon logo, and Lake Union Publishing are trademarks of Amazon.com, Inc., or its affiliates.

ISBN-13: 9781662515354 (paperback)
ISBN-13: 9781662515361 (digital)

Cover design by James Iacobelli
Cover image: © Frank Sun / Alamy

Printed in the United States of America

In loving memory of Mark Davis. Climb on, my friend.

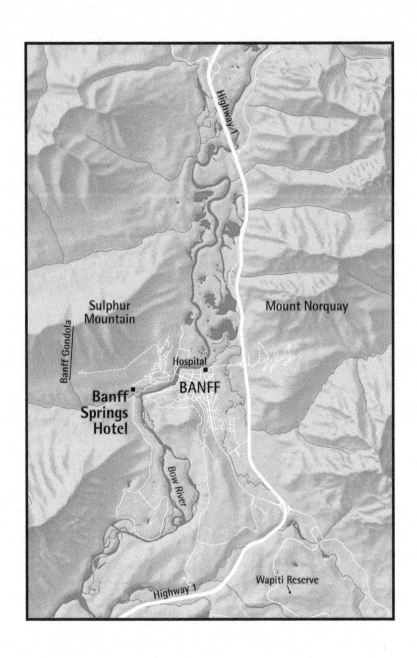

Cold.

You think you know it.

Maybe the word conjures pleasant thoughts? Tired feet in a mountain stream. A cherry Popsicle that stains your lips. Burrowing in your sleeping bag under a million stars.

You think you know what it does to you. Your teeth chatter. Your arms squeeze your body like a boa constrictor on a mouse. You cup your hands over your mouth to thaw them with your breath.

Stranded on the mountain in weather so cruel it would make the devil beam with pride, I know cold. There are no pleasant thoughts. The only part of me that isn't frozen is my will to survive. And even that's cracking.

As I close my eyes, the memory of blood pummels me like a storm. So much blood. Of course they think I did it. Innocent people don't run away. And I ran twice.

My lips feather like old tree bark. I try to breathe through my nose, but my nostrils are frozen shut. I know death is near because my thoughts are existential. I imagine the universe is a sphere. If you keep going long enough, you'll wind up where you started. How else could it be infinite?

Temperature is circular like that. As my skin turns to charcoal, I imagine the place where hot and cold meet, the extremes of both merging into one hellscape, then passing each other on the way back down.

My skin is burning. The air is so still I can't discern the glacier from the sky. Hell is supposed to be all fire and hot lava, but you don't know hell until you've been as cold as me.

PART 1
First to Die

CHAPTER 1
Julie

"One glass of champagne is not going to kill you!" Izzy teased as she reached across the table to fill my glass. She must have been on at least her third, because her cheeks shone shiny red like Christmas tree ornaments, and she was shouting even though our faces were so close I could smell the fruity undertones of her breath.

"Leave her alone, Izzy," Suki said, slapping Izzy's outstretched arm.

"Stop! I'm going to spill!" Izzy's eyebrows merged like fuzzy skis in snowplow as she balanced the throat of the bottle on the lip of my glass.

"It's fine," I said, holding the stem of my flute as champagne foamed over the top. "There are worse ways to go than death by champagne."

"That's the spirit!" Izzy beamed. I didn't normally drink during our ladies' lunches, but the patio was all dressed up in twinkly lights and tinsel. I didn't want to put a damper on the holiday cheer.

"To friendship," I said, raising my glass, because I thought toasting to friendship was something friends did.

"I'll drink to that!" Izzy said, clinking her glass against mine.

"You'll drink to anything," Suki teased, and Izzy smiled like it was a compliment. And maybe it was. Izzy had an uncanny ability to turn everything into a party—rainy nights were for Pictionary and Irish coffee, her book club had a wine pairing, she always brought the hot, new local craft beer to your backyard barbecue. My idea of kicking back after a hard day was a five-mile run around the lake. Which is probably why I always felt like the granola bar in your Halloween candy around these women who drank and laughed easily.

"The boys should be done by now," Christa, the last member of our party of four, said, peeking at her watch. "If Robbie came in last again, he'll be unbearable." The "boys" had gone to play golf, which you can do in December when you live in sunny Southern California.

"Well, with Jeff not playing, he had a fighting chance," Izzy said, and I couldn't hide my surprise.

"Not playing?"

The rouge on Izzy's cheeks spread down her neck.

"Sorry. I thought you knew?"

My husband was a very good golfer. He'd played since he was a kid. He wanted to play football, but his dad told him that golf would serve him better in business and in life. And Jeff knew better than to defy his father.

"I'm sure there's a simple explanation, I wouldn't worry," Christa offered, as someone who suspected there was something to worry about would.

"He might have told me," I said, because I honestly couldn't remember. I'd been a little checked out lately. Not depressed, exactly . . . OK, maybe a little depressed. Jeff wanted me to talk to someone. "For the marriage," he'd said. But I much preferred to run/bike/ski than to talk. Nature was my therapist. Checking out was the only way I knew how to keep my dark thoughts at bay.

"He's been grappling with some work thing, he probably just needed a rest," I said. Jeff's work had been intense lately. He'd been staying up long after I went to bed. A round of golf takes all morning, no surprise he would skip it when he had so much to do. Plus he knew I was out with these three. If he was cheating, which was the unspoken subtext of those concerned looks, he would have concocted a better alibi than golf with their husbands.

"Nice of him to give the other guys a chance," Suki said, not just to be kind. Jeff wasn't quite a scratch golfer, but the other husbands were overconfident, so he still managed to win most weekends without taking a handicap. Not that he cared about winning, that was my thing.

"I'll text him and find out where he is," I said, because they were all staring at me. I whipped up a quick Hey, coming home soon, where are you? then set the phone down on the table.

Jeff wasn't a big texter, so I felt only mildly annoyed that he hadn't responded before we drained the champagne and paid the check. I wanted to reassure my girlfriends that my husband was just fine, which, at the time, I thought was true. Driving west on the 101 freeway toward home on that cloudless afternoon, I was more worried about what I was going to do for the rest of the day than I was about Jeff. So he bailed on golf? There were plenty of other things he could be doing. He had other interests besides sports . . . unlike me.

After I retired from competition, I went back to school to finish my degree in kinesiology. I specialized in sports injuries because sports was all I knew. The only difference between me and my clients was that their best performances were in front of them, and mine were a distant memory.

I dialed Jeff's number as I got off at our exit. When he didn't answer, I imagined him sitting at the pool, combing through spreadsheets in his Ray-Bans and board shorts, his fawny shoulders soaking in the midday sun. My heartbeat quickened as I imagined coaxing him into the pool and out of those shorts. Just because he hadn't initiated sex lately didn't mean I couldn't. I was looking kind of pretty for a change. I had even ditched my Lululemon for a real bra and blow-dried my hair. Today would be the start of a new phase in our relationship, I told myself, one where we got close again. And I was right about the first part.

I met my husband at the bar at the Banff Springs Hotel. He was courting an investor out of Calgary for the tech company he'd just started in Southern California. I was celebrating my first-place finish in a biathlon competition in the neighboring town of Canmore, where

I lived and was training for my second Olympics. Alberta didn't have many Olympians, so I was a bit of a local celebrity. But it was me who was starstruck by him. I had never met a German Korean math nerd who could breakdance and do calculus. I was mesmerized by his wavy black hair and the way his full lips caressed his whiskey sour. He was to business what I was to sports—relentless in his pursuit of excellence. I understood his tendency to overanalyze everything from a potential investment to what toothpaste to buy. And he understood why a person who once measured her life in hundredths of a second had a hard time enjoying a midday glass of champagne.

"Hi, babe!" I called out as I walked into the house and put my keys on the hook next to Jeff's. His Tesla was in the garage, still plugged in from the night before. I felt a tingle of anticipation as I took off my sweater and tossed it onto a kitchen chair. We had lived in our four-thousand-square-foot McMansion with cathedral ceilings and parklike backyard for three years now, but were yet to populate it with the kids we both claimed to want. We'd chosen the Dos Vientos neighborhood in eastern Ventura County for its good schools and clean air and, yes, proximity to world-class golf courses and mountain biking trails. I'm not sure what we were waiting for to try to get pregnant, but I suspect our addiction to those trails and golf courses had something to do with it.

"Jeff? Where are you?" I opened the sliding glass doors to the backyard. We had a kidney-shaped pool with a hot tub in the cutout, but he wasn't in either, or sitting on one of the chaise longues. *What did he say he was going to do today?* My face got hot with frustration as I tried to remember. He wasn't a runner, and there was nowhere to walk to. He hadn't mentioned someone coming to pick him up and take him somewhere . . . *had he?*

I peeked in his home office, which was predictably tidy and disappointingly unoccupied, then kicked off my shoes and padded upstairs.

"Jeff?"

I was getting nervous now, though I didn't know why. Jeff was a thirty-three-year-old health nut with meticulous personal hygiene. He never got sick, rarely got mad, and unlike me, didn't indulge in self-destructive things like juice fasting or working out to exhaustion. He was überorganized and careful to a fault, and I couldn't think of a single logical reason why he wasn't answering me.

"Jeff, where are you?" My tone was hostile now, because how dare he make me worry like this! I marched into the bedroom. The bed was made, just like I'd left it. I was about to turn around to search the rest of the house when I noticed the closed bathroom door. We never closed the bathroom door. It was just us. The toilet had its own little cabin, and we loved how the light from the skylight spilled into the bedroom. *So why is the door closed today?*

I walked over to the bathroom door and pushed down on the handle. It was locked. *Who locks the bathroom door when they're home alone?* My trickle of nervousness turned into a wave of panic. I banged on the door with my palm.

"Jeff! Open the door!"

I was all nerves and adrenaline as I turned my body sideways and kicked the door handle with the blade of my foot. The latch gave way with a violent crack, but the door only opened a sliver. As if it had bumped up against something. There was nothing in the bathroom that wasn't bolted down, except our toothbrushes and a hamper that I knew to be empty because I'd emptied it that morning.

"Jeff!"

I pressed my palms against the door and pushed. The door fought back. Whatever was pressing against the other side was heavy but also had give, like a beanbag chair or sack of cement.

As I pressed my shoulder into the door, my gaze floated down to the tile, where an inky, crimson blister puffed up from the floor. My scream rose up from the deepest cavern of my belly as I collapsed to my knees.

"Jeff!" I shouted at the lump behind the bathroom door.

But he didn't answer.

CHAPTER 2
Izzy

I told myself I was only going to have one glass of champagne, but being around Julie always made me want to drink more. I don't know which of her perfect features made me feel most insecure. Her perky butt? Her cinnamon-cruller arms? Eyelashes that defied gravity? Honey-colored tresses that bounced without the help of hot tools? If she was grade A prime, I was Hamburger Helper. But my inferiority complex was not the only reason I hit the champagne hard when I was around her these days.

Our lakeside lunch spot was all decked out for Christmas, with tree trunks wrapped in tinsel and twinkly lights looped overhead. The fake snow on the awnings was a little over the top—it was seventy-two degrees out, who did they think they were fooling? Southern Californians have a complicated relationship with Christmas. Eleven months out of the year, we gloat about our weather, but come December we secretly wish we could trade places with our neighbors to the north.

I hugged the girls goodbye, then dipped into the bathroom to relieve my bladder. I'd told my husband I'd be home "around two," so of course my phone rang at two on the dot, just as I was crossing through the parking lot.

"I'm still at lunch," I lied, because I knew my husband wanted me home to take care of the kids, but I wasn't done taking care of myself. Plus after three (or four?) glasses of champagne, I thought it best to window-shop, or actual shop, for an hour or three before I got behind the wheel.

"Sorry," he mumbled. "Should I take care of dinner then?"

"It's only two o'clock," I snapped. But then I realized he was trying to be nice. "It's OK, I'll be home in plenty of time."

"Right. OK, enjoy your lunch."

If not for the alcohol coursing through my veins, I might have felt bad for leaving him home alone. Our twin boys were a handful. But most days it was my hands that wrestled with them. I once heard my husband tell a friend he couldn't come to poker night because he had to "babysit." "Um . . . it's called *parenting*," I'd reminded him, because I guess dads sometimes forget they are parents too? Especially when it's time to change a diaper or put the kids to bed. My husband's passive-aggressive sexism was not the reason I'd cheated on him, but it made me feel less like an ass about it.

"I'll make a lasagna later," I said, then immediately regretted it. It took me two hours to make a lasagna, if you included the time to scrub marinara sauce off the wall. *Ugh. Why didn't I just let him figure out dinner for a change?*

I knew the answer to that, of course—guilt. I'd made a promise to be faithful "till death do us part," and had broken that vow with shameful enthusiasm. I couldn't really call it an affair—we'd only slept together once—but in my mind, I was cheating every day. He was the one I thought about when I closed my eyes at night, while driving the kids to school, doing dishes, vacuuming, brushing my teeth, or any other task that required being conscious.

I crossed the street toward the shops. Downtown Westlake Village was like Rodeo Drive for Desperate Housewives, dotted with shiny boutiques with loungewear for every occasion—puffy sweats for après ski, shiny track pants for après Pilates, plush robes for après spa, silky pajamas for après sex. As I inhaled the extravagance of it all, a smiling snowman beckoned me inside the Lululemon with stick arms open wide. I wasn't going to buy anything—that seventy-dollar-per-person lunch accounted for the balance of this month's discretionary spending—but it was still fun to run my fingers through the rainbows of spandex pants and imagine what Julie or JLo might look like in them, because they were made for tighter bods than mine.

"Can I help you find a size?" a twiglike sales gal asked as she saw my hands devouring a violet crisscrossy crop top that someone with my jumbo assets could wear as a hat.

"Oh, it's not for me," I said, hoping to confuse her. *Was I shopping for a gift? Or disparaging the style?* She smiled and backed away.

Since I had my twins, my career as a real estate agent had slowed, but I still managed to hold on to a few listings. My occasional showings gave me desperately needed interactions with adults—otherwise the only nontoddling person I ever talked to was my husband. He was a good man, but the monotony of our life was taking its toll. In my dark moments—like after spending hours picking bits of nacho-cheese Doritos from between the couch cushions—I fantasized about separating, just to have some time for myself. But we were attached at the bank account now. And even under one roof, we could barely make ends meet.

I glanced at my watch. I knew I should get home, but I wanted to ride my champagne life raft just a little bit longer. As I imagined my lover calling like Calgon to take me away, my phone rang, and I felt a surge of excitement that maybe I'd just manifested him.

I plucked the phone from my purse and peeked down at the screen. "Hey, Jules," I said, hoping I didn't sound disappointed.

"Izzy?" She sounded upset. I felt my stomach tighten. I knew this day might come, yet I was wholly unprepared for it.

"Yes, it's me." I put a finger to my free ear to block out Dua Lipa, who was crooning from the speakers like a cat in heat.

"Oh my God, Izzy . . ."

She was more than upset, she was terrified. *Was it something else, then?*

"Hold on, I'm in a store. Give me one second—I'm stepping outside."

I pushed past a rack of hoodies and made for the door. I didn't realize I was still holding that purple bra-hat until the security system buzzed like I'd just given the wrong answer on *The Price Is Right*.

"Sorry," I said to Twiggy as I tossed the top at her protruding collarbone.

"OK, I'm here," I said, stepping out onto the sidewalk. "Julie, what's going on? Are you OK?"

Instead of an answer, I just heard sobs. Deep, guttural gasps that made me want to cry too.

"Jules, what's happened?"

"Izzy, I . . . it's Jeff . . . I . . . he . . . oh God!" I gripped the phone with both hands to stop them from shaking. My soaring heart rate must have metabolized all that champagne because I was suddenly stone-cold sober.

"Julie, take a breath and tell me what's wrong." My pulse was a drumroll. I felt every emotion at once—hope, terror, empathy, shame.

"Jeff is . . . he . . . oh my God, Izzy, there's so much blood."

And then there was just terror.

"Blood? What do you mean *blood*?"

"Izzy, Jeff is dead."

The sidewalk started spinning. I groped for something to hold on to, but there was only empty space. My heart would have broken for Julie if it weren't already breaking for me.

Because I loved Jeff too.

CHAPTER 3
Julie

"I don't think I can do this," I told Izzy when she arrived at my front door with a Crock-Pot of meatballs for the postburial reception. I didn't want to have people over. I wanted to lie down on my living room floor and sob into a pillow. But Izzy was insistent. "They'll bring food," she said. When I told her I didn't want food, she chided me. "People need to feel useful, Julie." And I guess those meatballs signaled she was one of those people.

"I forgot to bring a serving spoon," she said as she disappeared into the kitchen. I stood at the threshold as she foraged through my drawers.

"Can we tell them not to come?" My brave face was on its last legs. I'd barely slept since discovering Jeff dead on the bathroom floor, and my body ached like I'd gone sixteen rounds.

"You're not the only one who lost someone," she said softly. And I thought about Jeff's parents, who'd said their goodbyes at the graveyard, because why would they want to mourn with the person who couldn't even keep their son alive?

The worst part about losing your husband to suicide, besides the fact that he's gone and you have to spend the rest of your days trying to put your shattered life back together, is that everyone thinks it's your fault. The local newspaper drove the accusation home with its headline:

"Husband of Olympic Gold Medalist Takes His Own Life." As if I'd emasculated him with my former greatness. Husbands with loving, supportive wives don't shoot themselves in the head, conventional wisdom said. This was on me.

The second worst part of losing your husband to suicide is that you can't collect on the $2 million life insurance policy he took out when he bought your $2 million house. Insurance companies don't reward the beneficiaries of people who kill themselves, it's all there in the fine print. Luckily, Jeff was a successful tech entrepreneur, and we had investments and some money saved. Even without an insurance payout, I was confident I would be OK—heartbroken, but not broke.

"I'm just so tired, Izzy," I said as I handed her a ladle from the canister by the stove.

"I know, honey." Her eyes were rimmed with red. Jeff's death had rocked our whole community. But Izzy was too kind to cry in front of me.

"Thanks for your help. I don't know where I'd be . . ." I couldn't finish the sentence. She squeezed my arm to let me know I didn't have to.

We stood like that—her holding my arm, me choking on the lump in my throat—for a long, silent beat. Until, through the window, we saw the first car pull up.

"They're here," Izzy said, letting go of my arm. "Where are your plates?"

I opened a cupboard, then helped her carry my good china out to the dining room, because if your husband dying isn't a special occasion, what is? The front door was open, and funeral goers were already wafting in, arms laden with fruit platters and casseroles. Suki and Christa arrived wearing tea-length black dresses and carrying cold cuts, cheese, and flowers, their slack-jawed husbands in tow. I had questions for those husbands—*When did you know Jeff wasn't coming to golf? Did he call you? Did you try to call him? What did he say he was doing instead?* But the police had already interrogated them, and now was not the time for a reprise.

"Sorry for your loss," someone and everyone said. The condolences rolled in like a rising tide, steady and suffocating. Izzy's reminder that I wasn't the only one who lost someone echoed in my mind as I thanked them and hugged them all back.

"Julie, my heart is crushed. I am so very sorry," a French-accented voice said, and I did a double take because I couldn't believe who it was.

"Remy?"

"If you need to get away, you come see me, yes?" the manager of the Banff Springs Hotel said as he thrust a potted orchid into my chest. "I'll always have a room for you."

"Remy, I can't believe you came." What I really wanted to say was, I can't believe you *heard*, because Banff was fifteen hundred miles and an international border away. Had news of Jeff's death traveled that far, that fast?

"You are like family to me!" Remy said, and by the way his forehead buckled, I thought I'd offended him.

"No, of course. Thank you." I hadn't seen Remy since our wedding. He hadn't set us up, but he was the biggest enabler of our relationship. Jeff never came to my one-room apartment in Canmore. When we got together, it was always in his fancy Banff Springs Hotel room, at a discount generously provided by Remy, who was one of the few people outside my sport who understood it.

The biathlon is to the Olympics what the Komodo dragon is to the animal kingdom: exotic, fierce, and in a class of its own. As the prefix *bi* suggests, it has two components. The first is Nordic, or cross-country, skiing. The second is precision rifle marksmanship. You race to a shooting range in subzero weather with a rifle strapped to your back. Then, you empty your ammo into a target. Your score is the combination of your speed and accuracy. The biathlon originated in Scandinavia and Russia, where ski warfare was often the front line of battle. Swedish, Finnish, and Russian militaries staged contests to fine-tune their soldiers, and the sport was sprung. Canadians and Americans eventually wanted in on the action, and so it became an Olympic sport.

A native of Alberta, I grew up on skis. My parents left Canada for warmer climates when I was sixteen, but I didn't want to leave the snow. They thought my aspirations to compete in the World Cup that year were foolish. My father tried to beat some sense into me, but I was already stronger than he was, and after I proved it to him, he was all too happy to leave me behind. All I had when they moved away were my skis, my rifle, and a meager sponsorship. And a chip on my shoulder that got me out of bed even when it was thirty below.

The quaint, upscale town of Banff is twenty kilometers from working-class Canmore, and where my teammates and I sometimes went to kick back after a hard day's work. I was on a first name basis with all the staff at Remy's hotel, and they appreciated my hard work as I appreciated theirs. Remy, a former Olympic-downhill hopeful himself, treated me like royalty, comping drinks and meals he knew I couldn't afford. I didn't win that Olympic gold medal for him, but he was one of a handful of supporters who'd fueled my journey.

"It was kind of you to fly in for the service," I told my old friend. "Jeff would be touched."

"Don't forget my offer," Remy said. "Even if you just need a few days of mountain air."

I put down his orchid so I could hug him from my heart, then milled around with the other guests until darkness set in and people went back to their living loved ones. Christa and Suki cleared the food while Izzy sat with me on the overstuffed down couch Jeff had insisted we splurge on.

"I need you to sell my house, Izzy," I said to my Realtor friend. It would be a good commission for her, so I was surprised by her response.

"Let's just give the situation time to breathe," she replied, not grasping that the reason I needed to sell was that I *couldn't* breathe here, not anymore.

"I can't. He's everywhere." When I looked at the walls, I saw him on a ladder with a paintbrush in his hand, because he wanted them Arctic White, not Swiss Coffee. When I looked out the window, I saw him turning burgers at the grill. I couldn't bring myself to eat at the reclaimed-wood table he made with his own hands, or sleep between sheets that once clung to our naked bodies—not now, not ever. I didn't want to pile on my woes, so I didn't tell her the other part—that we had a big mortgage that wasn't going to pay itself. I didn't know exactly what our monthly nut was with HOA, insurance, property tax, and all the other expenses that came with a luxury home, just that there was a reason part-time physical therapists didn't live in houses like this one.

"If you don't like our furniture, we can stage it," I pressed. She could get rid of all of it, for all I cared.

"The furniture is not the problem." *There's a problem?*

"Don't you want the listing?"

She spoke to me like she was teaching the alphabet to a five-year-old. "Jules, someone died here."

"Yes. I am aware of that." I could feel my face getting hot. "And?"

"It's all over the papers. You and Jeff were not exactly below the radar. We need to give it time to settle down."

I never wanted to be famous. One of the reasons I'd agreed to move to California was that I could disappear. There were pop stars and Kardashians on every corner here. It should have been easy for a washed-up Olympian to fold into their shadows. That Jeff's death had made the front page was as surprising as it was maddening.

"How long?" I asked.

"Three months, at least. Then we can try."

I did a quick calculation in my head. The interest on our $1.5 million loan was probably twice my monthly salary. And I still needed to eat and keep the lights on. We had some equity in the house, but not enough to borrow against. I would have to pull from our savings for a few months. Not ideal, but not a catastrophe. As long as there were savings.

"I know this house is full of memories," Izzy said, kindly not mentioning the most noteworthy one. "I can help you find a rental if you really don't want to stay here."

And add to my monthly expenses? I thought but didn't say out loud.

"OK, all the food is put away," Suki announced as she and Christa emerged from the kitchen. "We froze most of it, but there are some cold cuts and cheese in the fridge."

"Thanks, you guys." I would have told them to take the food, but they'd brought a lot of it, and I didn't want to seem ungrateful.

They looked at Izzy, and she stood up to go.

"You going to be OK?" Izzy asked.

I nodded. I knew if I asked her to stay, she would. But I had tears to set free and a life to figure out and didn't want a witness for either.

"I'll call you tomorrow," she promised.

We hugged long and hard, and then I was alone. If Izzy wouldn't put my house on the market for three months, I would have to make a budget and a plan.

I went into Jeff's office and logged on to his computer. Jeff's desk was as organized as his brain. All his files were color coded, and his pencils, pens, and paper clips put away. The only decorative item on display was our wedding photo, which loomed large out of the corner of my eye.

All of our important passwords were in an online vault with a master password, which Jeff had made me commit to memory. I typed it into the browser, and our financials spread out in front of me like cards on a poker table.

We had four accounts: a joint checking with corresponding credit cards, a savings account, a brokerage account, and his business account. I signed in to our joint checking account—the one we used to pay for everything from gas and groceries to our mortgage and home insurance. The credit card was maxed, and the checking account balance was zero. I was a little surprised, but I figured Jeff must have moved our money someplace where it could earn interest, because isn't that what smart businesspeople do? I clicked the link to the savings account. I was *a lot* surprised to see it had only four dollars in it. *Had he moved the money somewhere else then?*

I logged on to Jeff's business account. He ran all his company expenses through that account, from payroll to office supplies. That account was worse than empty—not only was the credit card maxed, but the bank balance was $1,400 into overdraft.

My heartbeat quickened. Our last account was our brokerage account. We never touched this money. It was our cash reserve for emergencies—an earthquake, an illness, Armageddon. I opened the statement with trembling fingers. As the screen filled with numbers, my eyes devoured the data. Every single share of stock we once owned had been sold. The cash balance was sixty-two dollars.

I got a sick feeling in my stomach. My husband had taken his life with no warning and no note to tell me why. All I knew was that our money was gone. I was not only alone now, I was also penniless.

CHAPTER 4
Izzy

"Why do you think he did it?" Suki asked as our drinks arrived. She and Christa had stayed behind at Julie's with me to help clean up, and somehow, after we all left in separate cars, we wound up at a bar.

"He must have been unhappy," Christa said. Christa was a litigator. Stating the obvious was a job requirement, and also annoying.

"Yes, but why?" Suki pressed. She was a music teacher who played three instruments and spoke four languages, it was rare to see her stumped. "I mean, he kind of had a perfect life." I felt tears press against the backs of my eyes. Not just for the perfect life lost, but also for my part in destroying it.

I was attracted to Jeff the moment I laid eyes on him, as I imagined most people with a beating heart were. He was brilliant, funny, gorgeous, a terrific dancer. I had no intention of acting on my feelings. But that stolen dance at Christa's wedding last summer pushed me over the edge.

Julie was running some charity race the next day, so left after the speeches. And my husband had to relieve our teenage babysitter who turned into a pumpkin at midnight. It was both a case of right place, right time and wrong place, wrong time when Jeff and I bumped into each other on the dance floor, both flushed with wine and starved for affection.

The reception was at a hotel, so the next part was easy. I was a little nervous when Jeff charged the room to his credit card, but he assured me Julie never looked at their bank statements. I wondered what that was like, not having to keep tabs on your monthly spending. I knew having money didn't make Julie better than me, but I was still envious. And in that moment, I foolishly let the champagne running through my veins convince me I deserved a tiny taste of what she feasted on every day.

Jeff held my hand in the elevator and all the way down the hall. When we got to our room, he offered me the key with a gallant "Do the honors?" And I remember thinking, for a cheater, he was quite the gentleman. Until we got our clothes off. Then he was fifty shades of *Holy Shazam!* For the better part of an hour, I didn't know which way was up and I didn't care. It was more than great sex, it was a gift from the gods.

When we met for coffee two days later, we tried to blame our bad behavior on the booze. But when I reached across the table to make him pinkie promise to never speak a word of it to anyone, the sparks when our fingers touched nearly set our hair on fire. It wasn't just a physical attraction. We liked who we were with each other. I didn't have to be the timekeeper (*we gotta go!*), the housekeeper (*dishes in the dishwasher!*), the disciplinarian (*go to your room!*), the director of hospitality (*get dressed—we're going out!*). And he didn't have to be perfect for his perfect wife. Of course we vowed to never do it again. But that didn't mean we didn't want to.

Jeff was the son of an overachieving Korean mother who would have taken one look at me, with my plus-size hips and box-dyed red hair, and forbidden her son to ever see me again. While Julie was perfect on paper, I was the one who made him feel safe. Jeff married someone he considered his equal in looks, intelligence, and accomplishments. They belonged together, Jeff and Julie, down to the alliteration of their names. Or did they? Maybe there's a reason opposites attract. Marry your equal and you stay where you are. Marry your opposite and spend a lifetime learning about the space in between. As a couple, Jeff and Julie made sense. But everyone knows forbidden love is more fun than making sense.

"He had a great career, a great house, a great wife," Suki said, poking at the olive in her martini with her swizzle stick. "I don't get it."

"Sometimes things are not what they seem," Christa said, showcasing her special talent. And of course she was spot on. When Jeff had lured Julie from Canada to California, he'd promised her a life of luxury and ease. He bought her the nicest house in the nicest neighborhood, then worked like a dog so they could afford it. The pressure was relentless. Being good at what you did was not enough when your wife was literally the best at everything she tried. It had been suffocating. But so much that it would make him end his own life? I had a hard time believing that.

"I wonder if he was depressed," Suki, the sensitive one, said. "I mean, there's a reason they call it the silent killer."

"What do you think, Izzy?" Christa asked. At five foot ten, Christa was as formidable as Suki was petite. "You knew them the best."

Christa and Suki were staring at me with expectant eyes. I hadn't just betrayed Julie, I was betraying them too. They gave me friendship. I returned it with lies.

"No idea," I said, lying to their faces. I had an idea, namely that Jeff was dead because of me. I was the one who'd turned him into an adulterer. He was already feeling insecure about being good enough for his wife. Instead of reassuring him he was worthy, I'd made him less so.

My husband was waiting up for me when I got home, and I let him hug me even though I didn't deserve it. I lay awake into the wee hours, imagining Julie all alone in her bed, unable to escape the memory of Jeff's blood splattered across the walls while her so-called best friend went home to her living, breathing husband and kids.

I managed to sleep for a few hours and woke to the sound of rain. I couldn't stand the thought of Julie waking up to an empty house on this dreary day. The solution was so obvious, I couldn't believe I hadn't thought of it sooner. She would stay with us. We didn't need to use that third bedroom as an office. My husband had an office at work, and there was room for my desk in the family room. She might resist at first, but I'd insist. It was the least I could do for the friend whose life I ruined.

I got dressed and drove to Julie's. I was wearing sweats and sneakers in anticipation of getting Julie packed and moved in by the end of the day. If I'd been a crappy friend when Jeff was alive, I would make it up to her by going above and beyond now that he was dead.

I parked in her driveway, jogged through the rain, then knocked on her front door.

"Julie?"

I peeked in the window. It was dark. I could barely make out the silhouettes of the furniture.

I took out my phone and texted. I'm at your front door. A minute passed. Then a minute more. Still no response. I figured she was asleep. But if we were going to move her, we had a lot to do.

I reached under the planter and pulled out the spare key I knew Julie kept there.

Click. The dead bolt released. I opened the front door and stepped inside.

"Jules?" I called out, nice and loud. "It's Izzy. I'm here to kidnap you!"

The downstairs was completely still, so I went upstairs to look for her. The door to the primary bedroom was closed, as I imagined it had been since I'd moved her things into the guest suite. Julie didn't want to sleep in the room she'd shared with her husband ever again, and who could blame her?

The door to the guest bedroom was open. I walked down the hallway and rapped on the doorframe.

"Julie?" I peeked my head in. The bed was empty, as were the closet and all the dresser drawers I had filled with her clothes.

I padded down the stairs and into the kitchen. Jeff's Tesla fob was on the hook, but Julie's keys were gone.

The door to the garage was a few steps in front of me, so I walked over and pushed it open. I knew Julie hung her skis and winter clothes on the hooks on the far wall, but the wall was empty, as was her parking spot.

You didn't need skis or winter clothes where we lived. Which meant she'd gone someplace very far away, in the middle of the night, without telling a soul.

CHAPTER 5
Julie

I left Dos Vientos at four a.m. I didn't call to say I was coming, because what I wanted to ask was better done in person. My bank accounts were empty, but I had a gas card, and thanks to all the friends who'd come to pay their respects, enough cheese and lunch meat to get me to the North Pole. I wasn't planning to go that far, but it was comforting to know I could if things didn't work out.

The drive to my childhood stomping grounds was twenty-five hours in good weather, unmakeable in bad. If I didn't encounter any snowstorms, accidents, avalanches, or wild animals, I could get there in two days. Living in Southern California, it was easy to forget it was winter, but the reminder would be upon me soon enough. I hadn't checked the weather, because I was leaving this morning no matter what. Besides, I was no stranger to cold. It had never hurt me, at least not yet.

The route was as straightforward as the variables were unknown: get on the 15 freeway in California's inland empire, then take it all the way across Nevada, Utah, Idaho, and Montana. Cross into Canada at the twenty-four-hour point of entry in Sweetgrass. Head due north on Highway 4, then west on Highway 1. Jeff and I did this drive in reverse after we'd gotten engaged and were moving my stuff down to California. Everything about that trip was opposite—south instead of north, hot instead of cold, happy instead of sad, the beginning instead of the end. My only possessions of value at the time were my skis, my rifle, and my shiny gold medal. I was twenty-six. Jeff had just turned thirty. Three weeks before we left, when I'd asked him what he wanted for his big 3-0, he dropped to one knee, took my hand, and said, "Only you." I hadn't thought I was ready to get married, but the adoration in Jeff's eyes made it impossible to say no. So we packed my truck and hit the road. I loved my native Canada, but I had no plans to come back. Everything was bigger and brighter in America, including my future, because Jeff came with it.

We stayed with Jeff's parents in Santa Barbara that summer while we planned our wedding and shopped for a house. Jeff's parents were as involved in the wedding planning as my parents were checked out. My father's liver was failing from too much good living in Mexico, and my mother was afraid if they expressed any opinions, they would be expected to chip in. Jeff's parents had a beautiful house with a big yard and peekaboo ocean view. But Jeff insisted we get married in Banff. Jeff knew my friends on the ski team were as financially challenged as they were athletically gifted and couldn't come if we did it anywhere else. He wanted me surrounded by the people I loved on my wedding day, and his parents generously obliged.

My relationship with Jeff's parents was great at the beginning. His mother was fierce, and I understood immediately why her son was attracted to me. A first-generation American from Korean-born parents, Jeff's *umma* flexed her heritage like a peacock in mating season. Jeff had forgotten most of what he'd learned in Korean-immersion kindergarten, but that didn't stop Gloria from talking to him like he spoke the language fluently. Jeff's German American dad was as traditional as his mother was intense. I think Karl would have preferred his only son had married someone more feminine, but he respected my accomplishments as I respected his right to rib his son about having a wife who could bench-press more than he could.

My own parents were too caught up in their own lives to take an interest in mine, so we spent weekends and holidays with Jeff's. I enjoyed our closeness, and dared to let myself feel accepted and loved. But two years into our marriage, when we still hadn't given Gloria and Karl a grandchild, they started badgering us. At first their remarks were lighthearted ("Your genes are too good to waste, get going!"). Then they played the concerned card ("Is something wrong with your marriage? Is Julie working out too much? Maybe she should ease off. We're getting worried."). When we told them nothing was wrong, we were just not ready, they got angry. They'd spoiled us with an extravagant party so we would spoil them with bouncing babies. They were mad that we weren't fulfilling our end of the bargain, as we were mad that our celebration had come with strings attached.

The charcoal sky faded to ash as I crossed the state line into Nevada. I made it to Vegas as the last of the all-night gamblers were straggling back to their rooms to count their winnings or sleep off their losses. Memories of the long weekend Jeff and I had spent there started bubbling up . . . floating down the canals at the Venetian, counting the stars from atop the Ferris wheel at Circus Circus, making love on a ridiculous heart-shaped bed. We weren't gamblers, but Jeff insisted we come for the spectacle of it. By the end of the weekend, my camera roll was full and my cheeks hurt from smiling. It was the last trip we made together—one of only three since we'd gotten married.

As the Las Vegas skyline became a blur in my rearview, I stuck my arm out the window to try to feel something besides grief. Jeff was gone, but he was also everywhere. He was behind my eyes, dulling the outlines of the cars in front of me. He was in my ears, telling me to slow down, drive safe. He was in my throat, making it feel tight when I tried to breathe. He was part of me but lost to me, a mirage in the desert that never got closer no matter how fast I drove.

Sadness coiled around my heart. I opened and closed my fists on the steering wheel, trying to force the sensation out. Grief is energy. It has to move. *Open and close, open and close.* I flexed my fingers to move it through. If there was one thing I knew about pain, it was that it would pass. *Just keep going. Like we do in training. Suck it up. Breathe.*

Through my blurred vision, I saw a sign for St. George. I didn't want to stop, but my gas tank was near empty, so I took the exit. St. George was a hiker's paradise, dotted with some of the most striking canyons in the Southwest. Jeff and I had talked about taking a camping trip here, but we never found the time. My chest filled with regret about all the things we talked about doing but never did—karaoke night with friends, a trip to wine country, an African safari, making a baby. *What was so important that we could never find time to be happy?*

I pulled up to the pump and got out of the car to see a man with overalls and smiling eyes walking toward me.

"Fill 'er up, ma'am?" he asked.

"I'll do it," I said, and he put his hands in the air like I was robbing him at gunpoint. Jeff used to make that gesture too. "Why can't you ever accept help?" he'd ask when I insisted on making my own breakfast or carrying that heavy thing up the stairs. It hadn't occurred to me that he feared not being needed as much as I feared needing him. I may have left my parents, but they still ran my life.

I used the bathroom and got back on the road. The winter solstice was fast approaching. The days were short now, and the farther north I got, the shorter they would get. Darkness nipped at my tailpipe as the sun fought a shallow arc across the sky. Not only was it getting darker, but it was also getting colder. If the roads got icy, I would have to slow down. Not that it mattered—no one was expecting me. I knew it was foolish to leave my friends and my job, but California didn't make sense without Jeff. The only way to get over losing him was to go back to who I was before he came into my life. And so I drove forward and backward, toward the place that made me who I was, because what I'd become was too painful to face.

It was midnight when I pulled off the highway in Helena, Montana. I'd been driving for nearly twenty hours straight, and my neck was so stiff I could barely turn my head. The back seat was cold and hard beneath my sleeping bag, but I was grateful for the physical discomfort because it drowned out the other kind. *Why didn't he leave a note? Or tell me we were broke? And why were we broke?* I had messages on my phone, but I didn't look at them. It was unkind to leave without telling Izzy and the girls, but explaining why I had to would have meant revealing Jeff had left me penniless, and I wanted a better legacy for him than that.

I woke at six a.m. to a pale-gray sky heavy with snow. I felt a flicker of nervousness. My Subaru had four-wheel drive but no snow tires—I didn't want to get caught in a squall. I turned on my hip and pulled myself upright. Every inch of my body ached. My first coach liked to preach that "anyone can keep going when they feel good, but only champions can push through pain." So in my best imitation of a champion, I got back behind the wheel.

Montana was ranch country, and the two-lane highway was bordered by open space as far as the eye could see. Flurries broke through the clouds, melting on my windshield before my wipers could push them away. I didn't get a sunrise. Dawn was more like turning up the brightness on your TV screen.

I made a pit stop in Great Falls, which was known more for its fly-fishing than its coffee. The Canadian border was a hundred miles due north on a road so straight I could have driven it with my eyes closed. The border crossing was empty, and the agent was predictably surly, as anyone who spent their days in a four-by-four stall with nothing more than a stool and a space heater would be.

"What's the purpose of your trip?" the agent asked, his breath forming a cloud in the space between us.

"I'm coming home."

He looked at my passport, then at me.

"You're that skier," he said, like he'd just found a piece of candy in his pocket. I never updated my passport with my married name, perhaps because I'd worked so hard to make something of the one I was born with.

"Biathlete," I corrected him, because technically skiing was only half my superpower. He nodded, pretending to understand the distinction.

"Welcome home."

It had been overcast all morning, but as I drove onto Canadian soil, the sun came out to say hello. A tear of gratitude rolled down my cheek. I didn't have a house or any family here anymore, but my heart knew I was home.

I left my window open as I pulled onto the highway. Cold air numbed my skin. High above me, a bald eagle with wings as wide as palm fronds made lazy circles through a wispy cloud. I felt an instant kinship. For loners like that eagle and me, life would always be an individual sport. You're either given someone to take care of you, or the tools to take care of yourself. It was clear which category my eagle friend and I belonged to.

I rehearsed my request in my mind as my tires crunched over roads bumpy with salt. I wasn't looking for charity, just a place to disappear for a while. I didn't know my expectations were unrealistic. Because it's impossible to disappear when someone is watching you.

CHAPTER 6
Remy

I had just sat down at my desk with a croissant and a *café* when someone knocked on my door.

"Come in." *Merde!* I had so much work to do. Going to California had put me way behind. Plus my coffee was the perfect temperature and I had just warmed my croissant. If I had to get up to quiet the ruffled feathers of a guest whose bedsheets were scratchy or whose shower smelled like fish, my afternoon *goûter* would be ruined.

"Sorry to disturb you, Remy." It was Lily, the bouncy redhead from housekeeping. We had over one hundred housekeepers. I did not know all their names, but Lily made sure I knew hers.

"What can I do for you, Lily?" Lily was always asking for something. To go home early, come in late, take a day off to get a tooth pulled, her eyes checked, visit her boyfriend, her sick sister, her elderly mother, her dead grandmother's grave. Christmas was in two weeks, the hotel was going to be at maximum occupancy. She knew better than to ask for time off now.

"I just wanted to make sure you got my letter?" I felt a zing of agitation. There were only two reasons employees wrote letters to their bosses, and neither of them were good. The first was to complain about a policy, or worse—me personally. I treated her fairly. OK, maybe I grumbled a little when she asked for *yet another* day off, but I always found a way to accommodate her. As for the policies, I did not make them, only enforced them. But I still had to listen to my employees whine when they thought one unfair.

"You wrote me a letter?" My desk was a blizzard of spreadsheets, comment cards, invoices, unopened mail. One would think I had been gone for weeks, not just a few days. I was working my way through the piles but had not encountered a letter from her. I was about to ask her where she left it when she reached over and plucked it out of my inbox.

"A letter of resignation." And that was the other reason employees wrote letters to their bosses. "It's right here."

I took the letter from her outstretched hand. She clasped her hands in front of her waist while I read it. It was her two weeks' notice, effective a week ago.

"Why did you not email me?" I heard my voice rise in anger. She knew the holidays were all hands on deck. Banff was a beloved winter-vacation destination, and December to January was peak season.

She didn't answer, and it didn't matter.

"OK, thank you, Lily." I dismissed her with a nod of my head, and she closed the door behind her.

"Merde!"

I didn't regret moving to Banff. For someone whose first love was skiing, it was paradise. The snow was as light as powdered sugar, and there were views of mountains in every direction. There was no place on earth I would rather be. I just wish I didn't have to do this job to afford to live here.

I never aspired to work at a hotel. I was a skier. *Am* a skier. It was all I had ever wanted to do—from the moment I woke up, to the moment I went to bed, then all night in my dreams. I'd busted my *derrière* to make the Canadian Olympic team. But I didn't make the cut.

Some people fail because they don't work hard enough, but that was not my problem. I outworked everyone. When I wasn't on the mountain, I was in the weight room, pushing my body to exhaustion.

Others fail because they don't believe they can do it. That was not my problem either. I not only believed I would make the team, but I thought I would medal too. I had a collage with photos of myself next to magazine cutouts of my heroes—Ingemar Stenmark, Hermann Maier, Jean-Claude Killy, Erik Guay. Maybe I wanted it too much. Sometimes when you want something so badly, instead of attracting it, you repel it. Just like with people. I had made that mistake too.

When it was clear my times were never going to be good enough to make the Canadian national team, I packed up my skis and disappointment and went to France to work for the PGHM (Peloton de Gendarmerie de Haute Montagne), the elite mountain-rescue team in the French Alps. It's like ski patrol, but on steroids. The glacier below Mont Blanc beckoned daredevils from all over the world, who came to ski the steepest of the steeps. There were no chairlifts or trail markers, only cliffs and crevasses. I don't know who was crazier—the thrill seekers who pointed their skis down the mountain even though they knew it might be the last thing they would ever do, or me and my fellow rescuers, who risked our lives when they fell in the no-fall zones. It was demanding work, and the intensity was almost enough to make me forget the Olympics were happening without me. Venturing out onto the glacier in stormy, subzero weather is dangerous, even when you are trained, but it would have taken more courage to face my failure. I turned to saving other people because I didn't know how to save myself.

Not every rescue had a happy ending. Sometimes we were too late. Sometimes the injured died during transport. Mont Blanc took dozens of souls every winter. Some succumbed to head injuries. Some bled or froze to death. I'd seen as many dead bodies during those winter months as most emergency room doctors did all year.

I closed my email and opened our scheduling portal. I was already short staffed over the Christmas holiday. Now that Lily was quitting, I was perilously thin. Housekeeping is hard work and takes skill. There is an art to making a bed just so, and picking up after guests without invading their privacy requires discretion and grace. You also need a strong stomach. People do things in hotel rooms that they don't do at home. A room attendant must bear witness but never judge.

As I scoured the schedule to see which of my already overworked employees I could ask to work even harder, there was another knock on my door.

"*Entrez-vous!*" I called out, bracing myself for more bad news.

"Sorry to disturb you, Remy," Sydney from Sydney, my front desk clerk, said in her Australian accent, "but there's someone here to see you."

"A guest?" I assumed, because an employee would knock on my door themselves.

"I don't think so."

My coffee was cold and I'd lost my appetite, so I abandoned my crisis and my snack and followed Sydney into the lobby. With its domed ceilings and walls of stone, my workplace felt more like a castle than a hotel, and we kept the lights dim and the fireplace lit to complete the medieval vibe.

In my short life, I've repelled two things by wanting them too much. The first was the Olympics—a dream I clung to so hard I choked the life out of it. The second was not a thing, but a person. I had assumed she was gone forever too. But as I stepped into the lobby, I got a tingle of hope that maybe I was wrong.

Because there she was, standing at the front desk.

CHAPTER 7
Julie

The road to Banff was a sparsely trafficked two-lane highway carved through a forest of towering evergreens. As I climbed to two thousand, three thousand, four thousand feet, the snow on the ground grew thicker and thicker, until it coated the landscape like buttercream on a wedding cake.

It was just past three o'clock when the jagged outline of Cascade Mountain came into view. The sun hovered above the peak like a bright-red cherry atop an ice cream sundae, and I lowered my visor to shield my tired eyes. I'd been driving for nearly eight hours when I reached the gates of Banff National Park. You're supposed to buy a park pass if you're visiting any of the towns within the boundary, but I didn't know if I was staying, and I couldn't afford it even if I was, so I waved to the ranger like I was just passing through.

Driving into Banff was like falling into a Christmas card. The main road was flanked by pine trees that watched over the town like potbellied sentries in plush, emerald dress coats. Sparkly tinsel swirled around lampposts, and the rooftops were frosted with pristine snow. The sight of playful red ornaments peeking through pine needles usually made my heart swell with joy. But not today. Not anymore. My heart was a shipwreck at the bottom of the ocean, bloated with grief and ensnarled with questions I wasn't sure I wanted answered.

It hadn't fully sunk in that Jeff was dead. I still found myself taking mental notes of things I would tell him later—seeing a beady-eyed fox at the rest stop, hearing our wedding song on the radio—*twice*! And then I remembered that Jeff was gone, and there was no point making note of these things because they didn't mean anything to anyone but him.

The Banff Springs Hotel was at the far end of town, nestled in the shadow of Sulphur Mountain, named for the natural hot springs near the base. The exterior of the hundred-year-old building was a tumble of earth-colored stones piled unevenly toward the darkening sky. Haphazard, jagged turrets mimicked the asymmetrical silhouettes of the Rocky Mountains just beyond. There was a statue of some tubby white guy wagging a finger at you as you entered the roundabout. I suppose if you felt welcome there, you might not even notice it. But it loomed large for me today.

I drove up the incline and came to a stop at the main entrance. A valet rounded the front of my car and opened my door.

"Checking in?"

"No," I said, then corrected myself. "Maybe. I don't have a reservation. Can I just leave it here for a second?"

"Of course." He pointed to a spot a few meters in front of me.

"Thank you."

I pulled up and got out of the car. Fresh snow squeaked under my sneakered feet. I had boots, but they were buried at the bottom of a suitcase, along with my pride. It was a Canadian trademark to underdress. Fur-lined Sorels and overcoats were for tourists, not locals. As the doorman opened the door with his leather-gloved hand, he nodded at me like he knew what I was, but of course he was only partly right.

"Welcome to the Banff Springs Hotel."

I stepped onto the gleaming marble tile. Heat from the fireplace rolled over my skin as I drank in the sweet smell of cinnamon and pine.

The room was somehow both grand and cozy, with soaring ceilings and buttery leather couches that invited you to stay awhile. I counted six Christmas trees, all lit up and decorated with red ribbons tied in stiff symmetrical bows. A gingerbread house the size of a car was on display behind a black velvet rope—*look but don't touch!* My chest ached for Jeff. I didn't know I was crying until a salty tear dropped onto my upper lip. But I was trained to keep going. So I wiped back my tears and put one foot in front of the other until I reached the front desk.

"Checking in?" the rosy-cheeked desk clerk asked, her chestnut hair swirled atop her head like a cinnamon bun. Her bronze name tag told me she was Sydney from Sydney, but I was too spent to appreciate how adorable that was.

"No. I, um . . ." I paused. He told me I could come, but I still felt nervous. Things had not always been easy between us. But I didn't have any other place to go, and it was too late to turn back now.

Sydney from Sydney raised an inquisitive eyebrow. "How may I help you?"

"I'm here to see Remy."

As I spoke his name, the memories came flooding back. Piling into the bar with my teammates in our Team Canada jackets, knowing they invited people to stare and not minding one bit. Getting a round of fireballs sent over from the "gentleman in the blue blazer at the bar," whose French accent was every bit as charming as his smile. "I'm Remy," he'd said when he introduced himself, rolling his *r* as he extended a hand to shake. We would have invited him to join us even without the promise of free drinks. Yes, he worked at the hotel, but he was also one of us. A contender. Just because he didn't make the team didn't mean we thought less of him. We were all one injury away from the end of our careers too.

Visits to the hotel bar became a regular thing that winter. Working out six hours a day made us hungry as wolves. Remy was generous with us, comping appetizers when he was there, making his employee discount available to us when he wasn't. He made us feel welcome. Made *me* feel welcome. And special. And safe. I guess that's why I slept with him, because before I met Jeff, I'd thought that's what love was.

"I'll see if he's available," the smiling Aussie said, then stepped away from her post.

We were never boyfriend and girlfriend. Remy had a reputation as a ladies' man, and I'd assumed he slept with a lot of women. He never expressed feelings for me. Nor I for him. I always thought of us as each other's nightcap after our nightcap. So when I saw Jeff, sitting at the bar with a Bloody Caesar that looked more like a glass of salad than a drink, I made no attempt to hide my interest from Remy or anyone else.

I thought Remy was happy Jeff and I had made a love connection. He gave Jeff free room upgrades, sent complimentary champagne, smiled when I'd told him how great things were going. But the look on his face when he saw me today made me wonder if I'd misread his behavior. His expression wasn't one of surprise, but satisfaction—no, *victory*. At first I thought maybe I'd imagined it. But when he slipped his hand onto the small of my back and held it there a second too long, I knew I'd misjudged him. What I didn't know was that he was a better actor than any of my former fancy Hollywood neighbors, and that everything he'd said and done had been a performance just for me.

CHAPTER 8
Remy

When I saw her standing there, underdressed for the cold weather in her jeans and oversize sweatshirt, I thought I must be dreaming.

"Julie?"

She tried to smile, but grief was pulling at the corners of her mouth.

"Hi, Remy."

I kissed her on both cheeks, as was my usual.

"Sorry to show up unannounced."

"You know you are welcome anytime." I let my hand rest on her waist, just for a second. She crossed her arms in front of her chest, and I couldn't tell if she was cold or recoiling from my touch.

"Can we talk?" she asked.

"Let's go to the Sidecar." My office was a mess and smelled of stale coffee. I wanted to entice her to stay, not repel her.

"*Après vous*," I said, indicating for her to go ahead. She knew the way. The Sidecar had been our favorite hangout back in the day. Unlike the popular Rundle Bar, which was noisy and crowded après ski, the Sidecar was low key and intimate, the hotel's best-kept secret.

She paused at the door disguised as a bookcase, allowing me to open it for her. The cozy sitting room was predictably empty. She walked across the herringbone hardwood and slid into a booth.

"What can I get you?" I asked.

"I'm fine."

"How about some tea?"

"Tea would be lovely," she said to please me. "Thank you."

I took the walkie-talkie off my hip. "A pot of tea to the Sidecar please," I said into the radio. "And a bread basket too." My assistant manager responded with a succinct "Copy that," and I holstered the walkie and sat down across from my old friend.

"How are you doing, Julie?" I asked, even though I knew the answer. The hollows beneath her eyes were purple with exhaustion. She took off her hat and squeezed it to her chest.

"I need a job, Remy."

The statement was so absurd I thought I'd misheard her.

"I'm sorry?"

"Just for a few months, until my house sells."

"You want to work *here*?" The Banff Springs Hotel was a fine place to work, if you were unable to do what you loved full time. But Julie was an Olympian. Surely there were other jobs better suited to her.

"I can't stay in California. And I need the money." I understood one of those statements, but the other was unexpected.

"What about your clients?" Julie and I had not stayed in touch beyond the occasional thumbs-up on a Facebook post. But I knew she worked as a physical therapist, and I had no doubt she made decent money, better than she could make here.

She looked at me with desperate eyes. "I can't face them. Not after . . ." Her voice cracked, and she pressed her lips together to hold back the tears. I wanted to tell her Jeff's death was not her fault, that her clients knew that. But it occurred to me, the less I talked about Jeff, the better.

"Why don't you get a job at one of the resorts?" I suggested. "You would enjoy teaching skiing more than working at a hotel, no?" I would have loved to have Julie under my wing, but the thought of her doing anything other than what she was born to do broke my heart.

"You need a certification to teach on the mountain. Plus I'm not a downhiller." Technically both statements were true. She could get certified in a weekend, but only if a course was available—unlikely so close to the holidays. And while I was sure she could hold her own on any terrain, downhill technique was complex, and she had probably never learned it. When you are a natural at something, it can be hard to teach others who are not.

"What kind of job are you looking for?" There was no way I would let her shovel snow or pick up trash.

"Preferably one where I don't need to see or talk to anybody."

I was so entranced by the sight of her, I had momentarily forgotten I had a job opening, one I was desperate to fill. One that met her preferences perfectly. She wouldn't need to talk to guests or even many coworkers. In fact, the more invisible she was, the better. No one wants to fraternize with the person who cleans their *toilette*.

"I had an employee quit this morning," I started, then stopped myself. The notion of Olympic-gold-medalist Julie Weston Adler working as a maid was absurd. "But you don't want her job."

"I'll do anything," she said. "I'm not proud."

Her pronouncement was a slap in the face. I would have sold my soul to achieve what she had achieved. Yes, I had a staffing problem. And a potential solution was sitting right across from me. But I could not bring myself to offer her the job.

As I was racking my brain to figure out how else I might help her, the bookcase door to the lounge opened. It was Johnny, the bartender, with our tea and bread. He set down the cups, but as he went to pour the tea, Julie stopped him with her hand.

"Thank you, I'll do it."

Johnny looked at me, and I nodded. *"C'est bon."*

She slid my teacup in front of me. Amber liquid cascaded into the cup as she poured. I could have put her in the bar, as we could always use an extra cocktail waitress. But I didn't want her interfacing with our distinguished guests. That was how I lost her the first time.

"So?" she asked, setting the pot down without pouring herself a cup.

"It's in housekeeping," I said. "You would be a room attendant."

"You mean like a chambermaid?"

"We call them room attendants here," I said, because if she was going to do it, I wanted her to do it with dignity.

"That sounds perfect. I'll take it." I tried to tell myself this was a win-win. She was solving my problem, and I was solving hers.

"You don't have to live in staff housing, but it's easier—"

"No, I want to live on-site," she said before I could finish my thought. We had a few rooms in the executive-staff wing of the main building. They were cramped and dark, but she'd have one to herself. Unlike in the dorms, where she would have to share.

"I have a room for you," I said. "But it is very small—you are not going to like it."

"I'm sure it's perfect." She reached across the table and grabbed my hand. "I can't tell you how much I appreciate this, Remy." Her fingers were cold, but her grip was strong. I loved her duality of femininity and strength. She was a superstar. She could have gotten a job anywhere. Everyone needed seasonal help. But she came here, to *my* hotel. I couldn't stop myself from jumping to the obvious conclusion, because the only thing different about working at the Banff Springs Hotel was *me*.

"Happy to have you here." The sides of her mouth ticked up like she was happy too. And I let myself believe that we were finally walking into our destiny.

"When can I start?" Her eagerness swallowed up my apprehension.

"We can get you moved in right now."

CHAPTER 9
Julie

"Housekeeping!" Lily called out as she knocked on a hotel-room door. My maid mentor and I were dressed in matching slate gray uniforms that looked like scrubs. She wore hers a size too small, to show off a figure that rivaled those of my Hollywood-bombshell neighbors. Her red hair was swept up in a messy bun, and her upturned eyelashes seemed to go on forever.

"You're supposed to count to three before you enter," Lily said as she waved her card in front of the magnetic keypad. "But I have a life outside this job." She winked at me, like that life was pretty great.

"You ready?" she asked as the lock clicked open and the pea-size light turned from red to green.

She pushed open the door without waiting for my answer. The room was a junior suite with a king-size bed and a small sitting area. Lily walked around the foot of the bed and opened the blinds.

"You gotta see what you're doing," Lily said as the room flooded with sunlight. "Even though you might not want to." She laugh-snorted at her own joke, then walked back over to the bed.

"Always strip the bed first," she instructed. "That will tell you what kind of people you're dealing with."

"How do you mean?"

"Hotel rooms are made for sex," she explained. "It's not a question of *if* they're doing it, it's *how freaky* they're doing it." She wrinkled her nose, then lowered her voice. "There's evidence of the no-pants dance just about everywhere."

She pointed to an opaque streak on the headboard, and I made a mental note to never sleep in a hotel bed again.

"It goes without saying, whatever you do, don't take off your gloves."

We were both wearing royal blue latex gloves. There was a box of them in the cart parked outside the door. "Part of the uniform," Lily had said. And they just became the most important part.

"We cover the duvet with a sheet," she said as she pulled back the top sheet. "Don't be surprised if you find a little present underneath it. You can radio one of the floaters for a clean duvet if you have to. Stuff sometimes finds its way inside the pillowcases, too, so remove them slowly."

We worked together to strip the bed. I tossed the dirty linens into the cart, then got a lesson in how to make perfect hospital corners.

"We don't have fitted sheets. They're all the same, just different sizes." I watched Lily do the first corner. Then she did two as I did one.

"Don't worry, you'll get faster at it."

We put on fresh pillowcases, then karate chopped the pillows down the middle to make them puff out like butterfly wings.

"That's it for the bed."

We sprayed the mirrors with window cleaner and the shower with mold killer, and wiped down the wood surfaces with a pink solvent that smelled like grapefruit.

"If they leave clothes on the floor, put them on the chair," she said, picking a pair of pants up off the floor. "But make sure it's clean first. People love to do it on the chair."

I made a second mental note: no sitting on the chairs either.

"Speaking of, y'know." She didn't want to say the word, so I said it for her.

"Sex?"

"You're pretty, so occasionally you may encounter a guest who wants you to do things. We're not supposed to, but that's up to you."

"Wait, what?" The other stuff was disturbing, but this was obscene.

"Oh, honey," she soothed. We were close in age, but apparently she felt I needed mothering. "Hotels attract all sorts of weirdos. I once had a guy ask me to tie him up and whip him with a wet towel."

"You didn't do it . . . did you?"

"He gave me a thousand bucks," she said with a shrug, and I suddenly wondered if I should have asked Remy for a waitressing job. "Most people are cool. They leave you alone, you leave them alone."

I stayed in Lily's shadow for the rest of my shift. After that first clean, we mostly worked in silence. She shouted a correction here and there—"Don't forget to clean the soap well!" "Change the toilet paper roll!" "Radio room service to restock the minifridge!"—but otherwise she stayed in her head and I stayed in mine.

The best thing about the job was also the worst thing. It was hard. To turn the rooms over in the narrow window between checkout and check-in, we had to be like sharks, always moving. It was physical work. I was strong, but polishing fixtures until they shone took a different kind of strength. But between scrubbing grout and counting glassware, towels, bottles in the minibar, I didn't have time to think about Jeff. Best thing, worst thing. It all balanced out.

Most of the rooms we cleaned were unoccupied. A few guests sent us away. One older man let us clean while he read a book in the germ-infested chair. My shift was almost over—I had started an hour before Lily to fill out paperwork and get a lecture from the head of housekeeping—so I mentioned to Lily that I should probably go clock out.

"You know we only have one clean left," she said.

I didn't want to go into overtime on my first day. "Can you do it without me?"

"I mean, I could, but . . ." A slow smile spread across her face.

"But what?"

She tilted her head toward the door at the end of the hall: the penthouse suite.

"You're going to want to see this."

CHAPTER 10
Julie

"Come in!" a woman's voice boomed as Lily knocked on the door to announce our arrival.

"Brace yourself." Lily waved her key over the keypad—click!—and opened the door to the penthouse suite. I stepped over the threshold. It was more like an apartment than a suite, with a proper living room, dining room, kitchenette, powder room, and two bedrooms with en suite baths. You could live there all year round. Which apparently the current resident was planning to do.

"Hello, Mrs. Rousseau," Lily said to the spindly blonde sitting at the writing desk. The woman was dressed in a cashmere hoodie with matching flared leggings and fur-lined slippers. She looked to be in her early fifties, but it was hard to know for sure, as anyone who could afford this room surely had surgical help to keep from looking her age.

"Hello, Lily," Mrs. Rousseau said without looking up. She was typing on a laptop. I glanced down at her hands. Thick veins snaked toward fingers adorned with diamonds. *Not fifties—sixties, more likely.* The only other thing on the desk was a lowball cocktail in a beveled crystal glass. I figured it must have been whiskey because you don't drink iced tea out of a glass like that.

"OK to clean now?" Lily asked.

"I wouldn't have told you to come in if it wasn't."

Lily looked at me and ticked her head toward one of the bedrooms. I was just about to head in with my armful of clean sheets when Mrs. Rousseau spoke again.

"Who's your tagalong?"

"This is Julie. Today's her first day."

I turned around, expecting to see Mrs. Rousseau looking at me. But she was still staring at her screen.

"You know I don't like new people."

"Well, you're going to have to get used to her, because I'm retiring."

Mrs. Rousseau stopped typing and looked at Lily.

"Retiring? To do what?"

"I'm getting married."

"For money, I hope."

"No. For love."

"There's no such thing."

"Well, hopefully he'll make a lot of money then," Lily replied with a smile.

"If he doesn't, get out fast while you still have your looks," Mrs. Rousseau said sternly, to make sure Lily knew she wasn't joking.

Lily turned her back to Mrs. Rousseau and rolled her eyes. I forced a smile, even though talk of marriage and husbands made my heart drop into my shoes. I absolutely married for love. Yes, I'd met Jeff when he was a guest here. And I knew this to be a nice hotel and that most of the guests had money. But I didn't make assumptions. I was there, and I was broke. Turns out I'd been right to assume Jeff wasn't rich, either—at least not yet. As he explained the night we met, it was his angel investor, an Alberta oilman, who was footing the bill for his trips to Banff. "Megabucks Mackenzie," he jokingly called him. He explained how Megabucks flew him up from Southern California to drink expensive brandy and play golf with potential investors. Jeff would impress them with his killer golf swing, and Megabucks would take their money.

Jeff's company took off thanks to all those trips, and our love soared along with it. I assumed Jeff knew I meant it when I vowed to love him for richer or for poorer, but maybe I should have told him? Because now I couldn't help but wonder if he'd killed himself because he was afraid of disappointing me. The only other reason I could think of was that he'd been desperately, hopelessly disappointed in himself.

I followed Lily into Mrs. Rousseau's bedroom. Lily did three hospital corners in the time it took me to do one, but when she inspected my work, she smiled her approval.

"Nice job."

I'm embarrassed to admit how good that compliment made me feel. People assume Olympians are confident, and I suppose we are when we're winning. But there can only be one winner. Which makes for a lot of losers. And when medals and accolades are the only things that make you feel worthy, falling off the podium is like falling off a cliff.

"I'll do her bathroom," Lily said, whipping out a toilet brush. "Go do the second bedroom. No one's sleeping there—you just need to dust."

I had to cross the living room to get to the other bedroom, but Mrs. Rousseau ignored me like someone who is accustomed to hired help buzzing around. I expected the second bedroom to be empty, so had to choke back a gasp when I opened the door.

Lily was right, the room hadn't been slept in. That would have been impossible, as both beds were covered with clothes. And I mean *covered.* The bed closer to the door was for purses. Chanel, Gucci, Prada, Balenciaga, Louis Vuitton, Hermès—you didn't have to be a sophisticate to recognize the luxury brands. The other bed was a sea of denim, silk, and cashmere: jeans, leggings, turtlenecks, and crewnecks. Just beyond the beds, and also between them, blouses, blazers, puffers, and furs hung on expandable wardrobe racks, all extended to maximum length. Boots and shoes were piled high on every surface, including the windowsills. It looked like a high-end garage sale, minus the garage.

As I gaped at Mrs. Rousseau's outlandish riches, the pain of losing the life I had with Jeff rose up from the pit of my belly. It wasn't the clothes I coveted, it was what they represented—a life of ease, a man to take care of you, even if you could take care of yourself. I'd let myself be seduced by a man with a promising future, forgetting that I once had one too. *Had.* It was gone now. And took my self-worth along with it.

I knew it would take time to accept my new lot in life. That's why I came here, to start fresh. But memories of my former glory were not only still lurking, they were also about to get me in a whole lot of trouble.

CHAPTER 11
Julie

"What's the deal with Mrs. Rousseau?" I asked Lily over a plate of lemony shrimp scampi.

"Oh, you mean Lady Ceci?"

"Lady Ceci?"

"That's what we call her. She's a trip, huh?" We were in the staff canteen. All employees got one free meal a day in the spartan cafeteria-style eatery, and this was the first proper one I'd had since I left California.

"How long has she been staying at the hotel?" I asked, dipping my bread into the buttery sauce. For cafeteria food it was delicious, and I wasn't going to waste a drop of it.

"Oh, months. Five or six at least."

"Six months?!"

"She's going through a divorce. Her husband is loaded. Or *was* loaded before she started living here, ha ha. I think she's trying to stick it to him."

"Her suite looks like a department store," I said, trying to imagine how many elevator trips it had taken to get all that stuff up there.

"Yeah, well, don't go shopping in it," Lily warned, and I would later wonder if she was the one who'd put the idea in my head.

She talked about her upcoming wedding, and she let it slip that contrary to what she'd told Lady Ceci, she was marrying for love *and money*. I still wore my rings, but she didn't ask about my husband. I figured she intuited that something had happened to him. But her next question revealed she'd intuited more than that.

"So what's the deal with you and Remy?"

I felt myself blush. "What do you mean?"

"You kind of skipped the whole interview process. I figured you must be tight." She raised a knowing eyebrow.

"He's an old friend," I said, even though my red cheeks surely gave away that we were once more than that.

"Hey, no judgment from me. We all think he's a babe. *Zat acc-cennnt*," she said in an exaggerated French accent. "If I wasn't getting married, I'd be all over that."

We cleared our plates and said our good nights, and she returned to her quarters and I to mine. It was shocking how much my life had changed in the last seven days. I went from a mansion to a shoebox, hot weather to cold, from having a husband and friends to painfully alone. I wasn't sure which part was a dream—my three and a half years in California? Or being back here.

I changed out of my uniform and pulled on some sweats. My Team Canada swag reminded me what I'd achieved, and also what I hadn't. Yes, I'd won Olympic gold, but then I quit, before I had a chance to see how great I could become.

I met Jeff at the tender age of twenty-three. After dating long distance for two and a half years, I was afraid if I didn't go with him to California, I'd lose him forever. At least that's what I told myself. Perhaps, deep down, I was afraid of something else. Athletes are told, *There's no limit to how great you can be!* Problem is, when the sky's the limit, you never arrive.

There was another reason I followed Jeff to California. After the Olympics were over, my teammates all went home. But the only home I'd ever known had been sold long ago. I'll never forget the day my parents told me they were leaving, or how angry my father got when I said I wouldn't go with them. "Girls don't belong in sports," he said. "Get your head out of the clouds." Mom was too afraid of him to disagree, so I helped them pack the truck, then stood on the curb as they drove away. "If you want to come to Mexico, you'll have to pay your own way," Dad said through the open window. I was sixteen.

I couch surfed and flipped burgers until I had enough money to get a studio apartment. Then I worked my butt off. I wasn't trying to prove my parents wrong. I was trying to win them back. But they didn't come. Not when I made the team, not even when I medaled. Sometimes I wonder if I had fallen on my face, given them their *I told you so*, things might have been different. But it was too late now. They were gone. In my quest to make them love me, I'd driven them away. I thought they might come for Jeff's funeral, but the opportunity to hold my hand had never been something that called to them. So once again, I was on my own. But this time I had nothing to work toward, and no one to save me from myself.

I picked up my phone to check my text messages. There were a handful from clients, sending love and hugs. But most were from Izzy. We're worried. Where are you? Please call and let us know you're OK. I didn't want my friends to know I was working as a maid, because then I'd have to tell them why. Jeff spent all your money without telling you? they would ask, trying to hide their shock and disbelief. And what would I say then? Yes, he'd plunged us into financial ruin, but what did it say about me that I didn't notice? We'd vowed to stand by each other in good times and in bad. But when things were bad, he kept his struggle hidden. Was he protecting me from something? Or did I make it too hard for him to be vulnerable with me?

I dreaded the conversation, but it was unkind to make my friends worry. So I dialed Izzy's number. She answered on the first ring.

"My God, Julie! Where are you? Are you OK? The girls and I have been worried sick!" She sounded frantic. I tried to reassure her.

"Hi, Izzy. Yes, I'm fine." I probably should have added an *I'm sorry,* but her next question came too fast.

"Where on earth did you go?"

"I'm in Banff."

There was a beat of silence. *Does she not know where Banff is?*

"In Canada," I clarified.

"Sorry, yes, I know where Banff is, but what the heck are you doing there?"

I should have told her the truth. That my bank accounts were empty, that Jeff's suicide had filled me with shame, that I couldn't face my clients, or stay in the house we'd once shared.

"Just needed to get away," I said.

And there it was. My little white lie. I told myself I did it for Jeff, to protect his memory. Unfortunately, even tiny, well-intentioned lies are dangerous. Because they force you to tell bigger lies to cover them up. This first lie wasn't going to bite me. But the next one was going to swallow me whole.

CHAPTER 12
Izzy

"So I have news," I said as I sat down for Sunday brunch across from Christa and Suki. It was windy out, so we were seated inside, at a window table overlooking a sad little pond dotted with sad-looking ducks.

"What kind of news?" Suki asked, her amber eyes wide like Frisbees.

"Good afternoon, ladies," a waiter who came out of nowhere said. "Can I start you with something to drink?"

"We need a minute, thanks," Christa said, shooing him away.

"Well?" Suki said. "Don't keep us in suspense." They knew what this was about. They just didn't want to steal my glory by guessing.

"I spoke to Julie," I said. And they gave me their best surprised faces.

"What?"

"When?"

"Last night. You'll never guess where she called me from." I wasn't trying to tease them, but I didn't want to deny them a suspenseful thrill either.

"Hawaii?" Suki guessed.

"Paris?" Christa said.

And I wished I hadn't made them guess.

"Canada."

"Canada!" they both said in unison, loud enough for the whole restaurant to hear.

"She's staying at the Banff Springs Hotel," I clarified.

"Isn't that where she and Jeff met?" Christa asked.

And Suki got more specific. "And fell in love?"

That last part stung, but I tried not to show it. "Yes, while she was training for the Olympics." I'd learned this from Julie on one of our many walks through my neighborhood when the twins were in strollers. We didn't have a fancy double-wide, so it took a second set of arms and legs to push them around the block, and she'd generously offered hers.

"Poor Julie." Christa sighed. I choked back my guilt. Just because my own marriage was tanking didn't give me the right to tank someone else's.

I'd hoped my affection for the man I married would return after the boys got through their terrible twos, but no such luck. I didn't have time (or babysitting) to go to therapy, so I did what I could to help myself. The first batch of books I read suggested happiness was a God-given right, and I should pursue it at all costs. According to self-help gurus who never breastfed two babies at a time, my life was about me. "Your only obligation in life is to be happy," they wrote. "Fly! Be free!" While I found it an intriguing concept, I was responsible for two little lives who, if they could talk, would tell me that was a load of crap. If my life was only about me, it would rain nannies and limoncello shots. So I tossed those new age books and bought some newer age books. My second round of gurus suggested it wasn't my marriage that was the problem, but my attitude about it. "Want what you got," the wise writers wrote. "You don't have to change your life, just change your thoughts!"

I liked the sound of trading my self-pity for gratitude. I made lists of the things I liked about my husband. I did meditations where I spoke them out loud. I imagined my attitude as a coin I could flip. Tails was negative thoughts, heads was positive. All I had to do was keep choosing heads! Focusing on the positive worked for a little while . . . until I met Jeff. I grappled with the existential question of what was worse: to stay in a marriage when I was head over heels for someone else or break up my family so I could "fly, be free!" I didn't believe Jeff would leave Julie for me, but I didn't know how to stop myself from fantasizing about it. Which hadn't been fair to my husband, my kids, or me.

"Are you ready to order?" The waiter was looking at me.

"Prosecco?" I suggested. And Suki and Christa nodded.

"Glass or bottle?" he asked.

"Bottle!" we all replied.

"How long is Julie staying in Canada?" Christa asked after the waiter had moved off.

"Is she ever coming back?" Suki echoed.

"She didn't say," I replied. "But she's staying at a hotel, so I assume she'll be back eventually."

Suki had her phone out and was scrolling through the Banff Springs Hotel website. "Holy cow, it's expensive. It must be really nice."

I remembered what Julie had said about wanting to sell her house, but I figured that was about memories, not money. Because, unlike us, she and Jeff always had lots of it. He was a tech entrepreneur from Richie Rich Santa Barbara. And she was a decorated Olympian. How could they not be loaded?

"She deserves it after what she's been through," I offered. There was a time it would have made me feel jealous to find out my perfect friend was living at a luxury hotel. But in this moment, all I felt was an overwhelming desire to help and comfort her.

"We need to do something," Suki said, reading my mind. "You know, to cheer her up."

Suki was right. We had to do something. *I* had to do something. Jeff's suicide was my fault, after all.

"I have a crazy idea," I said without thinking it through.

"What?" they both asked.

"Let's go visit her."

"Oh my God, yes!" Suki squealed.

"When?" Christa asked.

"Next weekend?" I suggested. I couldn't go during the week, because of the kids, but a weekend trip was feasible. Certainly my husband could handle the boys for a couple of days.

"It's affordable if we share a room," Suki said, looking at me, because money wasn't an issue for Christa. "We can split it three ways."

"We have a gazillion airline points we can donate," Christa offered, even though her husband probably would have liked to keep those points for himself. "And I can't think of a better reason to use them than this."

"Should we call and tell her that we're coming?" Suki asked, and I shook my head. If we called, she might tell us not to come. If I knew one thing about grief, it was that you don't ask the grieving person for permission to be there for them, you just show up.

"No, let's surprise her."

CHAPTER 13
Julie

My room was small and oddly shaped, with low-hanging beams that begged you to bump your head. The narrow, paned window rattled when the wind blew . . . so pretty much all night long. But that wasn't the reason I couldn't sleep.

It was five a.m. when I finally stopped trying and got out of bed. My legs ached from lack of exercise. When you work out every day of your life, it's the days you do nothing that hurt. I hadn't had a proper run, ride, hike, or ski for three full days. My muscles were screaming. So I flipped on the light, pulled on my Rad Pants, jacket, hat, gloves, and boots, and headed out the door.

I took the service elevator down to the basement, then used my magnetic key to unlock the ski locker. I hadn't brought a favorite pillow or clothes for a night out, but I had packed all my sports equipment: my custom rifle, which I'd stashed under my bed, and three pairs of skis—wisp thin for skating, long and lean for cross-country, downhill for resort and backcountry. I plucked the long and leans from the peg, then slipped out the loading dock door onto the snow.

It was pitch dark. I clicked on my headlamp to light the way. I didn't want to damage my skis, so I carried them across the hotel parking lot toward the Spray River trailhead just beyond. The Goat Creek

Trail wasn't a loop, just a there-and-back, nineteen kilometers in each direction. The hotel was in the valley, so I would do the moderate four hundred meters of vertical gain first, then enjoy coasting back to base. I used to be able to do this ski in under three hours, but I wasn't in that kind of shape anymore. I promised myself I wouldn't beat myself up if I couldn't get to the top today, knowing that was an empty promise.

I got to the trailhead, then dropped my skis to the ground. I had skied this trail before dawn many a time, but this was the first time my heart was as dark as the sky.

I clipped into my bindings and started up the incline. The snow was hard and slick, with a thin sheen of ice on top. I forced myself to maintain a moderate pace—enough to keep warm, but not overheat. Normally I listened to music when I worked out, but I had forgotten my AirPods in California, so my soundtrack was the swish-swish of my skis chugging along the tracks. The left-right, left-right rhythm reminded me of windshield wipers, and I imagined myself equally measured and tireless. Cross-country skiing doesn't take a ton of technique like downhill does. It's all about the breathing. Quick inhales. Long exhales. All the breath out. "Make it a meditation," my coach used to say. In the olden days, these workouts were spurred by a prize at the end—a qualification, a medal, a kiss that warmed every square inch of my body. Today's prize was the opportunity to escape—not just my lies, but also my guilt. I'd not only missed the signs my husband was contemplating suicide, but it's also possible I drove him to it. Just like I drove him to other things.

Jeff tried to tell me he was struggling to feel close to me. He wanted to go to counseling, but I had worked hard to bury my pain. Being rejected by the two people who were supposed to love me unconditionally had left deep wounds, and I didn't want some counselor picking at them. "Fear of intimacy is nothing to be ashamed of," Jeff had tried to reassure me. "Let's just meet it head on." For months, he begged me to "let him in." And then one day he stopped. He never confessed to finding someone else to be intimate with, and I never asked. Pretending

I didn't see the growing fissure between us was easier than confronting my demons, so I'd put my head in the sand while our communication, and our marriage bed, had grown cold.

I was three-quarters of the way up the trail before I forced myself to turn around. I had an eight-hour shift in front of me, and had to get back to shower, dress, and eat. The snow was predictably fast on the way down, and I let myself teeter on the edge of out of control. My headlamp was pointed straight down toward the ground. At this speed, a rogue rock or twig could send me hurtling into a tree. It would be catastrophic to break a ski or a bone out here all alone, and I'd had enough catastrophes for a lifetime.

I got back to the hotel just as the sun was peeking above the mountains. I didn't want my friends to worry about me, so I took a quick selfie and texted it with the message in my healing place, then added a heart emoji for effect. The purple sky in the background was more moody than happy, but at least they'd know I was alive.

A few cars had exited the hotel parking lot since I'd embarked on my ski, but most guests were still either tucked in their beds, or at the breakfast table fueling up for a day of sport or sightseeing. I probably should have saved my one employee meal for later, but I was starving. So after I dropped my skis in the locker, I went straight to the staff canteen. Nobody talked to me, which was fine. I wasn't here to make friends. Just to survive until Izzy sold my house and I could figure out the rest of my life. Stay here? Move back to California? Nothing felt easy or right anymore.

I thought about the life I'd left behind. My clinic would have no trouble reassigning my clients to other therapists. I wasn't worried about them. I imagined the girls were back to their hectic lives—cramming to meet work deadlines, caring for kids, shopping for Christmas. When I'd spoken to Izzy last night, she said she understood that I needed some time away, and even offered to look in on the house until I came back. If I went back. Once she sold the house, I'd decide.

Unfortunately, my plan to wait and see was ill conceived. Because keeping your head low doesn't keep you safe when the target is on your back.

CHAPTER 14
Julie

I tucked a muffin and two granola bars in my jacket pocket, then headed back to my room to get ready for my shift. My door was locked, but clearly someone had been in here, as there was an envelope on my desk that hadn't been there when I left. That's the way of hotels. With a wave of an all-powerful master key, any of us can go into any room we want, even each other's.

I opened the envelope and read the short note. It was from Remy. "Hope you had a good first day. Come find me and let me know how it's going." *Did he deliver it himself? And why does the thought of him coming in here make me uneasy?*

I left the note on my desk as a reminder to stop in and see Remy after work, then took a quick shower and changed into my uniform. The first half of my shift was perfectly boring. Besides an unflushed toilet, the grossest thing I stumbled across was a plate of three-day-old poutine. Not all the food that people left uneaten had mold sprouting from it—some of it was untouched and relatively fresh: a whole turkey sandwich, a chicken potpie with crust still intact, a fruit plate under taut plastic wrap. As I slid a plate of crispy french toast in the trash, I wondered if I should have saved that staff meal for later.

I did everything Lily taught me. My hospital corners were getting sharper, my mirrors less streaky, and the corduroy tracks left by my vacuum would have made a snowcat driver proud. If I was going to work as a maid, I was going to be the best damn maid this hotel had ever seen, because wasn't that just like me? The work was simple but satisfying. As someone accustomed to monotony (box jumps, squats, crunches, repeat), I even kind of liked it. Plus unlike physical therapy, where results take weeks or months, a room goes from grimy to glistening in mere minutes.

I had rooms to clean on every floor, so I bopped around, attacking my schedule wing by wing. Mrs. Rousseau's room was once again on my list, so I decided to venture up there before the sun set in hopes of catching a glimpse of her view.

I rapped on the doorframe.

"Enter!" Mrs. Rousseau bellowed, and I pressed my key to the pad and poked my head in.

"Housekeeping?" I called out. For some reason it came out sounding like a question, and I wondered if I still hadn't accepted my present vocation.

"Yes, obviously," Mrs. Rousseau snapped. "Come in and get started."

I grabbed the clean sheets off the cart and stepped into the suite. Ceci Rousseau was at her desk, looking downright regal in a purple angora sweater and cream wide-leg trousers. Her laptop was open. I snuck a peek at her screen to see she was playing bridge.

"I'm going to start in the bedroom," I said.

"As you wish."

The king-size bed looked barely slept in. The covers were folded down on one side, and the other side was untouched. I felt a pang of sadness when I realized that's what my bed at home would have looked like if I were still there.

As I stripped the bed, a pair of fuzzy socks dropped onto the floor. At first I thought Mrs. Rousseau must have kicked them off in the night. But then I realized they were on the wrong side of the bed—the neatly made side. *How did they get over there?* It dawned on me that this might be a test to see if I actually changed the sheets, or just pretended to. I couldn't help but wonder what would have happened if I'd failed.

As I plucked the socks off the floor and laid them on the high-back chair, I wondered why a woman with Lady Ceci's refined taste would want to spend her days holed up in a hotel in Banff, all dressed up with nowhere to go. It's not like there was culture here. Yes, there were a few art galleries but not like in Paris or New York. There was a theater but no thespians of note, a concert hall but few concerts. There was an annual film festival, but that was only for a week, and mostly attracted outdoors people and hippies. Didn't Lady Ceci have any friends? Who did she talk to all day? Was there a secret society of people who live in hotels that I didn't know about?

I finished the bed, then balled up the dirty sheets and started back toward my cart. But as I crossed through the living room, Mrs. Rousseau called out to me.

"What's your story?" she asked without looking up from her bridge game.

"I'm sorry?" I wasn't sure what she meant by that, and I thought it better not to guess.

"Well, you're obviously quite pretty. What are you doing cleaning hotel rooms?"

I didn't know what being pretty had to do with one's station in life. But I offered a plausible and partially true response.

"Just wanted to spend some time in the mountains." I took in her high cheekbones and neck as graceful as a prima ballerina's. I imagined she was stunning in her day. No wonder she considered looks to be a currency. In that department it was obvious she had once been quite wealthy.

"Oh, please," she said. "I see that ring on your finger. Is he a monster?" The question was so horrific I thought I must have misunderstood it.

"Who?"

"Your husband. You're here to get away from him, am I right?"

"No, ma'am," I said. "My husband is not a monster." And then, to explain the squeak in my voice: "He's dead." It was the first time I'd spoken those words out loud, and they stung like a belly flop. I thought she would offer her condolences, like any decent human would, but decency wasn't her thing.

"Not very kind of him to leave you so poor you have to clean toilets." It was a cruel thing to say, crueler still because it was true. I summoned Olympic-gold-medal strength and looked her square in the eye.

"I can take care of myself." And there was no squeak in my voice this time.

"Meh," she harrumphed, and she went back to her game while I went back to work. She was wrong about Jeff. The unkind thing he'd done was not leaving me poor. I was fully capable of supporting myself. What was unkind was that he'd left me to forever wonder why he did it. What had hurt him so badly that he woke up and decided he couldn't go on? And how could I live the rest of my life without ever knowing if it had something to do with me?

I hadn't told the police about all our money being gone, but I wondered if I should. What if Jeff was being blackmailed? That would explain why he would deplete the accounts without telling me. And if what he had done was really bad, it would explain why he'd ended his life too.

I wiped down the mirror and shook off the thought. I had always known Jeff to be scrupulous, at least when it came to business.

As for our marriage, I wasn't so sure.

CHAPTER 15
Izzy

Guilt makes you do all sorts of reckless things—betray friends, lie to cover your tracks, spend money you don't have. Images of Lady Macbeth scrubbing imaginary blood off her hands assaulted my senses as I explained to my boys why Mommy was going to be away for a couple of days.

"Auntie Julie is going through a hard time," I said as I tucked them into their beds and smoothed unruly curls off their Kewpie doll faces. "So Mommy is going to go visit her."

"Why did she leave?" they asked. And I didn't know the real answer, so I didn't have to lie.

"She just needed some time away."

I kissed them good night, then switched off the light.

Packing for Banff was easy and hard. Easy, because I only had one drawer of winter clothes, so I didn't have to agonize over what to bring. Hard, because I only had one drawer of winter clothes, and the contents weren't up to the task. The weather forecast was for temperatures in the single digits. No way my puffer from Old Navy could handle that.

"Just borrow stuff from Julie," my hub said as he walked into our room and saw me staring into my half-empty suitcase. I felt a rise of irritation. There were four dress sizes between Julie and me. Was my husband cruel? Or just clueless?

I thought about backing out, but it was too late. We'd gotten the plane tickets on Christa's points, but it wouldn't be fair to ask the other girls to pay half the rental car and hotel instead of a third. Plus I was already a liar. I didn't want to be unreliable too.

I couldn't afford to spend hundreds of dollars on clothes I would wear only once, but I couldn't travel to Canada in cotton separates from Target either. I didn't even have a hat that covered my ears. As I scoured the web for bargains in the wee hours of the night (with none to be found), it suddenly occurred to me that I knew someone who owned high-tech layers that would fit me. And I could take them without asking because he'd never know.

I dropped the boys at their half-day preschool and drove to Jeff and Julie's. The sun was warm through my windshield, yet I had goose bumps all over. I didn't know why I was nervous. Julie had asked me to look in on the place. Plus the house was about to be my listing, it would be irresponsible of me not to stop by.

"Shoo!" I said to my nervous thoughts as I unclipped my seat belt and got out of the car. As I started up the front walk, rosebushes nipped at my arms. I made a mental note to ask the gardener to cut them back, then another mental note to make sure Julie still had a gardener.

I reached the end of the pavers and stepped onto the stoop. A spiderweb clung to the hanging fixture overhead. I'd take care of that later with a swat of the broom. Just because it was the only sign of life didn't mean I would let it linger.

The hide-a-key was in its usual spot under the planter. I let myself in just as I had the morning Julie left but pocketed the key this time. Now that the house was empty, it was foolish to leave the key in such an obvious place. Not that right under one's nose was necessarily a bad hiding place. As Jeff and I had dared to presume, sometimes it's the only place a person didn't look.

I closed and locked the front door behind me, then stood in the foyer for a long, solemn beat. It was ghostly quiet. Even the air was mournful. My eyes combed the space. The flowers on the kitchen island were starting to wither. Vibrant pink petals had shriveled and darkened. *To match my heart,* I thought . . . then pushed the thought away. I had no right to pine for Jeff. He was never going to leave Julie. All I'd lost was a fantasy.

I didn't try to stop my tears as I gathered the flowers and tossed them in the green bin. Then I cleaned the refrigerator. I didn't know how long Julie was going to be away, but I didn't want her to come back to sour milk. I was hurt that she'd left without so much as a goodbye, but I also admired her for it. Friends were great, but you were a fool to think they would ever put your needs in front of theirs. I'd proven that.

I took out the trash, then headed upstairs. I knew where Jeff's clothes were. I'd looked in all the dresser drawers when I moved Julie into the spare bedroom. Looking at Jeff's belongings was the next best thing to looking at him, and I'd pored through those drawers to mourn as much as help.

The good thing about high-tech outerwear is it all looks the same. Nobody would recognize that black Marmot down jacket as Jeff's, everybody has some version of it. His long underwear would be . . . well, long. But again, the sleeves that stuck out from under my sweater would look the same as everybody else's. I had no use for the peekaboo slit in the crotch, but no one would see that part. I only needed three pairs of merino wool socks, but I helped myself to four. I also took a plain black beanie, a fleece pullover, and a pair of waterproof gloves.

I didn't linger. Yes, it gave me a little thrill to run my hands over flannel shirts I'd once fantasized about sliding off Jeff's gently sloping shoulders. But these clothes connected him to Julie, not me. That cashmere sweater he'd worn to that party, that suit he'd worn to that reception, that polo he'd worn the night he proposed . . . those were Julie's memories, not mine. I may have gotten a tiny taste of him when he was alive. But in death, he was all hers.

There was a tote bag on a hanger. I plucked it off and stuffed my loot in it. I was about to head back downstairs when morbid curiosity got the best of me. I'd been afraid to peek in the bathroom the day I moved Julie's things into the guest room, but the cleanup crew had come and gone since then, *so why not look now?*

I told myself I was peeking in out of necessity. I was Julie's Realtor, I had to see what needed to be done to the place. But in truth there was something more nefarious luring me in there. I wanted to see where he'd done it. If there was anything left of him. A strand of hair. A drop of blood. A wisp of his soul.

The door was closed. I noticed as I approached that the handle was broken, drooping toward the ground like a fractured bone. I extended my hand toward the door. It wafted open on buttery hinges. I met my own eyes in the mirror. They asked me what I was doing in here. I looked away.

There was a faint smell of bleach. The walls and tile had been scrubbed clean. I bent over for a closer look at the floor. Was that a hint of pink in the grout? Did I really want to know?

I backed out into the bedroom. As I turned to go, my eyes landed on the nightstand. A book about organic chemistry told me it was Jeff's. There was something else on that nightstand too. I hadn't noticed it before, but its sleek profile caught my eye.

It was his cell phone.

I didn't think there would be clues about our affair in his texts—as far as I knew, there was only that one incriminating thread, when I texted that we needed to talk, and he texted back the time and place. And hopefully he'd deleted the exchange, as I had.

I knew his passcode—it was Julie's birthday. I'd seen him enter it when he paid for our coffees. I didn't want to look now, because if I did, I wouldn't have an excuse to look at it later. Not that I thought there would be photos of us. But it couldn't hurt to check. Julie didn't have anything left of Jeff but her memories. I didn't want them ruined by something she found on that phone.

So I plucked it off the nightstand and tucked it in the tote.

CHAPTER 16
Julie

By day five, I had settled into a routine: get up, work out, eat, shower, clean, scavenge for food, sleep, repeat. If I was lucky enough to get a tip, I would buy myself a proper dinner, either at the hotel or somewhere in town. Cold weather makes you hungry, and there was never enough food to fill the abyss where my heart used to be.

I had never done this type of work, and the experience was eye-opening. I was raised to think we humans were put on earth to *accomplish* things—build buildings, cure diseases, break barriers, achieve greatness in our chosen pursuit. But what was greatness? I always thought being great meant being better than everyone else. It's what drove me to ski faster, shoot sharper, even (dumb as it sounds) get my assigned rooms cleaner than any chambermaid before me. But if you're chasing greatness, you're always running toward a moving target—today's "great" is tomorrow's performance to beat. Love, on the other hand, doesn't run from you, it only expands. How different might things be now if I'd devoted myself to growing love instead of trying to be great?

I spent some tip money on a ham-and-cheese sandwich, restocked my cart, then continued my rounds. As I cleaned a window that opened to an endless sky, I thought about what it would be like to stay at this job forever. Some people worked as housekeepers their whole lives, quietly lifting people up with sparkling floors and clean beds. Whose contribution to society is more important? The record breaker? Or the person who makes you feel comfortable wherever you are?

I did my assignments in a slightly different order today and found myself at Mrs. Rousseau's suite an hour later than usual. We hadn't exchanged more than a gruff "good afternoon" since she'd nearly made me cry, and I dreaded the twenty minutes I spent in her company. I dared to hope that this time she wouldn't be home. *People don't come to Banff to sit in their hotel rooms,* I told myself . . . momentarily forgetting that Ceci Rousseau wasn't most people. She was constantly trying to test me—leaving money out to tempt me, hiding things under furniture to make sure I moved it when I vacuumed. The socks in the bed were not an isolated incident. At first I wondered if she was evil or just bored. But then I got my answer.

"Housekeeping!" I announced as I knocked on the door. *One one thousand, two one thousand, three one thousand . . .* Normally Lady Ceci had summoned me to enter before I even started counting. When I got no response, I felt my shoulders relax, relieved I could clean her room in peace.

I used my key card and stepped inside. My arms were laden with linens, so, as usual, I headed for the bedroom. When I walked through the open bedroom door and saw Mrs. Rousseau standing naked at the foot of the bed, at first I was confused. Her skin was the color of milk, not flesh. If not for the bright shock of red lipstick on her puckered scowl, her silhouette might have been camouflaged against the lath plaster walls. I had never seen my own mother naked, and the athletic bodies carved by hours in the gym looked nothing like the willowy mass of skin and bones standing in front of me. I was so surprised by the sight of her, it took me a full second to realize what I was looking at. And a second is a long time to be caught staring at someone naked.

"What are you doing! Get out!" Mrs. Rousseau snapped, then grabbed a pillow off the bed and hurled it at me.

"Sorry," I managed, then stumbled backward out the door. My face burned with embarrassment as I tossed the linens back on the cart and pushed it toward the elevator on shaking legs.

"C'mon, c'mon, c'mon," I said to the closed elevator door as I frantically pressed the button. I didn't think Mrs. Rousseau was going to come after me with a fireplace poker, though she'd arguably earned the right to take a swing at me.

Ding.

The elevator doors opened. My cart bumped over the threshold as I hurried inside. Should I tell someone? Lily? Remy? The head of housekeeping, who already disliked me for getting hired behind her back? I decided the best thing I could do was put my head down and go back to work. *So much for winning the award for Banff's Best Housekeeper.*

I slunk into the next room on my list, making triple sure no one was home. As I cleaned toothpaste off the bathroom mirror, I prayed Mrs. Rousseau would be too embarrassed to report me. Fifteen short minutes later, when I was summoned to report to the front desk, I knew my prayers had been in vain.

"Julie, report to the lobby *immediately*," Francesca, the head of housekeeping, said through the walkie-talkie on my hip.

"Copy," I said, a little confused why Francesca wanted me to come to the lobby, because wouldn't her office be a more appropriate place to fire me?

I shook off the thought, stowed my cart in a supply closet, and rehearsed what I would say: *She didn't answer. I assumed she wasn't there.* As I rode the elevator down to the ground floor, I checked my reflection in the mirror to make sure my hair and uniform were regulation neat. If I broke rule number one, I didn't want to be guilty of breaking rules number seventeen and eighteen too.

The Banff hotel was a maze, as impractical and whimsical as an old English castle. Gargoyles glared at me from jagged eaves as I walk-jogged under their disapproving stares. My armpits were sweating in that polyester uniform, but at least my cardio training kept me from also being breathless.

As soon as I entered the lobby—

"There she is!" Mrs. Rousseau shouted, pointing at me with a coffin-shaped nail. She was standing not with Francesca, but with Remy.

I kept my head low as I approached. Mrs. Rousseau's chin jutted up toward the sky as her stiletto heels dug into a carpet the color of blood. We had quite the audience—a couple coming in from the cold, a family admiring the gingerbread house, a bellman, Sydney from Sydney, and three other front desk clerks—all staring at me like I was a polar bear in the desert.

"Hello, Julie," Remy said in that singsongy French accent. Working days and nights had aged him, but he was still handsome, even with the threads of gray running through his jet-black hair. That dark suit gave him Don Draper vibes, and I imagined, when needed, he could be just as ruthless.

"Hello, Remy," I said respectfully. "Hello, ma'am." By the way Mrs. Rousseau was looking at me, I thought she was expecting me to bow. And I might have, if I thought it could get me out of this mess.

"I believe you owe Mrs. Rousseau an apology?" Remy said, his voice rising like a question. I had anticipated this and offered a heartfelt one without hesitation.

"Mrs. Rousseau, I made an unforgivable mistake. Walking in on you like that was a horrific violation of privacy. I was careless, and I am truly sorry for the distress I have caused you."

"Humph," she huffed, then swiveled her head to look at Remy. "Where do you find these people?"

"Julie is our newest hire. I regret she was not trained to the Banff Springs standard."

He looked at me, and I could tell from the glint in his eye that his disappointment was an act.

"She's an abomination. Not just careless, mouthy too." *Mouthy? That's a new one.* "There's really no excuse. I'm tempted to call corporate. I moved to this hotel to escape lowlifes and incompetents, not be surrounded by them."

My ears burned holes in the sides of my head. I wanted to reach out and strangle her. I clasped my hands together to keep from lunging for her throat.

"On behalf of the entire staff, I deeply apologize," Remy said.

The room was deathly still. Nobody breathed or moved. Lady Ceci's tongue-lashing was humiliating, but for her to insist on degrading me in the lobby for the whole world to see was a whole other level of wicked.

As Mrs. Rousseau crossed her arms in front of her chest, I wondered if she had always been this horrible, or if the divorce made her that way. We like to think of love and hate as opposites, but in reality, they are only a hair's breadth apart, one morphing into the other with a tiny shift of the wind. If love is energy, and energy is never created or destroyed, it's no wonder passionate love turns to fiery hate. The law of conservation demands it.

"I don't know where we go from here," Ceci Rousseau said. And Remy took the bait.

"As compensation for your distress, please allow us to treat you to a day at the spa. I will handle the bookings personally."

"That's the least you can do," Lady Ceci huffed.

"I'll send someone up with a menu of services and follow up in the morning." He pulled a business card out of his inside pocket. "Here's my personal cell phone number—don't hesitate to use it," he said as he scribbled his number on the back of the card. She practically held her nose as she plucked it from his outstretched fingers.

"My room still needs cleaning. I'll be in the bar." She looked at me like I was her personal servant. I looked at Remy. *Please no.*

"Julie will make sure it's spotless."

Lady Ceci harrumphed and stormed toward the stairs.

"She set me up," I said, once she was out of earshot. "I announced myself loud enough to scare the birds off the roof."

"She goes to happy hour every day. It's from three to five. Stays until it ends. If you want to clean when she's not there."

"Now you tell me."

I thought back to all the traps she had set—socks in the bed, a bracelet under the chair, twenty-dollar bills sticking out of the pockets of pants she'd left on the floor. I didn't know why this woman had it out for me, but if she wanted a war, she'd picked the wrong opponent.

CHAPTER 17
Izzy

"Don't you look warm and cozy," Suki said as we stepped out of the Calgary airport into the frigid night air. I was a Bakersfield gal and could tolerate temperatures hot enough to toast a dinner roll. But cold was a beast with an unfamiliar bite, one I was pretty sure could sever me in half.

"Where'd you get that fancy puffer?" Christa asked, eyeing the jacket I had just slipped out of my carry-on.

"And those boots?" Suki echoed as I pulled those out too.

"Begged, borrowed, and stole," I said. Two out of the three were true. The boots were "on loan" from Costco. They had a no-questions-asked return policy, and those babies were going back first thing Monday morning. As for Jeff's things, he wasn't getting those back, so that was outright theft.

The rental-car depot was right across the street. Christa had booked the midsize SUV, but when the Alamo clerk asked for a driver's license, my friend looked at me.

"What are you looking at me for?"

"I've never driven in the snow."

"Me neither!"

We both looked at Suki.

"Don't look at me—my license expired six months ago."

I reluctantly handed over my license. I'd driven in LA traffic with two screaming toddlers in the back seat, how much more treacherous could a little ice and snow be?

The roads were crunchy and uneven, but the SUV had good traction, and once we got on the highway, the driving was easier. Suki insisted we listen to Christmas music, so we jingled all the way, past trees that scraped the sky, and under little bridges made for animals to cross the highway without getting flattened.

"Do you think we'll see any mooses?" Suki asked.

"I hope not!" I said.

"I think the plural of *moose* is *moose*," Christa said.

"No," I corrected her. "The plural of moose is 'we're goners,' so let's not even think about it."

The girls laughed at my joke, and I felt light as a feather. I spent so many of my waking hours being someone's wife, or someone's mother . . . it felt good to immerse myself in just being a friend.

"Don't look now, but I think we're in a Hallmark movie," Christa said as we pulled off Highway 1 into the wintery wonderland of Banff. She wasn't exaggerating. It was so small-town charming I half expected a man with perfect hair and a blue-eyed husky to knock on the window to ask for directions. *Sorry to be a bother,* he would say in his lilting British accent, *but can you tell me where the Banff Springs Hotel is?* And I would smile and flutter my eyelashes. *Hop in, we're headed there too!*

"The hotel is across the bridge," Suki said, snapping me out of my movie fantasy. Mariah Carey's "All I Want for Christmas Is You" tumbled out of our car-stereo speakers as we rolled past chichi boutiques and hipster coffee shops adorned with twinkly lights. I didn't deserve anything for Christmas, yet I still dared to wish for two things: one more night with Jeff and to be a better person. That these two wishes contradicted each other did not concern or even occur to me.

"There!"

I followed Suki's pointing finger to the end of the block, where a medieval-looking castle made me wonder if I should expect to see Harry Potter or the Prince of Wales.

"That's the hotel?" Christa gasped.

"Isn't it cool looking?" Suki said.

"I thought it would be more . . ." For once, Christa couldn't find words, so I helped her.

"Of this century?" I guessed.

"I think it's amazing!" Suki gushed.

I had seen pictures of the lobby, but I was not prepared for its magnificence. The ceilings were high and domed like an amphitheater, but the exposed stone walls made it feel like a cave. The Christmas decorations were lavish but not over the top. It was homey and grand all at once, and I got a little misty as I took it all in. *How my boys would love that gingerbread house,* I thought. I imagined them darting under the velvet rope to lick the frosting off the walls, and I suddenly longed for them a little less.

We had a room with two double beds. Christa and Suki offered to share, and I took them up on their generosity. Despite the tragic impetus for coming, we were excited to be on our first girls' trip, which was one girl short of being complete.

"Shall we call Julie now?" Suki said.

I already had the hotel phone in my hand. "Calling now." The front desk clerk picked up on the first ring.

"This is the front desk. How may I help you?"

"Can you connect me with Julie Adler please?"

I heard the faint sound of typing. Then an incongruous response.

"I'm sorry, I don't have a Julie Adler."

"What's wrong?" Christa asked when she saw my brows merge.

"She's not here."

"Try her maiden name." *Oh, right, of course.*

"Sorry. We think she might be under Julie Weston?" I said into the phone.

A few more keyboard clicks, then:

"No, I'm sorry. No Julie Adler or Julie Weston." To fill the stunned pause, she added, "This is the Banff Springs Hotel—"

"Yes, we know," I said, a little too snappy. "Thank you."

I hung up. Suki was already punching something into her cell phone.

"Are you calling her?" Christa asked as Suki held the phone to her ear . . . then removed it a short second later.

"It went straight to voicemail," she said, looking down at the phone like it had betrayed her.

"I'll text her," I said. Jules, it's Izzy and the girls, I read aloud as I typed.

"Tell her we're here!" Suki enthused.

"I will. Ooh, she's typing!" I said as three dots appeared on my phone screen.

"What did she say?"

"One sec, she's still typing."

The dots stopped, then restarted. Then her text came through.

"You're with Christa and Suki?" I read aloud.

"Yup," I said as I texted back.

Nice. Where are you guys? Julie texted.

And I couldn't wait to tell her.

CHAPTER 18
Julie

Where are you guys? I texted. I imagined them sitting at a bar, gin and tonics at the ready, speculating why a successful businessman in a happy marriage would put a bullet in his head.

You'll never guess, Izzy wrote. I had just gotten off my shift and was riding the elevator down to my room. I was starving and not really in the mood for a guessing game, but I played along.

Finney's? Finney's was our go-to for a casual dinner after work. If I wasn't doing a twilight run, I would sometimes join them on the patio for crunchy pot stickers and spicy tuna rolls.

Nope. Guess again.

Ding. The elevator opened. I presumed they were out to eat. It was dinnertime—where else would they be?

BJ's? As I started toward my room, my stomach growled at the thought of BJ's spicy buffalo wings smothered in creamy blue cheese dip. I had missed breakfast because of a too-long workout that morning and was looking forward to sitting down for my staff meal just as soon as I showered and changed.

Ping. Izzy's reply popped up on my phone just as I reached my door.

Nope. We're HERE!

I didn't know where she meant by *here*, so I texted:
What do you mean here? I pressed my key to the keypad and stepped into my room. And as I kicked off my shoes, the response came in all caps.

THE BANFF SPRINGS HOTEL.

My key slipped from my hand as the blood drained from my face. *She couldn't be serious . . . could she?*
More dots appeared on the screen. I held my breath as I waited for her to say she was just kidding.

We were worried about you so we came!

Nope, not kidding.
More dots, and then: Did you have dinner yet? We're starving!
I got a sinking feeling in my stomach. I should have been overjoyed. My friends had gone to considerable effort and expense to make sure I was OK. But I didn't want them to see me like this, living in a room the size of a coat closet, working as a maid.
I had to reply. *But what to say?* I'd told them I was in my happy place, enjoying some rest, relaxation, and healing. I couldn't tell them my so-called happy place was making other people's beds and scrubbing toilets. *Ugh. Why did I have to send that selfie?*
OMG! What a wonderful surprise! I typed. Luckily a text didn't require any acting skills, because this surprise was not wonderful, and I wasn't much of an actor.

What's your room number? We'll come get you.

My heart sped up in my chest. There was no way I would let them
see my tiny staff quarters, not when they were in a well-appointed guest
room . . . one likely cleaned by me.

I'll come to you, I texted. Just need to take a quick shower.

As I shampooed my hair, I practiced different versions of how I
would explain my situation to them: *The truth is, I'm broke . . . our
financial situation is complicated . . . I took this job because I couldn't face
you . . .*

I dried off and pulled on my jeans and a sweater. I hadn't brought
any going out clothes, given that I hadn't planned, nor could I afford,
to go out. I didn't take the time to put on makeup or blow-dry my hair.
If I was going to tell my friends I was down and out, I might as well
look the part. Plus I was starving and didn't want to keep them, or my
stomach, waiting.

Izzy and the girls were in the east wing, four floors above me. I had
been too busy trying to learn my new job to think about the reason I'd
had to take it. I imagined once I told them all my money was gone,
they would be ravenous to help me figure out what had happened to
it, because who doesn't love a good mystery? Especially one about the
downfall of the local celebrity couple.

The door to their room was propped open, but I still knocked.

"Hello?" I said, peeking through the crack. "Anybody home?"

"Juuuuulieeeee!" Izzy bellowed as she opened the door and swallowed me in a hug. I was relieved to see that all three women were
dressed down in anticipation of a quiet night. They told me how wonderful I looked. I thanked them all for coming, then led them down to
the secret sitting room behind the door disguised as a bookcase (which
they thought was so cool) so we could talk in relative privacy.

"OK, tell us everything!" Suki said after I'd returned from the
Rundle Bar next door with a round of drinks that Johnny the bartender had given me for free. I'd also ordered a selection of appetizers.

The Sidecar didn't have table service, but Johnny would bring the food when it was ready. I'd flashed my work ID and told him to charge it to my account, but he said not to worry, everything was on the house, compliments of the manager. I hadn't told Remy my friends were here, but I was too grateful to wonder how he knew.

"Not much to tell," I said. For someone who was going to confess, I wasn't off to a very good start—bringing them drinks I was getting for free, insisting on treating when all I'd have to pay was the tip. They'd come all this way. I didn't want to bum their trip with my sob story.

"We know you're in hell," Izzy said. "We want you to know we're here for you no matter what." And there was my opening. All I had to do was walk through.

"Thanks, Izzy." I thought back to what I'd rehearsed in the shower. Five little words: *The truth is, I'm broke.*

"We love you," Christa said. I opened my mouth to speak.

"You're amazing and beautiful, and we feel lucky to call you our friend," Suki added. And then I couldn't do it. *They wouldn't feel lucky to know me if they knew what I was.*

Any reasonable person would have swallowed their pride and confessed all. But reasonable had never been my thing. There is nothing reasonable about chasing Olympic gold . . . or getting up at four a.m. to train in subzero temperatures . . . or thinking you can have it all—a triumphant career in sports, a beautiful home in a great neighborhood, a great big love. Daring to be unreasonable had gotten me everything I wanted. The thought of revealing that every single one of those things had been taken from me was positively mortifying. So, as per usual, I did the most unreasonable thing possible: I lied.

"Coming here has been really good for me."

My big ego had once been an asset. Fear of humiliation is a powerful motivator, even more powerful than hope. It's what got me up that hill when my body was screaming for me to stop, and ultimately, up on that podium. But now my massive ego was a problem. It refused to let me tell my friends how far I had fallen.

All you have to do is get through this weekend, my ego coaxed. *You're doing it for Jeff,* it insisted. *So no one will know he left you penniless.*

The food arrived—crispy nachos, garlicky bruschetta, ahi tacos, grilled mushroom caps stuffed with crab, poutine with feathery cheese curds. It was more than I'd ordered, and the bartender winked at me as he served it to assure me I wouldn't be paying for any of it. I dug into the poutine despite the niggling knot in my stomach that was about to grow tighter.

"Oh, by the way," Izzy said. "We tried to call your room, but they didn't have you under Adler or Weston."

"We know you're famous here in Canada," Suki said.

"Of course you want to be incognito," Christa added. "Given what happened." And I foolishly thought all I had to do was nod and smile.

"What name are you staying under?" Izzy asked. And panic prickled down my arms.

They were all staring at me. It would be weird if I didn't tell them—they were my friends. I only knew the name of one guest, so I blurted it out without thinking.

"Ceci Rousseau."

CHAPTER 19
Remy

It was my turn to go skiing.

I hadn't had a day off since I'd returned from California, and I was itching to get back on the slopes. It was not snowing, but the sky was swollen with clouds. Mountain weather was unpredictable. A gray sky could bring flurries or a full-blown blizzard. I would have preferred a sunny day for my first outing in over a week, but I'd skied in all kinds of weather. I would not be deterred.

I took the shuttle to the mountain and clicked into my skis at the base. I didn't have to wait in lift lines, the staff knew me and always let me cut in front. As I got on the chairlift between two snowboarders wearing headphones to shut out the world, I took a moment to breathe in what was happening in mine.

It had been a triumphant week. I knew when I saw Julie at Jeff's funeral that she would come back to Banff. This was her home. Jeff was the only reason she had gone to California. Now that he was gone, there was nothing keeping her there, and everything beckoning her back here—the mountains, the memories, *me*.

I hadn't expected her to ask for a job, but it wasn't a total surprise either. Julie was never one to sit around doing nothing. She liked to be—*needed* to be—busy. She wasn't spoiled like Ceci Rousseau, who had unwittingly done me a service with her tirade. It was not very often I got to play the hero, especially to *the* Julie Weston.

I didn't take it personally that Julie hadn't stopped by my office, even though I'd left a note on her desk asking her to. Her husband had been dead for only two weeks. She probably didn't want to seem overly eager. It would have been easy to engineer an "accidental" run-in in the back-of-house. Thanks to my employee spies throughout the hotel, I knew where she was pretty much every moment of every day. But I didn't want to crowd her. I'd made that mistake once before. I told myself to be patient, we had plenty of time. *Good things come . . .*

I wanted Julie to have her mornings free to work out, so I'd instructed Francesca not to give her the early shift. It was nice to see her back to her old, overachieving ways. She was never one to settle for an ordinary life. I was still asleep when she left for her morning skis, but we had a camera on the loading dock, and I'd seen her coming back a few days in a row now. If I missed her, the cafeteria manager always let me know when she arrived for breakfast, all snow kissed and rosy cheeked for her omelet and toast. I know it sounds like I was stalking her, but I'd spent the last three years missing her, I wasn't going to let her get away again.

The arrival of her friends was a surprise, and not just to me. There was no way she would have invited them. I had no intention of blowing her cover. In fact, once I learned they were here, I made sure she had the weekend off. Francesca, her supervisor, already suspected we were more than friends, no point trying to hide it. And what did I care? We would be together eventually, it had always been our destiny.

I had thought about stopping by the Sidecar to say hello, but I wanted her friends to meet me as her independently wealthy boyfriend, not a hotel employee. So when Johnny the bartender phoned me to say she had just ordered a round of drinks, I told him to give her whatever she wanted on the house—"compliments of the manager," *bien sûr*. I didn't want to hover, but it was important she knew I was looking out for her, like before. But this time, *I* would be the man with the promising future who got to keep her forever.

The chairlift slowed when we got to the top. I scooted out from between the snowboarders and banked left toward the trees. The marked trails were skied out, but I never skied the marked trails. There was always untracked snow in the forest, and my favorite pastime was finding it.

I ducked under the trail-closed barrier and dropped into the narrow couloir. The snow was deep here, which meant I had to go fast to keep from getting stuck. Skiing powder is different than skiing groomers. You have to keep your body weight over your skis, because if you lean too far forward, you could catch an edge and flip. And on terrain this steep, if you start rolling, you may never stop.

I had seen it countless times in Chamonix: skiers who came for the thrill of fresh powder, but went too fast and got into trouble. Some froze to death before we could get to them. Others lost control and skied right over a cliff. Unlike in a resort, where rescuers use sleds to cart injured skiers off the mountain, the front face of l'Aiguille du Midi is too steep for sleds. If a skier could not ski out on their own power after some oxygen and first aid—a splint for their broken leg, a tourniquet for their bleeding arm—we had to leave them there. Leaving people to die was the worst part of my job. We did what we could to ease their suffering. Some of my fellow soldiers carried whiskey. I carried a gun. How the injured party chose to go was up to them.

There was no turning in the couloir, so I was flying when I popped out at the bottom. I entered the forest like a rock from a slingshot. The trees dictated my turns, like the pegs on a Plinko board. The key to skiing powder is to stay relaxed, let your upper body do the work while your legs gently steer. You have to anticipate. Trying to turn too sharply can knock you on your *derrière*. And you do not want to fall where no one's going to find you.

I got into a rhythm. The trees were a blur of emerald and white as I whizzed by. I didn't realize it had begun to snow until I emerged from the grove. I didn't recall there being snow in the weather forecast, but then again, I also didn't recall checking the forecast before I left.

I did a few more runs off the backside, then called it a day. I had some paperwork to catch up on back at the hotel, including filing an incident report about Julie's run-in with Madame Rousseau. That woman had been a thorn in my side since the day she arrived. I looked forward to never having to see her scowling face again.

I had to wait twenty minutes for the bus and didn't get back to the hotel until almost noon. Normally, I went in through the staff entrance, but I was cold and my boots had grown stiff, so I went in through the front door.

"Oh! Hi there," a woman said as I stepped into the lobby. I didn't recognize her, but there was no reason not to be polite.

"Hello."

"Sorry, of course you don't remember me, it was a horrific day," she offered. I didn't know what to say, so I just nodded and forced a smile.

"I'm Isabel," she said, offering her hand. "Julie's friend. Most people call me Izzy."

"Ahhh, yes," I said, removing my glove so I could shake. "Remy."

I didn't remember meeting her, but no harm in pretending.

"I didn't realize you were here too," she said.

"No?"

"We thought Julie was all alone. That's why we came." She smiled. And I was confused. Did she think I was . . . *a guest?*

"We've known each other a long time," I offered.

"It was nice of you to come for the service."

"Jeff was a friend too."

"Are you from here?" *Could she not hear the accent?*

"Not originally." *Obviously.* "Julie and I trained together." That was technically untrue. She trained with the ski team. I trained *tout seul.* But we skied together unofficially sometimes.

"I see."

There was an awkward beat of silence.

"I'm just waiting for the other ladies to come down," she said. "Three women, one bathroom."

"Yes, of course."

"We're meeting Julie for lunch in town." She smiled a little too brightly. I dare say she was almost . . . giddy.

"Wonderful. Nice to see you, Isabel."

"And you as well."

As I turned to go, it hit me. Isabel thought my presence here meant I was *with* Julie, as in, *her boyfriend*. And given my hopes for the future, I decided not to correct her.

CHAPTER 20
Izzy

"Where's Julie?" Christa asked as she and Suki stepped out of the elevator.

"She's meeting us at the restaurant," I replied. Julie had told me she had an "errand," but I knew why she didn't want to hang out in the lobby.

"What's going on with you?" Suki asked. After ten years of friendship, she could read me like a book, and knew I was sitting on something tantalizing.

"Let's walk."

A light snow was falling as we stepped out into the roundabout. I knew from my weather app that it was –8°C. I didn't need to know what that was in American to know that it was freeze-your-tits-off cold. The restaurant was a fifteen-minute walk from the hotel. I was grateful for Jeff's puffer, and after the revelations of the last five minutes, suddenly felt a little bit less guilty about wearing it.

"What's going on, Izzy?" Suki repeated.

"Did something happen?" Christa asked. I took a quick look around to make sure no one was within earshot. "Why are you acting so dramatic?"

"C'mon, spill!" Suki said, so I did.

"Remember that French guy at Jeff's funeral?"

"What French guy?"

"The tall, dark, and handsome one."

"What about him?" Christa asked.

"I don't remember him," Suki said.

"Yes, you do," Christa interjected, sucking in her cheekbones and puffing up her lips.

"Oh, that guy!" Suki said.

"He was hot."

"What about him?"

"His name's Remy," I told them.

"OK," Suki said.

"And?" Christa asked. So I dropped my bomb.

"He's here."

"You mean in Banff?" Suki asked.

"Not just in Banff," I said, "staying at the hotel."

"So?"

Good God, do I have to spell it out for them?

"Why would some hot guy from Julie's past be at the same hotel two weeks after her husband died?" I said. "Unless . . ." I raised my freezing cold eyebrows. And then they got it.

"Oh my God."

"Oh. My. God."

"Right?"

"But it's so soon," Suki said.

"Too soon," Christa added. And I raised my eyebrows again.

"Wait," Christa continued. "You think it started . . ."

And Suki finished her thought. "While they were still married?"

"It would explain a lot," I said, knowing what I was implying was harsh but also totally credible.

"You think Julie . . ." Christa couldn't get the words out.

Suki shook her head. "No, Julie wouldn't do that."

"She and Jeff were solid," Christa said.

And I just shrugged. Because I couldn't say how I knew otherwise.

"Well, I'm not jumping to conclusions," Christa announced.

"Me neither," Suki agreed. "It's probably just a coincidence. This is an extremely popular winter-vacation destination."

I didn't bother trying to convince them—didn't have to. The events of the next twenty-four hours would reveal all.

CHAPTER 21
Julie

The girls wanted to go shopping. I hadn't asked for the weekend off, but Francesca had given it to me, so after my Saturday-morning ski, I joined them for lunch.

I told Izzy I had an errand to run so I could meet them in town. I didn't want to hang out in the lobby and risk a staff member saying something that might reveal that I was an employee—and a disgraced one at that. My tip money had run out, and it would have been torture to watch my friends eat Banff's most mouthwatering croque monsieur on an empty stomach, so I ate my usual late breakfast in the staff cafeteria before heading out.

"Aren't you hungry?" Izzy asked after I didn't order.

"I ate at the hotel," I said. "I've been up since five." And, unlike much of what I'd said to my friends since they'd arrived, both statements were true.

The girls insisted I have a coffee, which they paid for, and then we were off to the shops.

"It's like being inside a snow globe!" Suki enthused as snow dotted our parkas and eyelashes. If not for the dread percolating through my chest, I might have been charmed by these picture-perfect streets, all decorated for Christmas, but all I could think about was how to get through the weekend without my friends finding out I was a fraud.

The town was bustling with tourists. I heard dozens of languages—French, Chinese, Japanese, a swirl of Slavic tongues that I couldn't identify. I did my best to return my friends' smiles as we walked arm in arm down the sidewalk, peeking into shops selling all sorts of local treasures—art, clothing, keepsakes, jewelry. I couldn't buy anything, but it would have been strange if I didn't try on a few hats and scarves.

"Oh my God, I love that on you—it goes with your eyes!" Christa said as I wrapped a periwinkle pashmina around my neck. We were in an upscale boutique on Banff Avenue filled with luxury cold-weather items—goose-down jackets, shiny leather boots, earmuffs made of fox fur and mink. I never imagined something as insignificant as a new scarf could dampen the pain of losing Jeff, but being wrapped in cozy, featherweight cashmere did make me feel a little better, if only for a moment.

"Let's all get something to remember our first girls' trip by," Christa said.

"Maybe we should all get the same thing!" Suki chimed in.

"We're not getting matching outfits," Izzy vetoed.

"Not the whole outfit," Suki clarified. "Just one part. Like a scarf!" she added, looking at me. The scarf around my neck was $200. Which was $199 more than I had.

"I barely have room in my closet for the stuff I brought," I lied. "I'm not buying anything new." I took off the scarf and hung it back on the mannequin.

"Well, I hope you have something fabulous for tonight," Christa said.

"What's tonight?" I asked, trying not to sound nervous.

"We're taking you to Sky Bistro!"

"Our treat," Suki added before I could object. "Our husbands insisted."

Sky Bistro was a five-star restaurant atop Sulphur Mountain. You had to take a gondola to get there. It had views of the entire park. I had always wanted to go. But when I was training, I couldn't afford to eat anywhere that Remy's employee discount didn't apply. And when Jeff was here, we rarely left the hotel, but for other reasons.

"They promised not to complain about the bill," Izzy said. I knew this was a splurge for her, and my heart swelled with gratitude for the sacrifices she was making to spoil me.

"You guys are too good to me," I said, shame catching in my throat. "I don't deserve you."

"We can't imagine what you're going through," Christa said.

"We want you to feel taken care of and loved," Suki added.

My eyes welled with tears. Not just out of grief, but also out of guilt. Because you don't love people by lying to them. But I was in too deep now. And I wanted their friendship, not their pity.

"Well, if we're going to get something matching, how about something practical . . . like this?" Izzy said, modeling a fur-lined cowboy hat. She strutted across the boutique like a supermodel on the catwalk, and we all laughed.

Despite my disappointed feelings that I couldn't buy anything for my friends or myself, it was a good day—the best I'd had since Jeff died. Christa bought some crystals in a woo-woo spiritual-healing store, Suki bought gloves (because apparently she'd forgotten hers), and Izzy and I pretended that there was nothing we wanted or needed.

We were cold and wet from the snow when we got back to the hotel, so we split up to shower and change, with a plan to meet back in the lobby in an hour. I didn't know that anyone was watching me, so I stopped to grab an apple off the counter before heading to my room. As I unlocked the door and peered inside, I looked for signs that someone had been there, but saw none. I walked to the bedside table and checked my phone. I hadn't brought it with me to lunch, roaming was too expensive. Plus I was already with the only people on this earth I wanted to talk to.

I took a quick shower, then wrapped myself in a towel and peered into my closet. It looked like the sale rack at REI. I had a half dozen pairs of ratty Rad Pants, four pairs of snow pants with bibs. There was an assortment of sweatpants from Roots, base layers from MEC, fleece zip fronts from Columbia and Marmot, and of course my flashy Team Canada separates. But not a single thing suitable to wear to a nice dinner out.

I imagined the girls all dressed up in jewel-toned sweaters and pearls. I could just tell them the truth—that I'd left my nice clothes at home. It's not like I didn't own any. Of course they had told me we were going out to a fancy dinner while we were clothes shopping . . . so why hadn't I bought something to wear?

As I stared into my closet, my father's parting words echoed in my mind. "You'll never amount to anything." At my wedding, instead of acknowledging my impressive past, he took a swing at my unremarkable future. "Now that your best days are behind you, you're wise to marry someone who can take care of you." And it wouldn't have hurt if it wasn't true.

I wasn't movie-star famous, but I didn't want to be seen out at a fancy restaurant in a pilly pullover from L.L.Bean. For one night, I wanted to look beautiful, successful, worthy of the gold medal I once wore proudly around my neck.

I didn't have any clothes that would match my fancy legacy. But I knew who did.

And as luck would have it, it was happy hour.

CHAPTER 22
Izzy

"You look amazing," I said to Julie as she stepped into the lobby like Julia Roberts arriving at a movie premiere. *Being in love looked good on her,* I thought, but couldn't say out loud. The girls weren't ready to accept that Julie had cheated on Jeff. And it was hardly appropriate for me to be the one to convince them.

Discovering Julie had a lover made me feel a smidge less horrible for sleeping with Jeff, but that wasn't the only reason the discovery made me happy. I loved Julie. If there was another man in her life, she wouldn't be alone. I may have envied her, but I didn't want her to suffer. She was a beautiful, accomplished woman who'd helped me through some difficult months when the boys were babies. I would always want the best for her.

"Good Lord, woman, you put us to shame!" Christa gushed as she jumped up to give Julie a hug.

We were all dressed in our wintery best—Suki in a cream-colored cable-knit sweater, Christa in tartan plaid trousers, me channeling Catwoman in a black turtleneck and knee-high boots . . . but Julie was in another league. Her shiny, ruby-red leather pants were painted on impossibly toned legs, and her tanned complexion popped against a bright-white angora sweater as decadent as marshmallow fluff. She was a Greek goddess, and we were mere humans. *Same as it ever was.*

"Sorry I'm late," she stammered, and I had to look closer to see her eyes were rimmed with red. *Has she been crying?* Her hands shook as she pulled on her gloves. In our three years of friendship, she had never been late. And it wasn't like her to be rattled like this. But it also wasn't like me to willingly travel to a place where the average winter temperature was twenty below, so maybe we were in a brave new world, where everything was opposite?

"I had them pull the car around," Christa said. "Shall we go?"

Julie answered by heading toward the door, so we all followed her out. If she hadn't lost her husband two short weeks ago, I would have asked her what was wrong, but of course we all knew . . . or thought we knew.

The ride to the base of Sulphur Mountain was about ten minutes. The roads were slippery, so I took it slow, occasionally pumping the brakes like my dad taught me on our day trips to Pine Mountain. Julie was probably wishing she'd offered to drive, as Christa and Suki were surely wishing I'd asked her to.

"It's really coming down," Suki remarked to make me feel better about driving like a grandma. The steady swirl of snow was hypnotic, and I made sure to shift my gaze from the horizon to the road every few seconds to keep from falling into a spell.

"I don't remember seeing snow in the forecast," Christa said.

"It's probably just a squall," Julie said. "Hopefully it will pass by the time we get there."

We'd been warned the parking lot might be full, but we got a spot right up front, which I mistakenly took as a good sign. The snow didn't ease up by the time we got on the gondola, but it was just as well. I was afraid of heights, and the gauzy veil of white blocked my view of the gaping nothingness below.

"Isn't this amazing?" Suki exclaimed as the door of the Smart-car-size capsule closed and we teetered up the cable. The cabin had twin benches that faced one another, with room for two on each one. I didn't realize when we got in that it would turn around before heading up the mountain, so was stuck sitting backward for the whole seven-minute ride.

"I wish we could see," Christa said.

"I prefer not seeing," I said. I had a flashback to the Space Mountain ride at Disney World—the first and only roller coaster I'd ventured onto in my adult life. That ride started off with a slow ascent into darkness too. And then turned into the reason I never went on a roller coaster again. I knew this was a tram, not an amusement park ride, but I was still sweating like I was in spinning class.

"Don't worry, Izzy. It's perfectly safe," Julie assured me. "This gondola has been running for almost seventy years."

The thought of the cables suspending us in midair being twice my age made me feel worse, not better, but I just smiled and nodded like my heart wasn't doing its best impression of a drumroll. I thought I heard Christa say, "I think Banff is neat," but then again, she might've said, "I like ham and cheese." I was so focused on watching my life pass before my eyes I couldn't be sure.

"Izzy," Suki said, putting a hand on me.

I was too afraid to open my mouth and give the scream stuck in my throat the opportunity to jump out, so I just said, "Mmmm?"

"We're here."

She indicated the door, which had parted down the middle like the Red Sea (*Praise Moses!*), and I wasted zero seconds getting to my feet and scurrying out. If the girls exchanged an amused look, I didn't know or care, so happy was I to get out of there.

"We're a few minutes early—shall we go to the observation deck?" Christa asked, and before I could say, "I'll be at the bar," the ladies took off toward the cliff's edge.

"Izzy, come!" one of them shouted, beckoning me up a snow-covered staircase. "We want to take a picture!"

"Do I have to?" I asked, but Christa was already handing her phone to some rando, and I'd be a party pooper if I didn't join.

"Stand next to Julie," Suki ordered as I stepped onto the platform. If it had been a clear night, I could have seen mountain peaks in every direction. But instead all I saw was snow soup.

"You can't see anything," I objected.

"We still want a picture," Suki said.

"It's not every day you're on the top of the world with your besties," Christa added.

"Say Banff!" our photographer said, and we foolishly obliged. She snapped the photo as our mouths made the *ff* sound, and if you don't believe me when I tell you we all looked like beavers, do it in the mirror and see for yourself.

"Thanks!" Christa said, pocketing her phone.

I turned around to peer over the railing. The falling snow was transforming the landscape in front of my eyes, softening rooftops and tree branches, blurring the horizon so you couldn't tell the earth from the sky. If there was a more on-the-nose metaphor for "everything is temporary," I couldn't think of one. Snow falls, and the world is aglow with newness. Snow melts, and the earth reemerges. Jeff was a storm— exciting and new. But storms don't last. It's the earth, not the storm, that endures. I found myself wondering what my future held. Was this metaphor meant for me? Was it time to come back to earth now?

"Izzy, come on!" Christa shouted. "Our table is ready!"

I walked down the stairs and into the mountaintop bistro with floor-to-ceiling windows. Blond wood tables were adorned with crisp, white napkins rolled like egg rolls with silverware filling. Fresh flowers plumed from hourglass vases with alabaster sand at the bottoms. In its simplicity, the decor let the surroundings be the star, and I imagined, on a clear night, the view rose to the task.

"Right this way, ladies," the hostess said, clutching menus to her chest.

We were seated at a four-top in the middle. Sitting inside that glassed-in room was like being in a snow globe in a perpetual state of being shaken. We were ten thousand feet high, surrounded on all sides by a violent swirl of white. It was terrifying and glorious, kind of like falling in love. Yes, it was inappropriate for me to have fallen for Jeff. But the first step in forgiving myself was to name it. Betrayal was betrayal. There was no blaming the music or the booze. I didn't ask to feel those feelings. But I indulged them, and that was wrong.

The waiter took our drink order (a double for me). As I was trying to decide between pan-seared scallops and gnocchi cacio e pepe, a man in a dark suit tapped on a glass like the best man at a wedding.

"Good evening, everyone," he said once he got our attention. "Forgive me for interrupting, I am the manager, with some unfortunate news."

I braced myself for the announcement that they were out of gnocchi, but the news was worse than that. *Way* worse.

"In our twenty years of business, this has never happened," he continued, "but the weather forecast just updated this squall to a blizzard. Out of an abundance of caution, we're going to have to cut your evening short."

There was a beat of stunned silence. I looked at Julie.

"By 'cut the evening short' does that mean no dessert?" I was not only starving, but I was also counting on three whiskey gingers to hold my hand on the way back down the mountain. I hadn't even had my first one yet.

"They can't run the gondola if it's too windy," Julie said. "I think he wants us to leave now."

A chorus of chair legs scraping the floor confirmed Julie was right. People were putting on their coats. It appeared I was not only going to have to go down the mountain hungry, but sober too.

"Oh man," Christa muttered.

"Sorry, Julie," Suki said.

"Don't apologize," Julie replied. And a moment later they were all pulling on their hats and coats and looking expectantly at me.

"Right. Coming."

The line to get into the gondola was long but moved quickly. Thanks to me, we were among the last to get in. I rode forward this time, hip pressed to Julie's, hands balled into fists. As soon as our cabin left the platform, my stomach dropped to the valley floor.

I squeezed my eyes shut.

"You OK, Izzy?" Suki asked.

"Mmm-hmmm."

I settled into rhythmic breathing. *Five seconds in . . . hold for five seconds . . . five seconds out.* I was on my second round when a gust of wind slammed into the cabin wall, swinging us like a pendulum.

"Oh God!"

I slid into Julie, then she slid into me. Side to side we ricocheted, all while descending into a swirling white abyss.

"It's going to be OK, Izzy," Julie soothed, but I could hear the uneasiness in her voice. I looked up at Christa and Suki. They were holding hands. I reached for Julie's, and she gave mine a squeeze.

"We'll be down in a couple of minutes," Julie promised.

The night wind screamed like a wild animal. Cold air blasted through the seams of the cabin. My teeth were jackhammering. Just as I thought things couldn't get any dicier—

Fwump!

The cabin slammed to a stop. The pendulum turned into a corkscrew. I pressed my palm to the window to stop myself from spiraling onto the floor.

"What's happening? Why did we stop?"

Julie peered out the window. I followed her gaze. The twinkle of city lights had been extinguished to a blanket of dull-gray nothingness.

"Julie?"

"It appears we lost power."

But the news was worse than that.

"Not just to the gondola, but to the whole town."

CHAPTER 23
Remy

When I got promoted from head of catering to manager, I was trained what to do in case of an emergency—a fire, a power outage, a flood, a violent crime, the passing of a guest. Nothing catastrophic had ever happened on my watch, so I'd never needed to use that training. Apparently, I was overdue. Because that night I had to deal with not one, but *three* catastrophes, all at the same time.

The power outage was easy. There was nothing for me to do. The hotel had a generator that kicked in automatically. It would keep all the vital services running: elevator, lights, heat, electronic door locks, even the dishwashers and washing machines—though we were advised not to do laundry until we knew how long we'd be without power.

The guests would have experienced minor disruptions. Lights would have flickered, showers would have been interrupted as water pumps stopped then restarted, and guests would have been without internet while the systems rebooted. The security system—door alarms and cameras—would also go offline. Normally, I had eyes and ears on every corner of the hotel, but I was going to have to be in the dark for a while like everyone else.

Sixty seconds after the power went out, my cell phone rang as predicted. Someone from engineering was supposed to call within five minutes of the outage to make sure systems were operating as they should. We would go through a checklist together. Our priorities were guest safety and comfort, in that order.

I picked up my ringing phone. The display said *unknown caller*. Given that this had never happened before, I didn't know if I'd be hearing from the engineer on call or some higher-up off-site. I did know that the number one rule in any catastrophe was to stay calm, so that's what I made sure to project.

"This is Remy."

I sat down at my desk in anticipation of going through the checklist. But the person on the other line didn't say anything for several seconds. *Did they not hear me answer the phone?*

"Remy speaking," I repeated, a little louder this time. I was about to hang up, when I heard a tiny squeak. No, not a squeak, a voice. A woman's voice. One syllable. A word I could not make out.

"I am sorry, I cannot hear you. Say again?"

And this time I made out the word.

"Help."

My heart sped up in my chest. For a brief second, I was back in Chamonix, getting a call from a skier in distress. They all started the same way, with that word.

"Who is this?" I pressed the phone to my ear. The reply was barely audible.

"It's . . ." I wasn't sure what she said after that. It sounded like *me*, but no one but my mother would identify herself to me as *me*, and she would say *moi*.

I tried another way to identify the caller.

"Where are you calling from?"

"901."

Room 901 was the penthouse.

"Ceci?"

"Help," she repeated, a little more forcefully this time.

For a second I was confused how she'd gotten my private cell number. But then I remembered I had given it to her after her reprimand of Julie, so she could call me about the spa day I had promised her.

"Emergency," she said. And then I heard a gurgling noise, something between a moan and the sound of sucking water.

"Stay put, I am on my way."

I grabbed my key card off my desk and sprinted out of my office toward the elevator.

"C'mon, c'mon!" I cursed as I pressed the button. Ten long seconds later, the elevator finally arrived and shot me up to the ninth floor.

I pounded on Ceci's door. Despite what I knew the woman had done to Julie when she'd entered without being invited, I didn't wait for an answer.

"I'm coming in!"

I waved my e-key in front of the keypad and turned the handle as soon as the green light appeared.

"Ceci?"

I pushed the door open and stepped into the living room.

Then clamped my hand over my mouth to catch my scream.

PART 2
Second to Die

CHAPTER 24
Monique

Ten seconds after I'd put my frozen lasagna in the oven, the power went out. You'd think someone with my background would be prepared for something as ho-hum as a power outage, but not only did I have no idea where my torches and candles were, I also had nothing else to eat.

"Oh, come on," I shouted into the darkness, as people who live alone do. And it was *really* dark. There was no ambient light streaming in through the window from a distant streetlamp—those were out too. It appeared the whole block had gone dark. I know I shouldn't admit it, but I was a little uneasy. I wasn't afraid of the boogeyman, but if other people were, it could make for a long night.

"Hey, Siri!" I called out because my phone had a light that I could use to find a torch. But Siri didn't answer. My phone was not in the room. I was alone in the dark with no phone, an empty stomach, and a cold lasagna. To make the situation even more colorful, the unexpected squall was approaching near-blizzard conditions, rattling my windows and dumping snow on a roof that should have been replaced three winters ago. But I was too hungry to worry about that now.

I got up from the kitchen table and groped my way toward the stove. I was pretty sure there was a book of matches in the junk drawer. The only problem with a junk drawer was that it's filled with junk.

Finding anything in there was a challenge even when the lights were on. I opened the drawer, stuck my hand in, and began my probe.

"OK, matches, I know you're in there."

My hands worked their way from front to back, inventorying as they went. A screwdriver, a box of paper clips, a set of Allen wrenches. Behind those were a stack of Post-its, a Master Lock, a canister—no, *two* canisters—of bear spray. Left to right, then right to left. I was thorough and methodical. I was also unsuccessful.

"C'mon, matches, talk to me."

I didn't smoke and wasn't a scented-candle person. I only ever used matches to light the stove when the clicker went out after my pasta water overflowed. So they had to be near.

On a hunch, I reached into the cabinet over the range, and—
Bingo.

I didn't remember putting them up there, but it was logical that's where they'd be. I was nothing if not logical. I couldn't do my job if I wasn't.

I lit the stove, then gave my eyes a few seconds to adjust to the cool-blue light. Next task was to find my phone. I already knew it wasn't in the kitchen, and I hadn't been upstairs since I came home. *Where did I leave it?*

I peered into the dining room to see my jacket draped over the back of a chair.

"Gotcha."

My Arc'teryx shell was still damp from when I shoveled the driveway. In my job, I couldn't afford to wait for the local kid to come around with his plow. I also couldn't afford to be too hungry to function. So after I extracted my phone from the inside pocket, I walked back into the kitchen to do something about my growling stomach.

I turned off the stove, then clicked on the phone light to explore options for dinner that didn't require electricity. You're not supposed to open the refrigerator in a power outage, but I wasn't worried about letting out the cold air. Anything I didn't want to spoil I could take outside and put in the snow. Also, there was nothing in the refrigerator.

After contemplating how I might barbecue a frozen lasagna, I turned to the pantry. It was slim pickings in there, but I wasn't fussy. I was eating tuna out of the can with a side of ketchup chips when my phone buzzed with an incoming call.

"Montpelier," I answered, keeping the phone on speaker so I didn't have to stop eating.

"Is your power out?" the chief of police asked.

"Yes, sir. For about ten minutes now."

"Looks like the whole town is dark."

Tuna-scented oil ran down my fork onto my hand. I had a napkin somewhere, but the Telus bill was closer. "How can I help?"

Banff was a small town. We had a whopping eight police officers on staff. Technically I was a detective, but given the sparseness of our resources, I was expected to answer all sorts of calls, from bear sightings to bar fights. I imagined the chief wanted me to go do some hand-holding. People get scared when they're plunged into darkness.

"I need you at the Banff Springs Hotel, stat," the chief said.

"Argument over a minibar charge?" I guessed. My joke was an unsubtle attempt to rib him for calling his highest-ranking police officer for what I assumed was a minor scuffle, because we only ever had minor scuffles. The hotel had a massive gas-powered generator. Unlike my house, it wouldn't be cold and dark. I didn't say it, but the chief was doing me a favor by sending me somewhere I could get a real meal.

"I'm afraid not, Detective."

It wasn't like the chief to call me by my rank. I put down my ketchup chips.

"What's going on, sir?"

We didn't have much crime in Banff. We didn't even have a proper jail—just a drunk tank, and even that was rarely used. Besides the occasional pickpocket or petty theft, most of our calls involved relieving restless teens of the alcohol they'd stolen from their parents. My heart sped up at the thought I might finally get to use my degree in criminology to solve an actual crime.

Besides being a luxury hotel, the Banff Springs had a furrier, a jewelry shop, an art gallery, several boutiques, and a half dozen eateries. The clientele was wealthy and enjoyed a multitude of extracurricular activities, not all of them legal. I braced myself to hear there'd been a robbery or a drug deal gone awry. But this call was about something much, much worse.

"Homicide."

I thought for a moment I'd misheard him. This was Banff, not Toronto or Vancouver. He must have sensed my confusion, so he clarified.

"A hotel guest was shot in cold blood. I need you over there now."

I flipped my chips in the trash and grabbed my coat.

CHAPTER 25
Monique

Unlike that book of matches, my sidearm was exactly where I knew it would be, and I had it holstered to my hip in three seconds flat.

I backed my truck down the driveway, glad that I had taken the time to shovel. Not that my four-wheel drive couldn't have handled a foot of snow. I wouldn't have spent a year's salary on it if it couldn't. *My car broke down* was not an excuse for being late to work, because there was no being late to work. People's lives depended on it, never more so than today.

I put the truck in drive and made fresh tracks down my unplowed street. My neighborhood was speckled with modest, single-family A-frames, just like mine. There were no vacation rentals in Banff—you had to work here to buy a home here—so my neighbors and I all knew each other. I made a mental note to check in on Mrs. Potter (who lived alone) when I got back, not knowing I would be in no condition to help anybody when this night was over.

Snow assaulted my windshield as I drove down the hill into town. The bright-white flakes looked like a swirling constellation of stars against the dark night, and I suddenly felt like Luke Skywalker piloting toward the Death Star, emphasis on *death*.

There were three squad cars already parked in front of the hotel entrance when I pulled up. With my arrival, half the Banff police force was on the premises. That's only four officers, but typically the only time we all saw each other was at the company Christmas party.

I turned off the engine and stepped out into the snow. A valet opened his mouth to tell me I couldn't leave my truck there, but I flashed my badge before he could get the words out.

Officer Jason Jarvis, the veteran of the force, was stationed at the front door and met my gaze as I approached.

"Have you been inside, J. J.?"

"Not yet."

There was too much to do to leave a third of my manpower guarding the hotel entrance. "C'mon."

I beckoned him to follow me. Bookish, bespectacled officer Kyle Purdy was standing by the giant gingerbread house, hands clasped in front of his waist, waiting for my orders. I was the only one not in uniform—not having to put on that itchy polyester pantsuit was one of the perks of being at the top of the food chain.

"Officer Purdy," I said as Jarvis and I approached. Normally we called each other by our first names, but there were a lot of eyes on us and I thought it best to keep it formal.

"Good evening, Detective."

"Who else is here?" I asked.

"Stafford. He was first on scene." Simon Stafford was our newest officer, fresh out of the police academy. We called him "Babyface," though after what he'd seen today, that nickname would no longer be appropriate.

"Where's the crime scene?"

"Room 901, the penthouse. I'll find someone to take you there."

Purdy pushed his Harry Potter glasses up his nose as he moved off.

"What's up with this power outage?" I asked Jarvis, because of the four of us, he'd lived here the longest.

"I was hoping you knew."

Purdy returned with a pale, chestnut-haired woman whose name tag identified her as Sydney from Sydney.

"This is Detective Monique Montpelier," Purdy said, and I flashed my badge right on cue. "She was hoping you could take her to room 901."

"Yes, of course. Let me just go make a key."

"You don't have a master key?" I asked.

"I work the front desk. We don't have access to the guest rooms." Finding out who *did* have access to the victim's room was critical, so I put my best man on it.

"Purdy, I need you to get a manifest of guests with their corresponding room numbers. Make sure it shows when they checked in and their scheduled checkout dates. Scan the list and highlight anyone scheduled to leave tomorrow."

"Copy that." He started to move off, but I grabbed his arm.

"I also need a list of all the employees who have access to the guest rooms. Highlight anyone hired in the last two weeks."

"Got it."

"Presumably everyone who works here had a background check—"

"I'll get those too."

"Thanks, Kyle." I let go of his arm. He moved off toward the front desk as Sydney returned with my key.

"Jarvis, you're with me."

"Yes, ma'am."

Then, to Sydney: "Lead the way."

Jarvis and I fell in behind Sydney as she led us toward the elevator. Jarvis looked exactly like you'd expect a small-town cop to look: graying beard, sprouting potbelly, twinkle in his eye. He was no longer agile enough to get your cat out of the tree, but he'd hold your hand until somebody did. Officer Jason Jarvis, or J. J., as everybody called him, dedicated his life to serving and protecting the citizens of Banff. There had never been a more committed cop in the history of the RCMP, and if he were a ballplayer, he'd be a first-ballot hall of famer.

A few guests glanced our way, but their lack of concern suggested they presumed we were here because of the power outage, which by now was old news. I was grateful to have the power failure as cover for our presence. The only thing we'd gain by people knowing there'd been a murder was a whole lot of panic.

Ding.

The elevator doors opened, and we filed inside. Sydney pressed the magnetic key to the keypad, then handed it to me.

"I programmed it to work all week, so you can come and go as you need."

"Thank you." I don't want to say I was excited to run my first murder investigation, but yeah, I was excited. I felt calm but energized, nervous but hyperfocused. Every cell in my body was on high alert. I had trained for this. I was ready.

"How long have you worked at the Banff Springs Hotel, Sydney?" I asked as we rode up the elevator. The poor girl looked terrified. Not likely she knew anything that could help my investigation, but there was no reason not to get to know her a little.

"About eighteen months."

"This must be quite a shock for you."

"We haven't been told what happened, ma'am."

"No?"

"Only that one of the guests had a medical emergency." *Interesting.* I would have thought news of a homicide would have traveled quickly among the staff.

Ding.

The elevator doors opened. Officer Simon Stafford was standing at the end of the hall with a trim, dark-haired man in a suit. By the irritated look on the man's face, I knew Stafford was doing his job and not letting him in the room.

"I can take it from here, Sydney. Thanks."

Jarvis started to follow me down the hall, but I stopped him with my hand.

"I need you stationed here," I said. "In case anyone wanders up to this floor."

"Copy that." I thought he'd be disappointed to be relegated to elevator duty, but his eyes registered relief.

I walked over to where Stafford and the irritated-looking man were standing.

"Officer Stafford."

"Detective."

"I'm Detective Monique Montpelier of the RCMP," I said to the dark-haired stranger. "And you are . . . ?"

"Remy Delatour," he said, rolling the *r*'s at the beginning and end of his name. I knew of, but had never met, the manager of the Banff Springs Hotel. The word around town was that he was a bit of a player. As I stood in front of him, looking into those baby blues and breathing in the warm vanilla notes of his cologne, it was easy to see what all the fuss was about.

"Have you been in the room?" I asked, pushing those other thoughts aside.

"I was the one who found her."

"And you called 911?"

"Yes."

"Approximately what time was that?"

He looked down at his phone. "5:33 p.m." I glanced at Stafford, and he nodded that he understood we would verify that with dispatch.

"How did you know she needed help?"

"She phoned me. On my mobile. At"—he peeked at his phone again—"5:27." We would verify that too. But also—

"You give hotel guests your cell phone number?"

"Madame Rousseau was not a typical guest." I was curious what he meant by that, but I was eager to examine the scene. I did have one last question.

"How was she when you got here?" If Mrs. Rousseau had seen her attacker and told Delatour, this case might be open and shut.

"Dead, I'm afraid." But no such luck.

"As I'm sure my colleague Officer Stafford informed you, we have to seal off the room now." *In other words, go away,* I almost said, but stopped myself.

"I understand," he said, though the fact that he didn't move suggested that he didn't. I turned to Officer Stafford.

"You were first on scene?"

"Yes, ma'am."

"Anything strike you?" I wanted to ask his first impressions before he forgot. He hesitated before answering.

"Stafford?"

"It was not quick and painless." He coughed into his fist to cover the tremble in his voice. Simon Stafford was a burly guy, a former hockey player who might have gone pro if his Achilles hadn't snapped. He had the bones of a draught horse and hands as big as boxing mitts. It was unsettling to see him rattled.

"Noted."

I prepared myself for the worst as I put the key to the lock. The light went from red to green. I opened the door.

Despite being a cop for almost twenty years, I had never been on a murder scene. I was prepared for the sight of blood. What I wasn't prepared for was the smell of it—sour, metallic . . . like rotten apples mixed with old car parts.

I saw the crumpled form of the victim on the floor by the desk. Given that EMTs had already declared her beyond help, the body was supposed to remain untouched until the medical examiner got here to determine the cause and time of death. I had a flash of panic. *Am I supposed to call him? Or did Stafford do that?* This was new territory for all of us, but I still cursed myself for not knowing the protocol.

I turned my attention to the victim. She was a slight woman in her early sixties with shiny, platinum blond hair. Darkening blood encircled a gunshot wound in the center of her chest. Her hands and arms were covered in blood, as if she'd tried to tamp the bleeding. There were crimson handprints everywhere—on the carpet, the drapes, the sofa, the phone. Stafford was right. There had been nothing quick and painless about her death. Someone either wanted her to suffer or was a piss-poor shot.

Other than the smears of blood, the room was tidy. A fleece blanket was neatly folded on the side of the couch. Twin throw pillows were fluffed and symmetrically placed. There was a full glass of wine next to an open laptop on the writing desk. Just one glass. Did that mean she wasn't expecting company?

I took out my phone and photographed the scene, then stepped into the hall to talk to Stafford.

"Did you call the ME?" I asked, even though I should have known the answer.

"Chief did that." *That's right. First on scene calls the chief of police. He calls the medical examiner and his star detective. Or rather, his only detective.*

Remy Delatour was still standing next to Stafford. It was unclear what he was waiting for, but I decided to take the opportunity to ask him one more question.

"Do you have any idea who could have done this?"

And when he hesitated before answering, I knew that he did.

CHAPTER 26
Julie

"We're going to die here on this mountain, aren't we?" Izzy asked through terrified sobs. Her gloved hands were balled into tight fists, her eyes bulged with terror. We'd been stopped in midair for over ten minutes, bouncing and swaying like a playground tetherball.

"Surely the gondola can withstand a little wind and snow," Christa said with her typical confidence. There was nothing "little" about the blizzard we were in, and the wind was damn near hurricane strength. But I opted not to say so.

"Definitely," I said, trying to match Christa's optimism. Unlike when you're experiencing turbulence in an airplane, there was no pilot to reassure us that what was happening was normal and would pass. We were left to worry and wonder.

"I mean, there must have been storms like this before?" Suki asked.

The three women were looking at me like I was some sort of expert on winter.

"It snows here all the time," I said. "Sometimes even harder," I added for good measure.

"You said the gondola has been here for almost seventy years," Christa reminded me.

"That's right."

"Then it's held in worse weather than this," she reasoned.

Without people in it, I thought, but didn't say out loud. I was no engineer, but the strain on the cable when the cabins were full had to be significantly greater than when they were empty. They had evacuated the restaurant all at once. *That's a lot of full cabins.*

"OK, but if the power is out, how do we get down?" Suki asked.

"I would imagine they have a generator," I replied, because if they didn't, that would be very bad for us.

"So why isn't it on?" she pressed.

There were several possible explanations: they didn't know how to work it, it's out of gas, the gas was frozen—diesel fuel freezes in subzero temperatures. If it's not treated, it turns into a giant petrol Popsicle.

"Oh my God, do you think it's broken?" Izzy's eyes were as wide as truck tires.

The generator is broken was also a possibility—but I didn't want to say it.

"Firing up a generator takes time," I said, hoping it was true.

"Takes longer if they don't have one," Izzy shot back.

"Of course they have a generator," Christa said. "They wouldn't leave people to die up here."

And then, not two seconds after Christa had spoken the word *die*—

"Oh God, oh God, oh God!"

A gust of wind lifted our capsule into the air and—

"Ahhhhhh!"

Dropped it like a hot potato. We bounced so high we hit our heads on the ceiling.

"Ow!" Suki cursed.

"Are you OK?" Christa asked.

"I bit my tongue." Suki stuck out her tongue so we could see it. "Ithz it bleeding?"

I leaned over for a closer look. There was a line of blood where she'd bitten it, but I didn't think she would bleed out.

"I think it's OK."

The snow was falling in sheets now. I had experienced squalls before, but never while suspended in midair.

"Why ithz thithz happening?" Suki lisped, and I had to wonder the same thing. I wasn't what you might call a God-fearing person. I didn't pray or believe in karma. My coaches had taught me that good fortune is the result of hard work. It's your talent, training, and perseverance that determine your lot in life, not some supernatural force. A poor result is the product of insufficient preparation—*full stop*.

"I can't get pregnant," Christa blurted, as if this was her last chance to confess that not everything came easily to her. "We've been trying for two years, even before we got married."

Nobody said anything. Christa was the one who always got what she wanted because she went out and grabbed it by the throat. It was disorienting to imagine her struggling, and we were all rendered speechless.

"I don't want kidzzz," Suki said with her tender tongue. "Never did." She said it like an apology. Perhaps because she was a schoolteacher and feared it seemed blasphemous.

"Funny how the universe works," Christa said.

"Not alwaythzz that funny," Suki replied, putting a consoling hand on Christa's shoulder.

The wind screeched like brakes on an aging tractor trailer. As snow pummeled the windows of our tiny capsule, I suddenly wondered if my coaches had been wrong about we humans exclusively controlling our destinies. Because right now, the universe wasn't just toying with us, it was furious. I looked down at my designer clothes—*Ceci Rousseau's* designer clothes—and had to consider the possibility that our perilous situation had something to do with me.

I looked up at the panicked faces of my friends. They'd traveled over a thousand miles to be with me in my time of need. If it was confession time, I owed them mine. Not just about why I'd come to Banff, but all the lies my ego had made me tell since I'd gotten here.

I didn't know if it would assuage the universe, but I owed it to my friends to give it a try.

"You guys," I started. "I have something to confess too."

And as they all looked at me, I braced myself to be not only widowed, but friendless too.

CHAPTER 27
Monique

Banff doesn't have its own ME, and given the weather, I knew it would be tough to get one here. As I steeled myself for a long night of waiting, I got a whiff of good news. Calgary's chief medical examiner was on his way to Lake Louise, the town just west of Banff. When my boss connected with him, he was just fifteen minutes away on Highway 1. As I waited for him in the hall outside the crime scene, I went over what I knew.

The hotel manager had identified the victim as Mrs. Cecile Montgomery Rousseau. His nonanswer when I'd asked him if he knew who may have done this had piqued my curiosity. While I'd been tempted to press him about his suspicions, I thought it better to wait until I had more facts. *Who was this woman? What was she doing in Banff? And who might have a motive to kill her in cold blood?*

Delatour told me "Ceci" had been a hotel guest since sometime in June. When I'd remarked that six months was a long time to stay at a hotel, he explained that she was going through a divorce. I'd tried not to jump to conclusions. Contrary to popular belief, it's not *always* the husband. Even when he's a soon-to-be ex-husband. But I wouldn't be doing my job if I didn't check him out.

I didn't want Delatour hanging around when the medical examiner arrived, so I had Officer Stafford escort him back to his office to make copies of Ceci's room charges. I wanted to see her spending patterns and if they had recently changed. I also wanted to know who was paying her bills. Love and money are the top two motivators of violent crime. Those billing statements would tell me a lot about both.

The elevator dinged open, and a dark-complected man in a snow-dusted parka stepped out into the hall. This wing of the ninth floor had only the one suite. It was unlikely any guests would wander up here, but I had stationed Officer Jarvis by the elevator just in case. The ME showed his credentials to my man, and a few seconds later was shaking my hand.

"Rajan Parhar," he said, wiping melted snow from his brow. "You must be Detective Montpelier."

I nodded. "Sorry to interrupt your vacation, Dr. Parhar."

"Don't apologize," he said as he slid out of his coat. "The way this weather is shaping up, you may have saved me a miserable night on the side of the highway."

"Are the roads that bad?"

"And getting worse." It was a comment I should have paid more attention to, but I had other things on my mind.

Dr. Parhar pulled a lemon yellow gown over his sweater, stretched a pair of booties over his shoes, and slid his hands into a tight-fitting pair of rubber gloves. "Are you coming in?" he asked, right before covering his nose and mouth with a stiff, white N95 mask.

"Oh. Um . . . I don't have PPE." I wasn't squeamish about getting up close and personal with Ceci Rousseau's dead body, but once again, I didn't know the protocol. *Am I supposed to watch? Help? Or give him space?*

My question was answered when he reached into his kit and pulled out an extra pair of gloves, booties, and a mask.

"You don't need the gown. Just don't lean up against anything."

"Right. Thanks." I pulled on the protective gear and followed him into the suite.

"How many people have been through here?" he asked. And I was a little embarrassed to tell him I didn't know.

"The hotel manager for sure," I started. "He's the one who found her. Simon Stafford was the first police officer on scene. Two EMTs arrived shortly after that, but when it was clear there was nothing they could do, he sent them away."

"Did they try to revive her?"

"I'm not sure." I cursed my inexperience. I should have had a log of who'd been through here and what action they'd taken. "I didn't get the call until Stafford determined it was a homicide." As soon as I said it, I knew it sounded like an excuse for not doing my job. And also, that I had offended Dr. Parhar.

"I see. Well, hopefully I can still be of assistance."

Suspected it was a homicide, I should have said. Not *determined.* Making the determination was *his* job. Good Lord, couldn't I do anything right?

"I'm grateful you're here," I said, even though the damage had been done.

"Victim is a woman in her early sixties," he said aloud as he wrote, "found in a supine position, fully clothed."

I took out my phone. "You don't have to take notes," he said. "I'll give you my report." So I put the phone away.

"No tears in the fabric, no visible bruising or other signs of struggle." He picked up her arms one at a time and bent them at the elbows. "No rigor mortis in the extremities."

He wiggled her jaw. "Slight rigidity in the jaw." He made another note, then took a penlight out of his kit and shone it in her eyes.

"Corneas are beginning to cloud." He pulled her lower eyelids down. "I don't see any petechiae." He glanced up at me. "Means she wasn't strangled," he offered. And I nodded like I knew that.

He put down the penlight and pulled two thermometers from his duffel—a square digital one to measure the room temperature, and an old-school mercury one to measure hers. "Ambient temperature is 18.5 centigrade. Victim's internal temperature is . . ."

He rolled her onto her side. "Can you give me a hand here, Detective?"

I held the victim steady while he pulled down her pants.

"35.1," he announced as he extracted the rectal thermometer from her butt.

I knew that average body temperature was between 36.5 and 37.5, and for some reason felt the need to say so. "So slightly less than normal."

"We don't know her normal," he replied. And I felt my face redden. He dropped the thermometer into a baggie. "You can let go now."

I removed my hand from her waist. He left her propped up on her side as he picked up his clipboard.

"When was she last seen alive?" he asked, his pen poised to write down my response.

"The hotel manager said she called him at 5:27 p.m., but was unresponsive when he got here six minutes later, at 5:33 p.m."

He glanced at his watch. "That's credible."

Credible didn't mean factual, but it was helpful to know Delatour might have been telling the truth.

He put down the clipboard and leaned over the body. "Cause of death appears to be loss of blood from a gunshot wound," he said, shining his torch into the gaping hole in her chest. His fingers bumped their way down her spine. "Bullet entered her midthoracic, approximately four centimeters to the right of T6—"

"Wait. She was shot in the back?"

"That's right. You can tell by the presence of fine soot here on her blouse. And the shape of the bullet hole."

"How long could she have survived after sustaining a wound like that?"

He shrugged. "Takes a while to bleed out."

"It would be really helpful to know what you mean by 'a while,' Dr. Parhar."

"I know you want to pin me down, but I can't give you a number. Death was not instantaneous, we know that. Could have been a few minutes, or half an hour, or more."

I flashed back to Stafford's first impression of the scene: *It was not quick and painless . . .*

"Shall I continue?" Dr. Parhar asked.

"Yes, please. Sorry."

"After entering the midthoracic, the bullet appears to have exited above the right breast."

"Exited?"

"Yes. The bullet went clean through. Came out right here," he said, pointing to a feathery wound just below her clavicle.

"So the bullet is somewhere in this room!" I said, a little too enthusiastically.

"It's wherever she was shot," he hedged. "But, yes, chances are it's somewhere in the suite. If I had to guess, I'd say the bedroom."

"Why the bedroom?"

"Look at the handprints. They get darker toward the bedroom door."

"You think she was shot in the bedroom, then dragged herself out here to call for help?" I asked.

"It's a good hypothesis," said the man with a hundred times more experience.

"Right now I'm more concerned with *who* shot her, than where," I said, because I was eager to make an arrest and didn't have the experience to know it was all connected.

"Bullet might tell you that," he said with a shrug. "You never know."

CHAPTER 28
Monique

"When's your forensic team coming?" Dr. Parhar asked as he stood up and took off his mask.

"This isn't Calgary, Doctor."

"Meaning?"

"I'm it."

He looked at me like I was bike tires on a monster truck.

"How long have you been doing police work?" he asked, not just to be conversational.

"Ten years in Banff. Eight years in Vancouver before that."

"Oh. So you know what you're doing." My job for the Vancouver Police had been all desk work. That's why I'd come to Banff, to get out in the field. But I didn't tell him that.

"This is my first murder," I confessed, even though he'd probably already figured that out.

"Can I make a suggestion?"

"Please."

"Work fast. Having a murderer on the loose makes people nervous."

Before I could ask if he was one of those people, Officer Purdy knocked on the door.

"I have those records you asked for." He held up a stack of printouts.

"I'll be right out."

Dr. Parhar was packing up his kit. So I took the opportunity to ask, "Any other words of advice?"

He spoke without looking at me. "Trust your instincts. In the absence of experience, they're all you've got."

"Right."

He abruptly stood up. "I'll arrange to have the body transported to the morgue here. I suggest you hold on to it for a week before you turn it over to the family."

"Why a week?"

"Because that's when my vacation is over."

And I guessed that was his way of telling me I shouldn't bug him with questions until he'd gotten his share of fresh powder.

"You can keep the booties," he called over his shoulder as he exited the suite. And that was his way of telling me he thought I needed all the help I could get.

I followed him out into the hall, then took the guest and employee records from Purdy. There were over a thousand pages. I had flashbacks to my desk job, which was all paperwork, all the time.

"How are you at treasure hunts?" I asked Purdy. He looked at me blankly.

"Detective?"

"Somewhere in that suite is a bullet . . ."

I slipped off the booties and offered them to him.

"And you want me to find it," he said, somewhat gleefully.

"You have gloves?"

He responded by pulling a pair out of his pocket.

"Try not to touch anything," I said.

"Copy that."

Officer Purdy slipped on his gloves and my booties, then disappeared into the room. Purdy was a good cop. He knew his way around a gun and spent more time at the shooting range than all of us put together. Not that we ever shot at anything. But I knew weapons were a hobby of his. He would have been the right man for the job at hand, even if he weren't the only man for the job at hand.

I didn't have to hang out in that hallway, but I couldn't very well pore over confidential records while sitting at the bar, so I plunked down on the floor to look at what Purdy had rustled up.

Given that there were no signs of struggle, the murderer had to have been someone who'd either been invited up there or had a key. I wanted to know the names of everyone who had access to the ninth floor. That would include some (but not all) employees, registered guests, and any guests of guests. Guests of guests would be anonymous, but the other two groups I could track. And thanks to Purdy, I had a list of all of them.

Going through the list of registered guests would take hours, so I put that aside and started with the staff. The Banff Springs Hotel had seven hundred and twenty-two employees. Outside the executive staff (sales, business development, upper management), most of the employees were seasonal, arriving for training in either October (for the winter season) or April (for summer). Most stayed on for six months to a year, but a few stayed longer, and a few didn't work out. I didn't assume the killer was an employee, but it was the smallest group of people with access to this part of the hotel, so that's where I decided to start.

Of the seven hundred and twenty-two employees, only ninety-eight of them had all-access keys. They fell into four categories: management, room service, security, and housekeeping. I went through those ninety-eight names one by one to see if anything jumped out at me. As expected, except for management and security, which only comprised eighteen of the ninety-eight, all the other employees were seasonal. Forty-two started in October. Thirty-two had been hired in the spring, and five over the summer. Number ninety-eight of ninety-eight, a Ms. Julie Weston Adler, had been hired one week ago.

I paused on the name. It was familiar to me, but I couldn't place it. *How do I know that name?*

I picked up the stack of background checks. Each one was a page. There wasn't much information in them. They just indicated if a given employee had ever been arrested and/or convicted of a crime. Purdy had put them in alphabetical order. Adler's should have been on the top. But it wasn't.

I flipped to the bottom of the pile to see if Ms. Weston Adler was with the *W*s. She wasn't. The pages were numbered, but I counted them to make sure none were missing. Every employee had an affiliated background check, except for one: Ms. Julie Weston Adler.

"Detective?" I looked up to see Officer Purdy standing in the doorway. "You're going to want to see this."

I put down my stack of papers and followed him into the suite.

"She may have died here in the living room, but the trail of blood appears to originate in the primary bedroom," Purdy said, echoing what Dr. Parhar had observed. "So that's where I began my search."

He waved me into the bedroom. There was a stone fireplace across from the bed. Purdy pointed to the floor right in front of it . . . to where a spent bullet was lying on the carpet.

As I snapped a picture, Purdy offered his theory.

"See this nick in the fireplace?" he said, pointing to a fresh-looking chip just below the mantel. "I'm guessing after the bullet went through the victim, it bounced off the stone onto the floor."

"Go on."

"Can I pick it up?" he asked.

I was going to take it into evidence, not leave it there, and I already had a picture of where it had been found.

"Yes."

He scooped it off the ground and turned it over in his palm. It looked more like an old penny than a bullet—that trip through the victim's chest had done quite a number on it.

"Do you know what kind of bullet it is?" I asked.

"Nah, it's too mangled. But that casing should tell us."

He pointed to a spot under the bed—where a shiny copper shell casing was waiting to be discovered.

"Good eye," I said as I snapped a photo, then slipped on a glove to pick it up. He held out his hand, and I placed it in his palm.

"Interesting," he murmured as he examined it.

"What?"

"It's from a .22 LR."

"LR?"

"Long rifle. Like you use for shooting squirrels." *Wait, what?*

"Someone brought a rifle up here?" I tried to imagine somebody attempting to sneak a gun the size of a baseball bat through the lobby.

"Yeah, but you wouldn't waste that bullet on a squirrel."

"Why not?"

"It's a Lapua Polar."

"What's a Lapua Polar?"

"Expensive. Made in Germany. Their logo is right there on the side of the casing." He pinched it between his thumb and forefinger so I could see.

"If not for hunting squirrels, what's a Lapua Polar bullet used for?"

"Target shooting. Biathlon, mostly. They're engineered to perform in cold weather."

And I remembered how I knew that name.

CHAPTER 29
Julie

"You guys, I have something to confess too," I said. There were a lot of things I needed to tell them. And the way the wind was swatting our plexiglass cabin around like a cat with a ball of yarn, I feared it was now or never.

So how far to go back? I'd been lying to Izzy, Suki, and Christa since the moment we met. I paraded around town with my gold bangles and Chanel bag like I was some sort of superstar. But I was no superstar. I was a quitter. Everything fancy I owned was from Jeff. I'd done the exact same thing I'd judged Ceci for doing: married into it. Which was probably why I despised her. She reflected back at me what I didn't like about myself.

People assume decorated athletes are rich, but the endorsement and sponsorship money I'd made as a professional athlete dried up the minute I hung up my skis. All I had to show for my decade of competing was a single gold medal. I was proud of that medal, but it should have been the beginning of my career, not the end. BMW and RBC were ready to pay me big money to wear their logos on my chest. That's the funny thing about sponsors. In the beginning, when you're broke and need help, no one will give you a nickel. But once you've clawed your way to the top, they line up to pay your bills. The less you need them, the more they give you. And they were ready to give me the world.

But instead of accepting my hard-earned pot of gold at the end of the rainbow, I walked away. Because of Jeff.

I wasn't resentful, not at first. I had been training seven days a week since I was sixteen. I needed a break. I threw my energy into planning a wedding and a California-cool life. I shopped for a ring, a dress, a house, new friends to show them off to. I went back to school, got a degree, a job. And then there was nothing else to chase. I had "arrived." Except being dependent on a man for a lifestyle was never something I'd aspired to. So not "arrived" . . . *settled*. I masqueraded around town like Cinderella at the ball, when in reality I was the coach that turned back into a pumpkin.

I knew it wasn't fair to blame Jeff. It had been my choice to leave Canada to marry him. But by letting him take me away from everything that made me *me*, I turned him from my prince to my oppressor. The few times I floated the idea of going back to Canada to compete for another Olympics, he freaked out—"I'm building a company here! I've been working my whole life for this! You can't just ask me to walk away from everything I've built!" But that's exactly what he'd asked me to do: walk away from a career. He seduced me to hitch myself to his wagon, and I let it pull me instead of pulling myself. And even though I did it willingly, he was my coconspirator.

I hated being dependent on a man for my quality of life. It wasn't long before the self-loathing turned to rage. I tried to take it out on my workouts—pushing to the point of exhaustion, hoping I could drown out my emotional anguish with physical pain. But my disgust with myself grew and grew. Jeff felt my anger. How could he not? I may not have pulled the trigger that fateful day, but I still killed him. If he'd been depressed, I was the one who'd made him that way.

I didn't know if confessing all would help Suki, Christa, Izzy, and me out of our current predicament, but I decided it was time to spill. They might not have known I was living a lie, but the weather gods did. I was going to tell my friends what I really was. A liar, a thief, and the person who made my husband so miserable, killing himself was the only way to escape.

But before I could utter another word, Izzy interrupted by shouting at the top of her lungs. "I did a really bad thing! Really, really bad. I'm a terrible person and a terrible friend."

All eyes went from me to Izzy. And then, right after she spoke those words, as if her willingness to spill her secret were the trigger the universe was waiting for, the gondola started to move. And she was so overcome with relief she didn't see the pall of horror that had descended over my face.

"Oh my God! We're moving!" Christa shouted. "We're actually moving!"

And then everyone was laughing and hugging like whatever terrible thing Izzy had done had been forgiven and forgotten. Except for me. Because I knew what it was.

CHAPTER 30
Monique

"Tell me about Julie Weston Adler," I said to the hotel manager as I stood in front of his desk. Stafford was standing behind me, Jarvis was still on elevator duty, and I'd sent Purdy, my new ballistics expert, to the security office to pull tapes from the camera trained on said elevator.

"I printed Mrs. Rousseau's charge history," Mr. Delatour said. "All four hundred pages of it. Would you like to see it?" He leaned over and pulled a stack of papers from his laser printer.

"Right now I want to talk about Ms. Weston Adler."

"What do you want to know?"

"Let's start with how she came to work here," I said.

"I had an opening in housekeeping, so I hired her." His tone suggested that he thought this line of inquiry was a waste of time, but my instincts disagreed.

"What I don't understand is, why would a former Olympian take a job as"—I looked down at my notes to make sure I got her title right—"a room attendant?"

He made that face all French people do to indicate they couldn't care less. "You'll have to ask her." Either Remy Delatour had cast himself as the tough guy in an imaginary police procedural, or he had something to hide. If I were in a betting mood, I'd put my money on the latter.

"I'm asking you," I said, trying to match his tough-guy energy.

"She needed a job, I guess."

"You didn't run a background check."

"Is that a question?"

I rephrased.

"Why didn't you run a background check?"

"I didn't have to. Like you said, she's a former Olympian."

"Did you know Mrs. Adler personally?"

"Of course I knew her personally. She worked for me."

"What about before you hired her? In her Olympic days?"

"She came here sometimes," he said, then tried to explain it away. "The Nordic Centre is in Canmore."

"So you were . . . friends?"

"She was very busy with her training," he said. Then he probably realized I would find out he'd been at her wedding, so he added, "But, yes, we were friends."

"She needed a job, so she came to her old friend."

He made that couldn't-care-less face again.

"I gather Adler is her married name," I said. "What do you know about her husband?"

"You mean besides that he's dead?"

And that was news to me.

"I figured you knew, being a cop and all."

I looked at Stafford. He was already googling on his phone. "Husband of Olympian takes his own life," he read aloud.

I got a prickly feeling on the back of my neck.

"How did he do it?" I asked Stafford.

"Says he shot himself. Just two weeks ago."

That prickle spread down my arms.

"So her husband shoots himself, and she comes back to Canada to work for you."

"That seems to be the chronology," the Frenchman said, pronouncing *chronology* like *chronoll-oh*-jhee.

"Is she working tonight?"

"I'll have to check her schedule."

I sat down in the chair. He took the hint, got on his computer.

"No. She's off tonight."

"Did you see her?"

"What, tonight? I don't remember," he said. And I would have believed him if he hadn't added, "I see a lot of people."

This conversation was going nowhere. Perhaps others would be more forthcoming. I looked down at the list of employees. Interviewing them one by one would take all night. As I tried to decide who to summon first, my phone buzzed in my pocket.

"What's up, Purdy?"

"Hey, boss," he said. "I'm here in the security office, going through the surveillance footage."

Delatour's claim that he had called 911 at 5:33 p.m. had been confirmed by dispatch, so I'd told Purdy to work his way backward from there, call me if he saw anything unusual.

"And?" I asked.

"There's something you need to see."

CHAPTER 31
Izzy

I didn't know if confessing my sin would save us from certain death, but I had to do something. I had already prayed and peed my pants, there was nothing else left to try. Suki and Christa had summoned the courage to spill their secrets—why shouldn't I? Perhaps it was far-fetched to think our lives depended on it, but I couldn't risk staying silent if they did.

"I did a really bad thing!" I shouted before I lost my nerve. "Really, really bad." I was going to tell them everything—how I'd slept with Jeff, and all the lies I'd told to cover it up. I didn't care if they never forgave me. I just wanted us to get off this mountain alive.

"I'm a terrible person and a terrible friend."

My marriage was a disappointment, I would say. I'd been miserable and desperate for attention. We were drinking, but I knew better. He didn't want to, but I made the first move. I seduced him. The confession was on the tip of my tongue. But before I could spit it out—

Ka-chang!

The cabin shuddered as the cable came to life. We heard the sound of a motor running, of gears grinding. Our bodies lurched in unison as our capsule took flight.

"We're moving!" Christa shouted. "We're actually moving!" And we jumped up and hugged. As tears of relief streamed down our faces, the old adage that some things are better left unsaid hit me like an avalanche. No good would have come from me confessing my affair. Yes, it was wrong to lie, but that didn't make it right to tell.

Christa and I held hands for the entire ride down the mountain, counting the seconds until we arrived at the base. The moment the door opened, we all tumbled out in a heap.

"Hallelujah!" I cried out, raising my arms toward heaven. All around us, the other restaurant goers were cheering and laughing. I would have kissed the ground if it weren't so damn cold.

We followed the crowd off the platform and into the parking lot. The snow was up to my shins and rising like bread dough. Julie must have read my mind, because she held out her hand, palm open.

"I'll drive," she offered, and I happily handed her the keys.

"Yes, please." Her face was drawn. Her eyes were distant. I understood how the ordeal would make her long for Jeff, just as it had made me miss my loved ones, so I gave her space to feel her feelings . . . not knowing they were about something else.

The road hadn't been plowed, so the ride down the hill was slow going. Julie handled the conditions like a pro, keeping the car in second gear on the steep parts and accelerating into the turns. I thought her steely expression was concentration, but I should have known better.

"My God, the whole town is dark!" Suki said as the road straightened out at the base of town. It wasn't just the streetlamps and traffic signals that were out. All the restaurants and shops were dark too.

"Has this happened before?" Christa asked.

"Not that I'm aware of," Julie said.

The darkness was unsettling. I pushed back thoughts of the apocalypse as we drove down streets buried in snow. I reminded myself that if aliens were invading, there was no way their first stop would be Canada. The Canadians were the nicest people on the planet. They were kind to foreigners, had free health care, and were quick to offer an apology, even if it wasn't their fault.

The sidewalks were largely empty, except for a smattering of people gathered in the middle of the block.

"What's going on over there?" Christa asked.

As we approached, I saw the telltale yellow arches of a McDonald's. Two people in fur-hooded jackets were handing out white paper bags. I leaned out the window and shouted at a passerby who had just received one.

"Hey! What's going on?"

"They're giving out hamburgers!" came the joyous reply. "So they don't go to waste." *See what I mean about Canadians?*

"Oh my God, I'm starving," Suki said. "Can we stop?" And five minutes later we were parked and standing in knee-deep snow, eating cheeseburgers and fries.

"This is wild," Christa said, licking the salt off her fingers. "I've never seen so much snow in my life."

"Nature is amazing," an awestruck Suki said.

I looked at Christa's and Suki's smiling faces. And I felt something I hadn't felt for a long time. I'm not sure, but I think it was gratitude. Gratitude for these friends, this trip, laughter, hot food on a cold night. Why did it take nearly losing everything to make you feel grateful for what you had? I never ate McDonald's. Yet these paper-wrapped burgers were the best thing I'd ever tasted. It wasn't the food that was different. It was me.

As we climbed back in the car, I thought about what a horrible mistake it would have been to have told Julie about Jeff and me. Confessing only brings relief to the confessor. The kindest, most caring thing I could do for my friend was to keep my mouth shut, let her remember her husband not as a cheater, but as someone who loved her with all his heart. Which I had no doubt was true. I was a blip. She was his forever. I had no right to take that from her.

But I should have known from the way she avoided my gaze that I already had.

CHAPTER 32
Monique

The security office was across the lobby and three hallways down from Remy Delatour's office. I studied the hotel manager's face as he escorted Stafford and me there. Did he know what we were about to see? And why wasn't he more eager to help? There was a murderer on the loose in his hotel, he should be bending over backward to help us. Why was interviewing him like pulling teeth?

Officer Purdy was waiting outside the office when we approached.

"You find something interesting, Officer Purdy?"

"I'll let you be the judge of that." He indicated for me to go inside, then filed in behind Stafford and Delatour. I could have asked the prickly hotel manager to stay outside—everyone was a suspect at this point, including him. But I needed his cooperation and didn't want to risk putting him even more on the defensive.

The security office was wall-to-wall monitors. I counted sixteen. Thirteen of them were broadcasting live images—of the lobby, the loading dock, the hallways, the restaurants. Three of them were cued up to play back what Purdy had discovered.

"This is Jerzy," Purdy said, indicating the goateed security officer sitting at the controls.

"Hello, Jerzy."

"Ma'am."

"Jerzy has been working at the Banff Springs Hotel for sixteen years."

"I imagine you've seen it all," I said.

"Not all. But quite a bit."

"I'll let Jerzy walk you through the timeline." Purdy took a step back, so I had a clear view of the monitors.

"Normally we would have had no idea where to start," Jerzy said, in an accent that made his *w*'s sound like *v*'s. *Polish, maybe?* "But Mrs. Rousseau has been here for many months. I've come to know her habits."

He pressed play on a recording showing the entrance to the busy Rundle Bar. I saw a family of four filing out. Then a couple holding hands drifting in. And then—

"There she is, exiting the bar."

I recognized the slim frame and platinum bob. The footage was time-stamped 4:40 p.m.

"Is that time stamp right?" Stafford asked. God bless him, he was taking notes.

"Yes. Always."

"Does she go to the bar every day?" I asked.

"Without fail. Happy hour is three to five," Jerzy explained. "Normally she stays until the end, but today she left early." I didn't know if that last part was relevant, but I nodded to Stafford to make a note.

Jerzy paused that video, then pointed to the next monitor, where he had a different camera roll cued up.

"Here she is two minutes later, at 4:42, entering the west elevator," he said as he pressed play. "We don't have a camera in that elevator, but we can pick her up exiting on the ninth floor."

He paused that video and directed our attention to monitor number three. A fish-eye lens on the ninth floor showed her walking to her room, opening the door, then disappearing inside. The time was 4:43 p.m.

"OK, so we know she left the bar at 4:40 p.m. and got back to her room on the ninth floor at 4:43 p.m."

"We also know she wasn't alone," Jerzy said.

My heartbeat quickened. No one had accompanied her back to her room. Did that mean someone was there waiting for her?

Jerzy pressed rewind. I watched the time stamp on the video roll backward: 4:42, 4:41, 4:40 . . . He froze the tape at 4:39, as someone who wasn't Ceci was entering Ceci's room.

"Who's that?"

He rewound the tape a few more seconds, then played it at half-speed as a woman dressed in a slate gray housekeeping uniform exited the elevator pushing a cart.

"A room attendant?" I asked Delatour, and he nodded.

All eyes were glued to the video as the room attendant unlocked the door to Rousseau's suite and pushed the cart inside. I always thought housekeepers left their carts in the hall, so I asked, "Is it normal to push the cart into the room like that?"

"It's not unheard of," Delatour replied. *So not normal.*

Jerzy scrubbed forward. 4:41, 4:42 . . . We once again saw Mrs. Rousseau enter at 4:43. Jerzy let the video roll at four times normal speed. 4:44, 4:45, 4:46 . . . At 4:47, the door opened. Jerzy slowed the playback to normal speed so we could see it was the housekeeper pushing her cart back into the hall.

"Holy shit," I muttered.

"That's what I said," Purdy echoed.

"Did anyone else come in or out of that room after that?"

Jerzy and Purdy exchanged a look.

"What?"

"We don't know," Purdy said.

"What do you mean *you don't know*? Can't you run the tape?"

"The tape got erased."

"What?! How?"

"The system reset after the power outage," Jerzy said. "A chunk of the footage was deleted. Honestly, we're lucky to have this."

"How big a chunk?"

"We lost an hour. From five p.m. to six p.m. It's back online now."

Under normal circumstances, a camera malfunctioning during the exact same time frame as a murder would have sabotage written all over it. But I knew that when computer systems were improperly shut down, unsaved data was sometimes lost.

"Can we get it back?" I looked at Purdy. He looked at Jerzy.

"I'll look into it, but not likely."

"OK, so let's recap," I said to my team, focusing on what we could confirm. "The room attendant entered the room at 4:39. Mrs. Rousseau came back to her room four minutes later, at 4:43. They were in there together for four minutes, until 4:47. Mrs. Rousseau called for help at 5:27, is that right?" I asked Stafford, knowing he'd been keeping notes.

"That's right," Stafford confirmed.

I flashed back to the blood-soaked room. It was forty minutes between when the housekeeper exited and the victim made that phone call. We knew from the bloody handprints everywhere that she had been bleeding for a while. Dr. Parhar had said it could have taken a half hour or more for her to bleed out. There was no way of knowing how long it had taken her to pull herself off the floor and get to her phone. Or if Delatour was her first call. It's possible she'd tried to call others in that time. I made a mental note to check her phone records to see if we could account for at least some of those forty minutes.

"Do we know the identity of the housekeeper?" I asked, squinting at the grainy footage.

Jerzy tapped on his keyboard to zoom in on the image. The house-keeper's face was pixelated, but recognizable to someone who knew her.

"Mr. Delatour?"

"That's Julie Weston Adler," Delatour said. *Wait. What?*

"I thought you said she was off duty."

146

"She was."

"So what was she doing in uniform?"

Delatour didn't answer.

"Mr. Delatour?"

"I don't know."

There was no question Mrs. Rousseau had been shot in her suite—we had the spent bullet and the casing on the scene. Julie Weston Adler was the last person seen going in there . . . in her uniform, when she was off duty. And she'd still been in the room when Rousseau got back. I had one blind spot—those twenty-seven minutes between when the security cameras failed and the victim called Delatour. But even with that break in the surveillance footage, the evidence that Julie Weston Adler had done this was overwhelming. Enough to take the next step.

"I'm going to need Ms. Adler's address," I said, looking at Delatour as I dialed my phone.

"She lives here, at the hotel," Delatour said. "Most of the employees do."

The chief of police answered on the first ring.

"Detective?"

"How quickly can you get me a search warrant?"

"I'm dealing with a citywide power outage."

"I have a suspect. If I find what I'm looking for, I can make an arrest tonight."

Banff was a tourist town. Christmas was coming. We needed someone in custody.

"Give me ten minutes."

CHAPTER 33
Remy

The warrant to search Julie's room came in on my private fax machine. Detective Montpelier, or "mont-*peel*-yur," as she improperly pronounced it, was standing over me like an umbrella in a rainstorm, waiting for it to roll off the machine. She ripped it out of my hands the moment it finished printing.

"I'm going to need you to let us in that room," she said, waving the paper in front of my face.

"Of course."

I did not mean to be uncooperative. I wanted their suspect in custody, but not for the same reasons the police did. I wasn't afraid for myself or my guests. We weren't dealing with a serial killer here. Ceci's death was personal. Anybody who knew her could tell you that. The police wanted to catch the killer to keep people safe. That was their job. It was my job to run a hotel. Once news of the murder got out, the guests would panic. The only thing that would stop a mass exodus was an arrest, so if I could help them make one, I would.

The Banff Springs was one of the only hotels in town with enough generator power to keep all the lights on and the drinks flowing, and the place was hopping. I belonged in the lobby, mingling with guests, charming them to come back next year. But I couldn't trust anyone else to babysit this search. I wanted to be there when they found what they were looking for, as I knew they would. I'd been in there and seen it myself.

I had also seen what they'd just watched on video. I wasn't stalking Julie. I just wanted to talk to her, to let her know I'd chatted with her friend Isabel, but not to worry—I hadn't, and would never, say anything about her working here. I also wanted to make sure she didn't tell her friends I was her boss, so that in a few weeks, when my money came in, we could come out as the power couple we were destined to be. People forever associate you with the job you had when they met you. I didn't want to be known as that failed athlete turned hotel manager who got lucky with an investment—even though that's what I was. If our future life was going to include these friends, I wanted them to see me as a catch, not a consolation prize.

So I went to talk to her after she'd returned from shopping with her friends. When I saw her getting into the elevator wearing her uniform and pushing a cart, I almost called out to her. But then the doors closed. I watched the digital display as the elevator climbed, two, three, four, five, six . . . all the way to the top floor. Ceci's floor. She wasn't on the clock. I was confused why she would go there. Until I wasn't.

Julie's room was two hallways and three turns from my office. I took the detective and her posse through the back-of-hotel, where only staff members are allowed. There was no need to parade them through the guest areas and churn up concern.

"Here we are," I said as we reached Julie's room. Detective Montpelier pushed past me and pounded on the door. I knew Julie wasn't home, but I kept my mouth shut. The less you say, the less they can pin on you. And while not an accomplice, I was not innocent either.

"This is the RCMP—open the door," Montpelier shouted. When there was no answer, she stepped aside so I could unlock it.

"Wait outside," the detective ordered as the light went from red to green. She and her two goons had their guns drawn, and I was all too happy to get out of their way.

"RCMP!" Montpelier shouted into the room. "We're coming in!"

The next part happened fast. I stood with my back against the wall as the three officers charged into the room like racers from the starting gate.

I heard their boots thumping across the carpet, the sound of doors opening with force.

"Closet clear!"

"Bathroom clear!"

I heard dresser drawers opening and closing, the hollow whoosh of clothes hangers scraping across a metal bar.

"Detective!" one of the dogs shouted. And the scuffling abruptly stopped.

There was a beat of silence. *Did they find it?* I peeked in the door to see that, in fact, they had.

"This is Chief Hendricks," a voice boomed out of the detective's open mic.

"I need an arrest warrant, and I need it now," Detective Montpelier told the chief. "I found the murder weapon." And I knew as bad as things had been for Julie Weston Adler, they were about to get a lot worse.

CHAPTER 34
Monique

I never watched boxing or UFC. The idea of someone beating another person into a bloody pulp for sport was vulgar and inhumane to me. I always thought athletes like fencers, archers, target shooters, and biathletes were different: disciplined, skilled, nonviolent. But when I saw that .22-caliber rifle under Julie Weston Adler's bed, I questioned my assumption. Perhaps it says something about a person if they are drawn to a sport that entails mastering a deadly weapon? Or maybe the process of mastering it conjures fantasies of using it in other ways?

I asked Delatour to put hotel security on room 901 so I could have Jarvis back, then gathered my three-person team outside the suspect's room. The idea that Julie Weston Adler would come back to the scene of the crime seemed crazy, but so did murdering a woman in cold blood. I had no idea what Adler's next move would be, only prayed to God it wasn't to kill again.

"This is our suspect," I said, pulling up a picture of the former Olympic biathlete on my phone. I used her hotel-ID photo because it was the most recent, but there were hundreds of others to choose from—on the podium with medals around her neck, shooting a rifle identical to the one we'd found in her room, walking down the aisle to wed her now-dead husband. And what about that dead husband? His death had been ruled a suicide, but given this new development, was it worth a closer look?

With the issuing of the arrest warrant came an APB to all the police forces within a hundred kilometers of Banff. Because of the power outage and subsequent shutdown of the hotel's security cameras, we had no idea when, or even if, the suspect had left the hotel. But if she had, it was unlikely she would get very far in this storm. Still, we wanted her picture on the walls of every precinct from Calgary to Kicking Horse. The good news about the mountains is that there's only one way in and one way out. Assuming you're traveling by car—which, in this particular suspect's case, was not a given. The Canadian Rockies were full of adventure trails. They weren't for the faint of heart, but neither was chasing Olympic gold, so we couldn't rule them out as an escape route.

There were countless unknowns and no time to waste. The longer we took to act, the farther our suspect could travel. Of course it was also possible that she was still right under our noses. We were already here, so that's where we would start.

"OK guys, we need to track the suspect's movements after the murder," I said. "It's possible she left the premises, but we can't assume it. We have no indication that she's armed or dangerous, but even if she is, you're trained for this. I have full confidence that if a situation arises, you'll know what to do."

Stafford—perhaps subconsciously—reached for his sidearm like you pat your pocket to check for your keys.

I looked at my veteran. "Jarvis, I need you to start talking to staff. Start with the front desk clerks and work your way backward through the hotel. Did anybody see her this evening? What time? What was she wearing? Who was she with? You know the drill."

He nodded. "Copy that."

"Go."

Jarvis jogged off down the hall. Born and raised in Banff, J. J. knew as much about the town and this hotel as anybody. Easygoing and personable, he was well suited to the task of getting people to open up.

"Purdy, I need you in the security office watching all the entrances," I said. The main building had nine doors to the outside. I'd thought about having Sydney disable Adler's key—they can reprogram them remotely—but that might tip off our suspect and send her running off into the storm. No, better to have her inside the hotel, where we could corner her and make the arrest.

"If you spot her, do not leave your post. I need your eyes on the monitors until she's arrested."

"Copy that." And then he, too, was off.

"Stafford, you're staying here."

"Outside her room?"

"No, in it. Look for clues to where she might have gone. Check the pockets of her coats, her trash can, her dirty-clothes basket. Collect any handwritten notes, photographs, receipts. I want you to become an expert on Ms. Julie Weston Adler."

"And if she comes back while I'm in there?" he asked. And the answer was simple.

"Make the arrest."

CHAPTER 35
Monique

I had a bloody bullet. I had a rifle capable of firing said bullet. I had video of the owner of that rifle sneaking into the victim's room less than an hour before she was found dead. While we couldn't see the rifle in the video, that laundry cart was big enough to accommodate it. So I could explain how she'd snuck the weapon in and out. There was only one thing I didn't have: a motive. So while my staff cased the place to track down Julie Weston Adler's whereabouts, I went to work on why she'd done it.

Just like it takes two to tango, it takes both a suspect and a victim to formulate a motive. To convict someone of a crime, it's not enough to know if your suspect is capable, you have to know what your victim did to provoke them. Which meant learning about the victim.

Delatour had said that Ceci Rousseau went to the bar every afternoon for happy hour. So I took myself to the bar. The place was hopping. There was one empty stool by the servers' station, so I took it.

"What can I get you?" the bartender said as I sat down on the padded leather stool. I glanced at his name tag to see his name was Johnny.

"I'll have a Coke." He bent over to grab a glass. The woman to my right was clutching a mojito, her back to me as she canoodled with her fella. I would have preferred to talk to the bartender in private, but there was no time to wait.

As bartender Johnny put the Coke down in front of me, I placed my badge on the bar top.

"What's that? Are you a cop?"

"Detective Monique Montpelier. I was hoping to ask you a few questions."

"I'm kind of busy."

"You can work while we talk."

An order was coming in. He glanced over to look at it.

"What do you want to know?" he asked as he reached for a glass.

"There's a woman who comes here every day for happy hour," I said, careful to use present tense. I hadn't told anyone but my guys someone had died here. That was the chief's job.

"You don't mean Ceci?" he asked as he opened a bottle of beer and set it on the servers' station.

"So you know her?"

"Everybody knows her."

"So she's popular."

"I wouldn't say that."

Another drink order came through the machine. He turned his back on me to tear the paper off the ticker.

"What's her drink?" I asked as he pulled a bottle of gin from the top shelf. I wanted to see how well he remembered her. Also, I was curious.

"Who, Ceci? Manhattan, usually. Sometimes she has me make her an old-fashioned. To match her hair, she likes to joke."

"So she's a jokester."

"When she's not chewing someone a new asshole," Johnny said, squeezing a lime into that gin and tonic. He slid the drink toward a waiting cocktail waitress.

"Does she give you a hard time?"

"Nah, we get on pretty good. She's nicer to men. It's women she likes to rough up."

"Any in particular?"

He took a towel off his waist.

"There was a waitress here—her name was Madelaine," he said as he wiped the counter. "Pretty girl. On the young side. If Ceci was in her section, she would send me to take the order. They eventually moved Maddy to the Chop House." The Chop House was the steak house in the hotel. I'd never eaten there—it was two stars above my price range.

"So Mrs. Rousseau was rude to her?"

"More than just rude. She would accuse her of bringing the wrong drink, or spill it and say it was Maddy's fault, stuff like that."

"Are you talking about Ceci Rousseau?" a woman said, and I looked over to see front desk attendant Sydney from Sydney standing over my shoulder. She had let down her hair and changed out of her blazer. I guessed she was off duty and here for an after-shift drink.

"Do you know her?"

"Not really." She hesitated, like she wanted to tell me something but wasn't sure she should.

"I'm hearing that she wasn't such a nice person," I said, to open the door she had cracked. She waited for Johnny to move off, then leaned in close.

"Did something happen to her?" Sydney was the one who'd escorted me to the ninth floor when I first arrived. She said she'd been told there was some sort of emergency. I was relieved that so far that was all she knew.

"I can't comment on an open investigation."

And then she said something that surprised me.

"Did she hurt someone?"

My pulse quickened. *She knew something.*

"What makes you ask that?"

"She has a temper. Just the other day, she called some poor room attendant down to the lobby and yelled at her in front of everybody."

"Who's everybody?"

"Guests, staff, the manager."

"You mean Remy Delatour?" She nodded, and I found it . . . *curious* that he'd never mentioned that.

"What was the argument about?"

"I'm not sure. I just know Ceci was furious. She called the poor woman all sorts of names."

"Did she try to get the room attendant fired?"

"Remy wouldn't do that. He knows guests can be crazy. He has our backs."

"Do you know who the room attendant was?"

"Yeah, the new girl." I raised an eyebrow. I needed her to say her name.

"Which new girl?"

"I think her name is Julie." And if my heart skipped a beat when she said her name, it skipped two more after what she said next. "A couple of the other staffers told me she used to be famous."

"Famous for what?"

"They said she was in the Olympics or something." *Boom!* I pulled out my phone and showed her a picture.

"Yeah, that's her," Sydney confirmed.

And I had my motive.

This case was all but open and shut. The only thing left to do was arrest Julie Weston Adler. As I went to put my phone back in my jacket pocket, it buzzed in my hand.

"What's up, Jarvis?"

"Boss, you're not going to believe this," he said. "But our perp just walked through the front door."

CHAPTER 36
Julie

He tried to tell me. Not just after he'd slept with her, but also before. "This isn't a marriage," he'd said. "We need to try harder." He accused me of shutting down, running from hard conversations, not loving him anymore. And two of those three things were true. I loved Jeff with every bone in my body—which was why I did those other two things.

I had a teammate named Todd who was crazy about dogs. If he saw a dog on the trail, he would always stop to pet it. All his spare toonies went to dog-rescue charities. He even had a dog-of-the-month calendar inside his locker. One day I asked him, "Why don't you get a dog, Todd?" And he put up a hand and shook his head. "I can't go through the pain of losing another one. It's too hard." And I understood.

Jeff and I were long-distance lovers for the first two and a half years of our relationship. We didn't even live in the same country until we got engaged. And then it was a whirlwind of house shopping, wedding planning, merging our friends and our lives. During those first few months in California, life was an amusement park and Jeff was my guide. But after we got married and there were no more roller coasters to ride, all that was left to discover was each other. My husband had a vision of us as two trees growing side by side, branches and roots all intermingled. He wanted to know my deepest thoughts, my dreams for the future, what moved me, what scared me. Problem was, what scared me was *him*. I'd been vulnerable once—loved with my whole heart, as all children do with their mom and dad. And like my friend Todd, I couldn't do it again.

Jeff was in a pressure cooker at work. He needed to vent, fret, be held by loving arms. But the more he tried to climb into my heart, the more scared I got. He needed something I couldn't give him. Something my best friend had in abundance.

Izzy was passionate, generous, caring, and the most fun person you could ever hope to meet. Her arms were always open, it's no wonder Jeff fell into them. Fate may have stopped her from confessing, but I knew what she had done. It was so obvious now. Jeff had been trying to tell me for weeks. There was only one reason my husband would get a hotel room the night of Christa's wedding. Yes, I saw the charge. The only thing I didn't know was who had joined him. Until now. If the one-night stand had been a cry for help, I'd refused to answer it. Just like I'd refused to see the signs of the other thing he'd done.

The storm in my head was as fierce as the pounding snow as I drove down the hill into town. Izzy had betrayed me, but hadn't I betrayed her too? I pretended I was invincible, while my world was crumbling. The lies between us were like rot on wood. If we tried to strip them away, would there be anything left of our friendship?

The girls were still buzzing with excitement and relief as I drove us to the hotel. I didn't know what to say to them, so I kept my mouth shut.

"Good evening," the valet said as I pulled into the drive.

"Good evening," I said, even though it wasn't.

I got out of the car. The snow was falling from every direction all at once, stinging my face and blurring my vision. It was as dizzying as what had just happened, and as surreal as what was about to happen next.

"What a crazy night!" Christa said as she and Suki climbed out of the back seat.

"Could it get any crazier?" Suki asked, thinking her question was rhetorical.

"I don't know about you ladies," Izzy said, "but I need a drink."

"Hot toddies!" Christa said. "I'm frozen to the bone."

I was the last to step into the lobby. My friends waited for me at the threshold. They were scheduled to fly out in the morning. I just had to get through a few more hours of pretending I wasn't in the jaws of a blizzard of lies.

"I'm soaked—I'm going to go change," I said. "I'll meet you there." So much had happened in the last two hours that I had almost forgotten I was wearing Ceci's clothes. I didn't want a guest or coworker to recognize those red leather pants. It was scary enough that they might recognize me as a fellow employee.

"Want us to order for you?" Suki asked.

"Vodka soda."

Suki gave me the thumbs-up. As they started up the stairs, I banked toward the elevators. One step, two step, three steps, then—

"Hold it right there!"

A uniformed RCMP officer with a Grizzly Adams beard stepped out in front of me, one hand on his holstered gun, the other extended like a crossing guard stopping traffic. For a second I thought he was talking to someone else. I almost looked over my shoulder to see if there was a worse criminal behind me. But then another cop—a woman in Patagonia pants with a badge on her hip—stepped in front of him.

"I got this, Jarvis," she said to the uniformed cop. Then to me, "Mrs. Adler, I need you to put your hands on your head."

I placed my hands on the back of my head like I was doing a sit-up. In a flash, the woman cop had them cuffed behind my back.

"Julie Adler, you're under arrest for the murder of Cecile Rousseau," she said, and the floor fell out from under me. Hearing those three words in one sentence—*arrest, murder, Rousseau*—was not shocking, it was nonsensical.

"You have the right to remain silent . . ."

She grabbed my arm. As she spun me around, I saw Izzy, Christa, and Suki staring at me from the stairway to the bar. Their expressions were pure astonishment. As I imagine mine was too.

"Anything you say can and will be used against you in a court of law," the policewoman continued. She was pushing me toward the exit. I wanted to cry out—*What do you mean* murdered? *And why on earth would you think I did it?* But for some reason I was as mute as a mime.

Her fingers dug into my arm. She was strong, but I was stronger. Not that I considered resisting arrest. I was too stunned to do that.

"You have the right to an attorney . . ."

I felt a hundred eyes on me—desk clerks, valets, guests, the three women I once called friends were all staring.

"Please," I finally managed. "You've made a mistake."

And I was telling the truth. I wasn't responsible for Ceci Rousseau's death. But I couldn't say the same about the next one.

PART 3
Third to Die

PART 5

CHAPTER 37
Monique

My first arrest was a sixteen-year-old kid who stole a mickey of Jack Daniel's from a liquor store. He was underage, and this was not the sort of crime we pressed charges for here in Banff, so after sticking him in the drunk tank for an hour, we let him go. I don't know if he learned his lesson, but I never saw that kid again.

Since then, in my ten years on this force, I'd locked a few dozen other perps in that jail: a handful for fighting (separate cells), an assortment of drug dealers and shoplifters, a vandal, a homeless guy we nabbed so he wouldn't freeze to death on the street. But Julie Weston Adler was my first murderer, and I was determined to do it by the book.

"Watch your head," I said to my suspect as I guided her into the back seat of Jarvis's police-issue Ford Explorer and shut the door. J. J. was the one who'd spotted her, so I wanted to give him the honor of hauling her in. The chief had instructed us to wait for him outside the hotel and was on his way. It was cold, but we were amped as we stood by the hood with our hands jammed in our pockets and our faces flushed with pride. Our rinky-dink team had cracked a murder case in under two hours. It was nothing short of a miracle.

"Nice work, Officer Jarvis," I said to my veteran cop. I didn't know if it had been instinct or divine intervention that led him to look up at the exact moment our suspect had stepped into the hotel lobby, but his timing had been perfect.

"Got lucky" was his modest reply.

"It was still a heads-up play," I said, then offered my fist for him to bump. When his gloved hand tapped mine without a hint of enthusiasm, I knew something was wrong.

"What's going on, J. J.?"

I thought maybe he was disappointed that someone he'd admired had turned out to be a killer. J. J. and Julie Weston Adler were both Alberta natives. I imagined he knew who she was long before tonight, maybe even was a fan. But his melancholy had nothing to do with his hometown hero falling off her pedestal. It was more personal than that.

"I think this may be it for me," he said, his eyes betraying his forced smile.

Officer Jason Jarvis was the beating heart of the Banff police force. He had not only seen the town morph from a rough-and-tumble mountain hideaway to a premier tourist destination, but he had helped transform it. The stories of him chasing coke dealers and meth heads back to the big city were legendary.

"You can't retire now," I said. "We just bagged our first big perp!"

He smiled at the word *perp*, so I smiled too.

"It's the perfect time," he countered. "Why go out with a whimper when I can go out with a bang?"

His smile faltered, and I wondered if seeing a murder scene had shaken him.

"Take a few days off," I suggested. "See how you feel."

He fiddled with his beard. For a man in his sixties, he looked surprisingly young. He acted more like a man at the beginning of his career than the end—always early for work, willing to take the most unpleasant assignments . . . and with a smile.

"I have three grandkids now—did you know that?" he asked. "Two in Toronto and one in Revelstoke."

I did know, so I nodded.

"The wife is always whining that we never see them."

And then I realized he had already made up his mind. He was just looking for the right moment to tell me.

"You've had an admirable career, Officer Jarvis."

"Leaving in a blaze of glory," he joked.

"If I had known this was your last hurrah, I would have let you make the arrest."

"It's all good. I've done more than my fair share."

Just as I thought I might have to find a tissue to dab my eyes, the chief pulled up in his police-issue SUV.

"Chief's here," I said, pointing. We walked over to greet him as he got out of his car. To my surprise, he was in full dress uniform and freshly shaven.

"Good evening, sir," I said. We were not normally formal with each other, but his appearance, and the events of the night, were stark reminders that police work is serious business, even in a small town like ours.

"As if a citywide power outage wasn't enough," the chief groaned, shaking his head.

"Do they know what caused it?" Jarvis asked.

"Tree fell and took out the transformer, triggered an automatic shutdown of the whole grid. They're working on it. Hopefully we'll be back on line by morning."

"Well, that's good news," I said.

"Speaking of good news, where is she?" the chief asked.

I indicated Jarvis's car with my head. "Cuffed and ready for transport, sir."

"You sure about this, Detective?" I didn't want to use the word *sure*, but yeah, I was confident.

"The evidence is compelling."

"I hope so," he said, then looked down at his midriff. "Is my shirt horribly wrinkled?"

It was, but I shook my head no.

"You look sharp as a tack, sir."

"I have to do a press conference."

"About the power outage?" I guessed.

"Both. Word got out."

I was only a little surprised.

"Who leaked it?"

"Probably someone who saw us rolling the victim out in a body bag. Doesn't matter. We have a suspect in custody, best to just get it over with." He pulled at his shirtsleeves. "Damned shirt must have shrunk since I last wore it."

"I have the same problem, sir," J. J. said, tugging at the waistband of his coat. I didn't want to interrupt the male bonding, but I was eager to wrap this up.

"I can process the suspect," I offered. But the chief shook his head.

"She's not going to the drunk tank, Detective."

"Sir?"

"Our jail's not secure enough for a murder suspect. We can't even turn the lights on right now. She's going to Calgary."

"You mean in the morning?"

"No. Now."

The snow was falling so hard you could barely see your hand in front of your face. Calgary was over a hundred kilometers from Banff. In these conditions it could take half the night.

"But sir—"

"The decision was made by someone higher up than me." The chief's tone was stern, like he wasn't happy about it either. "Once she's processed, I'll do the presser. They don't want the public knowing there was a murder until she's behind bars." And I imagined that was ordained by someone higher up too.

"I volunteer to drive, Chief," Jarvis said, stepping forward.

"Officer Jarvis, that's not necessary—" I interrupted. I didn't want to send any of my men out in this storm, especially the one who'd just said he'd had enough.

"I've been driving these roads for almost fifty years," Jarvis said. "In all kinds of weather."

"All right then, Officer Jarvis," the chief said. "She's your perp. Don't dillydally. I want to make my statement and get out of these clothes. Pants got small too," he added, shaking his head.

I couldn't let J. J. go alone. Not with a murder suspect, not in this weather.

"I'll ride shotgun."

Jarvis opened his mouth to object, but I was his superior. It would be disrespectful for him to contradict me.

"Call when you get there," the chief said. "And good luck."

"Thanks," I said, not knowing luck would not be enough.

CHAPTER 38
Izzy

"This way, please," the frat-boy cop said as he escorted Suki, Christa, and me into a banquet hall that looked like the forbidden sitting room at your grandmother's house. The carpet was an aggressive swirl of crimson and indigo flowers, and the domed ceiling was high enough to fly a kite. On the far wall, heavy emerald drapes were cinched by tasseled gold rope. There was a pair of wingback chairs in front of a fireplace framed by a mantel with gargoyles carved into its underbelly. The walls may not have had ears, but the fireplace did.

The hunky policeman directed us toward the rectangular cherry-wood dining table in the center of the room, which was lacquered so heavily you could see the reflections of our terrified faces in the top. We sat down in silence. None of us dared utter a word. Our friend had just been arrested for murder—*murder!*—while we watched from above like spectators at the Kentucky Derby. I had thought being trapped in a gondola during a blizzard would be the low point of the trip, but things had gone from bad to horrific.

"I'm Simon Stafford of the RCMP," the cop said, sitting down across from us. "I'm just going to ask you a few questions, if that's all right?"

We all nodded. I knew *RCMP* stood for *Royal Canadian Mounted Police*, because I'd looked it up after seeing a trooper at the airport. "Just like Dudley Do-Right!" I'd said to the girls, but neither of them had watched enough cartoons to get the reference.

The cop smiled at us, revealing teeth so perfect I knew they must be fake. It was presumptuous to assume he was a former hockey player, but his forearms were as thick as bread loaves, and this was Canada. If you called central casting and asked for someone to play young Wayne Gretzky, this was the guy they would send.

"Where are you visiting from?" Young Gretzky asked.

"Ventura County, California," Christa said, taking charge like the lawyer she was.

"What brought you all to Banff?"

"We came to see our friend, Julie Weston Adler," Christa replied. She was sitting in the middle, so not only qualified to be our spokesperson but also perfectly positioned.

"And how do you all know Ms. Adler?"

"We're friends from back home."

"In California?"

"That's right," Christa said. "She's Canadian, but she moved to LA when she got married."

"Her husband's dead now," Suki blurted, and Christa and I both looked at her like she'd farted in church.

"Is that why she moved back to Canada, you reckon?"

"Oh, she didn't move back," Christa said. "She's just on vacation. Here, at the hotel."

The police officer made a face, like what Christa had said confused him.

"I think she has a boyfriend here," I offered. "That's why she came." I could feel Christa's and Suki's eyes on me, but I didn't meet their accusatory stares. "His name is Remy," I added. "He's French." And the hockey cop perked up.

"Remy Delatour?"

"I don't know his last name."

He went on his phone, pulled up a picture of the handsome Frenchman.

"Is this him?"

"Yes," I said confidently. The cop's arms flexed as he made a note on his pad.

"Has your friend Julie Adler ever mentioned a woman named Cecile Rousseau?"

We all shook our heads no.

"Or Ceci Rousseau?" he asked. And Suki perked up.

"Yes! That's her fake name!"

"What do you mean *fake name*?"

"Julie's famous. She won a gold medal at the Olympics. So she checked in to the hotel under a fake name," Suki explained.

"I see." Officer Simon Stafford tapped his pen on his pad like he'd rather be playing hockey.

"Why did you arrest her?" Christa asked. Her tone was aggressive, and for a second I thought she might have hurt the cop's feelings.

"She's a suspect in a murder investigation."

"Do you have evidence?" Christa pressed.

"I'm not at liberty to discuss the evidence—"

"Because we can vouch for her, she was with us all day."

"You'll have an opportunity to provide an alibi—"

"You can't just go arresting hotel guests." Christa was getting heated now. I kicked her under the table, but she ignored me. "I know we're not in America anymore," she went on, "but we still have rights."

Then the cop said something that surprised us.

"She wasn't a hotel guest. She worked here. As a chambermaid."

And we all stopped squawking.

CHAPTER 39
Remy

I was in my office when they arrested Julie. I didn't want to watch. Julie had gone from champion to chambermaid to charlatan, all in one week. What an epic fall from grace.

With the downfall of the woman I once adored came the destruction of a dream I'd held close for over seven years. I knew why Julie didn't want me when we met: I was a lowly assistant manager at a hotel, whose past was more promising than his future. Jeff was an MIT graduate being courted by some of the richest men in Canada. Of course she chose him. I bet on him too. Not just to get the girl. I bet on him with every penny of my life savings. If he was going to get rich, I was going to get rich right along with him. I figured, if he was smart enough to win Julie's heart, he was smart enough to make me a millionaire. And once he did, I'd be everything Julie wanted—the whole package, with the bank account to match.

I was disappointed when Julie told me Jeff had proposed, but once they were engaged, I stepped into the role of dutiful friend. I knew she would eventually tire of him. Jeff may have been smarter than me, but Julie and I were a much better match. We had a common Canadian heritage, and a shared love of sports and the great outdoors. Training for the Olympics had taught me patience. I knew she'd come back. And when she did, I would be worthy.

When Jeff started coming to Banff every month, at first I thought it was to see Julie. But she was just the sideshow. The primary purpose of his trips to Alberta was to court big oil money, much of which vacationed here in Banff. Jeff had big ideas and needed deep pockets to fund them. Once he got what he wanted, he took the money, and the girl, and ran.

The technology Jeff was working on was called quantum dots. Quantum dots are man-made nanoscopic crystals that can bend light. While scientists were theorizing they could be used to make solar panels, Jeff was already making them. His prototype was five times more efficient than any solar panel on the market, at half the price. His tech had the potential to put utility companies out of business. That's why one of the big ones was ready to pay hundreds of millions to buy it.

Calgary was a gas-and-oil town. But that didn't mean the people who got rich off it weren't also pursuing other ways to get rich. Call it diversifying, hedging your bets, or just plain greed, they wanted what Jeff was selling.

And so did I.

Jeff's lead investor was an Alberta oilman who sold shares in his drilling projects to accredited investors. Green tech was new to "Megabucks Mackenzie," but he fashioned himself as a cowboy, and the green-energy market was the Wild, Wild West. He loved to talk about how "there's gold in them thar hills," and investors were lining up to get their share.

Jeff's cowboy benefactor was a shameless risk-taker. Like me, he quickly tired of resort skiing. When I offered to take him to the backcountry, he eagerly accepted. I guided him through some of the best skiing of his life. The views from the top of the glaciers were magnificent, and the powder was sublime. We had a couple of harrowing experiences—a tumble into a tree well, a mini avalanche we had to outrun. But I took care of him. And he took care of me.

The invitation to participate as an investor in Jeff's company came after I guided Mac through a death-defying couloir with a near fifty-degree pitch. He was so elated to have made it out alive, he extended an invitation that he promised would change my life. He was keeping the investor group small, he'd said. Only a chosen few. And he chose me.

To be an accredited investor, you need to have a seven-figure income or a high-powered job. I had neither of those things. But I did have some savings. And my ski buddy was willing to make an exception. As long as I didn't tell anybody. The government restricts who is allowed to participate in high-risk investments like this one. The intent is to keep unsophisticated people from getting in over their heads. Mackenzie could get fined or sued for including me. So we kept it our secret.

Mac predicted the return could be as high as ten times what I invested. I was no stranger to risk. One might say I craved it. So I handed over all the money I had in the world: 300,000 Canadian dollars.

That was a little over three years ago—right before Jeff and Julie got married. I never told Julie I was an investor in her husband's company. Not even Jeff knew. And not just because I'd promised Mackenzie I wouldn't tell. When I became a multimillionaire, I didn't want Julie to know I'd relied on her husband to make my fortune. And I didn't want him to have the satisfaction of knowing it either.

It had been several weeks since I'd spoken with Mac, and I owed him a call. I didn't know how Megabucks Mackenzie Rousseau would react to the news that his wife had been murdered, but I picked up the phone to find out.

CHAPTER 40
Monique

Driving in falling snow can be hypnotic. You have to sit high in your chair so you can see the road underneath you. Otherwise it feels like you're in a video game, piloting your spaceship through an asteroid field. You can get lulled into thinking *game over* means *insert another quarter*, when in fact the consequences of messing up are much more permanent than that.

I glanced at the speedometer to see we were going fifty kilometers an hour. The speed limit was ninety, but fifty still felt fast, given the conditions. I understood why the commissioner wanted us to bring our murder suspect to Calgary, but I wished he could have waited until morning.

Jarvis held the wheel of his souped-up Ford Explorer loosely with both hands, like driving in a blizzard was no big deal. Even still, I forced myself to be a second set of eyes for him, making sure I could see the mile markers along the side of the highway that indicated we were still on it. I would say there wasn't another car in sight, but that would be meaningless, given that we couldn't see.

As the windshield wipers thumped in time with my nervous heart, I glanced in the rearview. Our suspect sat perfectly still, staring out her window with her handcuffed hands tucked in the small of her back. Julie Weston Adler looked as much like a murderer as Ted Bundy looked like a serial killer—which was to say, not at all. But the pieces all lined up. She'd put on her uniform to sneak her rifle up to the ninth floor in a laundry cart, entered the victim's room with a key only she and a handful of others on the premises had, waited for the victim to return from happy hour, then shot her at point-blank range in the back. I had a bullet that matched the weapon under her bed. Half the staff witnessed the two arguing in the lobby. This was as close to a no-brainer as you could get. So why did I feel uncertain?

I studied her expression. She didn't look angry, scared, or even sad. She looked . . . indifferent. Like this was neither the worst thing that had ever happened to her, nor the most challenging. I reminded myself that as an Olympic gold medalist, Julie Weston Adler knew how to beat the odds. And I suddenly felt a wave of panic. My evidence was strong, but it was circumstantial. There were no eyewitnesses. I had a gun, but even if her prints were on it, that didn't mean it had always been in her possession. Dozens of other staffers had access to her room. Who's to say one of her coworkers didn't take it when she wasn't home? And then there were those twenty-seven unaccounted-for minutes when the power was out and all security cam footage was lost. It would be a stretch to argue that someone had time to sneak into her room, steal her gun, then go to the ninth floor and shoot someone, but it could raise reasonable doubt. Getting a conviction would come down to my story against hers. Me against her. And she was a formidable adversary.

As insecurity danced in my chest, Julie Adler raised her eyes and met mine in the mirror. There was not a trace of fear in them. She couldn't say the same about mine.

"Are you OK back there?" I asked, not to be nice. I wanted my suspect to know I was not intimidated by her. Yes, she had rights. But I was in control.

"Just fine, thank you." Her voice was calm and polite. Was she acting? Or a psychopath?

"We're processing you in Calgary," I said. I didn't have to let her know where we were going, but there was no reason not to.

"That's fine. There's no one waiting up for me."

It was an obvious reference to her dead husband. Was she trying to bait me? Or win my sympathies?

Jarvis's eyes were glued to the road, but I could tell from his expression that he didn't approve of me talking to her. She was a murder suspect. If I improperly solicited a confession, it could hurt the prosecutor's eventual case.

I turned my focus back to the road. A mile marker floated by. I glanced at the speedometer. Unlike Julie and me, Jarvis did have someone waiting up for him. Is that why he had sped up?

"Roads are good," he said, reading my mind.

"The visibility sucks," I countered.

"There's nothing to run into out here."

He was almost right. No one was foolish enough to venture out in this weather. Every man, woman, and child was tucked in their bed. But people were not the only residents of Banff.

Banff National Park is a breeding ground for elk, or wapiti, as the locals call the deerlike animals that sometimes venture into our parks and school playgrounds. Once, one even walked through the McDonald's drive-through. Normally it was the park rangers who were called to shoo them away, but occasionally we got the honor.

The average female elk is five feet tall at the shoulder, but the bull is closer in size to a moose. Out here in the Rockies, where food is plentiful and there's space to run and grow, male elk can get as large as twelve hundred pounds. At two meters wide, their antlers have the wingspan of an eagle, and they're as formidable as they are sharp.

If I could see, I would have known we were passing right by the national wapiti reserve. I would have noticed that a tree had fallen on the fence and created a four-foot-wide opening—wide enough for even the largest elk to walk through. And if I were really paying attention, I would have seen that one just had.

Elk are smart. While you'll occasionally see one on a backcountry road, or on Banff Avenue if McDonald's is open, they know better than to wander out onto the highway. Unless it's snowing too hard for them to see the highway.

Fwimp-fwump, fwimp-fwump.

The windshield wipers tried to clear a sight line, but their efforts were no match for the conditions. The headlights only made things worse, illuminating the kaleidoscope of snow instead of the road.

It was Julie who saw him first. Maybe being in the back seat gave her a better angle. Or maybe her reflexes were quicker and her senses more keenly attuned.

"Watch out!" she shouted, leaning forward in her seat.

I found her eyes in the mirror. Before they were blank. Now they were raw terror.

By the time Jarvis and I realized we were going to hit it, it was too late.

The SUV hydroplaned as Jarvis slammed the brakes.

Thunnnnk!

The sound was like a crash of thunder—above us, below us, and in the air all around.

The airbag slammed into my chest. I couldn't call out. I couldn't breathe.

And then I was upside down. No, sideways. No, rolling.

I clawed at the airbag. *Can't . . . breathe . . .*

The seat belt dug into my throat as we rolled and rolled.

We hit something hard.

My brain slammed against my skull.

I felt pain.

I felt cold.

And then I felt nothing.

CHAPTER 41
Julie

I felt it before I saw it. That's how it always was for me out in nature. Jeff used to joke that I must have a sixth sense, because I always knew when an animal was lurking. I felt the eagles overhead, the snakes in the grass, the bobcats in the bush. When you're a guest in their home, it's wise to be aware if you've overstayed your welcome.

I never saw elk out on the trails, but I knew they had big energy. The one we killed that night was an eight-foot-tall bull. I felt his presence like you feel a storm cloud moving in. At first that's what I thought it was: a whirling dervish of snow kicked up by the wind. But then the antlers took shape, as spindly as a spiderweb, and I knew we were on a collision course that would not end well for him or us.

I sat up and shouted.

"Watch out!"

But it was already too late. The bull was charging toward the car as we were speeding toward him. We were like two trains on the same track, barreling toward an inevitable crash.

I was seat belted in. My hands were cuffed behind my back. It was crazy uncomfortable riding with handcuffs pushing into my lower back, but boy was I grateful for that seat belt now.

I braced for impact. My muscles became an exoskeleton as I flexed them all at once—pecs, abs, latissimus dorsi. I clenched my teeth so I wouldn't sever my tongue. The only thing I couldn't protect was my head. But if this crash was coming for my head, at least it would be over quick. I wasn't a person of faith, but I remember thinking the words *I surrender*, because even my hardened body would need God's mercy to survive this.

The mass of fur, flesh, and bone descended on the hood like a bomb exploding. I raised my knees to my chest to make a human cannonball.

And then I went for a ride.

The SUV tumbled roof over chassis, roof over chassis—three, four, five, times. Gravity was a ravenous beast, pulling us into its gully. If we were near the wapiti reserve, the highway was elevated here. It would be a long drop.

The roar of crumpling aluminum and steel swallowed us like an earthquake. As I spiraled toward certain death, I felt a flash of panic that I'd played my cards all wrong. I'd spent my whole life trying to earn the love of two people who couldn't love me back, then pushed away the one person who did. Why wouldn't I let Jeff see my wounds? And why did I think I had to be perfect for him to want to stay with me? As answers floated just beyond my reach, the car slammed to a stop, and I was thrust back into my body with a crash as deafening as a sonic boom.

I gasped, and cold air flooded my lungs. The seat belt bit into my collarbone. I was still in my seat—the chest strap had held tight. I tried to reach up and loosen it, momentarily forgetting my hands were cuffed behind my back. My head felt strangely heavy, and I realized I was upside down—a lump of flesh and bone suspended by a taut nylon strap.

I turned my head left and right. Wiggled my fingers. Wiggled my toes. Licked my lips and swallowed. I rolled my ankles, straightened then rebent my legs. To my astonishment, everything still worked. I was hanging like a bat in a cave, but I was alive.

My chest strained against the seat belt as I took a deep breath. I exhaled and watched the steam rise not above my head, but below it, toward my upside-down midriff. After a few more deep breaths, the pounding in my chest softened and the sounds of the night revealed themselves. I heard the creak of the car settling. A low whistle of wind. I knew the windows were broken from the cross breeze of frigid air. Right in front of me, I could see the headrests of the front seats, but no heads.

"Hello?" I called out. My voice was tight with fear. "Are you guys all right?"

No answer. Dread seized my heart.

"If you can hear me, I'm going to come help you."

I closed my eyes and said a silent prayer that my captors weren't beyond help. Then I got to work helping myself.

I was on the left side of the car, behind the driver, so knew the button to release the seat belt was by my right hip. I slid my cuffed hands along the small of my back, then extended my fingers to probe for the mechanism. After a few seconds of groping, my index finger found the button. I maneuvered my shoulders for maximum leverage, then pushed straight down—or rather, *up*—to release the buckle.

Click.

My upside-down head thumped down onto the spongy cloth roof as the seat belt retracted. I let my legs fall sideways, then rolled over onto my stomach. Bits of safety glass crunched under my weight as I inchwormed toward the gaping hole where the window used to be. I flexed my neck muscles to raise my chin as I wiggled out of the overturned vehicle into the snow.

The ground was cold and wet against my exposed belly. I rolled onto my side, then tucked my knees toward my chest and hoisted myself up to kneeling. The handcuffs dug into my wrists as my kneecaps sank into the snow. I didn't realize I was panting until I saw my breath like puffs of smoke in the night air. I was one of three people who'd tumbled down that hill. I braced myself to see what had become of the other two.

I stood up on shaking legs. The canopy of branches above my head diffused the falling snow, but also shrouded me in near total darkness. I wanted my hands in front of me, not behind, so I slid my cuffed wrists down my butt and stepped backward through the opening between my arms—kind of like jumping rope backward, except the rope was my two arms connected by a steel chain. My fingers were cold, so I slipped my hands under the ribbed waist of my jacket to thaw them.

As my fingers tingled and came back to life, my eyes began to adjust to the darkness. Bits of snow-soaked sky leaked through the treetops, casting the scene in eerie charcoal light. It was a few short steps to the driver's side door, which was dented but still intact. I waded toward it through the knee-deep snow, then crouched down and peered through the shattered window. The seat belt had done its job. The bearded cop was firmly strapped to his seat. The bull's antlers had done their job too. Two were wrapped around his throat like tines of a fork. One was planted in his chest like a sword through the heart.

I stumbled back. My shoulder connected with a tree trunk. I pressed my body into it to keep myself upright. A wave of nausea rose up from my belly as hot tears stung my cheeks. I'd seen all sorts of injuries during my time on the ski team—broken bones, bloodied faces, noses black with frostbite. And confronted the lifeless form of my own husband on our bathroom floor. But the gruesomeness of this death gutted me.

I took a sharp breath in and forced it out through my mouth. This was not the time to fall apart. There was another person in that mangled SUV. And if she was trapped or hurt, I was the only one who could help her.

I forced myself to look at the carnage. Like the SUV and the people in it, the elk was upside down, sandwiched between the hood and the ground. His front legs were folded under his body. His bloodied back legs were pointed straight up toward the sky.

I walked back toward the wreckage. The beast's massive head blocked my view of the passenger seat. I waded through the snow toward the front of the vehicle. As I rounded the hood, I saw the bull's antlers fanned out inside the cab. I shuddered as I imagined them slicing through the windshield, impaling everything within their reach. I knew that the odds of the other cop surviving were miniscule. And also that I needed to go and see.

I squeezed my handcuffed arms to my sides for warmth as I passed the bull's massive backside. Even in death he was magnificent. The king of the forest. *Forgive us, beautiful beast. May you rest in peace.*

I reached the passenger's side door and squatted down to peer in the mangled opening that used to be the window. The female cop was still in her seat, held firm by her seat belt. Somehow—miraculously!—the elk's antlers had spared her. Her eyes were closed, her mouth agape. I reached out and put my cuffed hands an inch from her parted lips. And felt a whisper of warm air.

She was alive.

And I had to figure out how to keep her that way.

CHAPTER 42
Julie

The snow was relentless, and the temperature was dropping. I didn't know how long it would take for the police to realize two officers were missing, but in this weather, every second counted. Freezing to death was not the only threat. We'd taken a big tumble. If the policewoman had internal injuries, getting her to a hospital was urgent. I had to get her out of there, and fast.

I did a quick visual examination. The hood of the SUV was compressed like an accordion, but the cab was largely intact. The thousand pounds of bull elk on the hood had stopped the roof from collapsing when the car flipped. If not for him, we all would have been crushed.

The woman cop's upside-down face was turned toward me. She had a nasty gash on her cheek. Gravity had caused the blood to run up her face, toward her eye. It was caking in her eyelashes like mud on truck tires. Her arms dangled above her head. The left one hung straight, but the right was bent at a funny angle—either dislocated, broken, or both. The lap belt held her upper thighs close to the seat. I peered into the cavern to see her lower legs still intact and her feet snug in their boots. She was in bad shape, but not so bad that I couldn't move her.

I leaned into the compartment to look for a way to call for help. The police radio was in pieces. I imagined both cops had cell phones, but it was too cramped and dark in there to crawl around looking for them. I couldn't frisk the male cop's pockets—he was so entangled with the elk I didn't know where his body stopped and the animal's began. As for the policewoman, when I dipped into her jacket pocket, I found her wallet, but no phone. We'd rolled for at least fifty meters. If her phone had fallen out a window, it would be two feet deep in snow. And even if I found it, what was the likelihood it wouldn't be smashed? Or that we would have service? There was no cell tower near here—residents had been complaining about that for years. No, there was no calling for help. I would have to do this myself. Handcuffed. In a blizzard.

I breathed into my hands to warm them. The woods were deathly quiet. I closed my eyes to think. This was an emergency vehicle. It would be equipped with supplies—*in the trunk maybe?*

"I'll be right back," I said to my unconscious captor, then waded through the knee-high snow toward the rear compartment. The back window was gone, so I lowered myself onto cuffed hands and knees and crawled inside. There was a hard case the size of a carry-on suitcase strapped to the bottom—my top—of the trunk. I unclipped it and pulled it out into the snow. I had no idea what would be in there, or what I was looking for, just hoped I would know it if and when I saw it.

I pushed the box under the cover of a big pine tree, then opened the hard plastic lid. On top were a pair of gloves and a black, wool toque. I took them out and put them on immediately. Underneath those was a smattering of tools—screwdriver, wrench, tack hammer, duct tape. There were flares—which would have been useful if we weren't in a blizzard—bear spray, Band-Aids, antibacterial ointment, a roll of gauze, an EpiPen. None of these things were helpful to me. But I did find three things that were.

The emergency blanket was the thin foil kind. Not only would that help keep her warm, but it was smooth and would slide easily over the snow. There was no rope, but there was something that could substitute for one: jumper cables. I was about to close the box when I saw one more useful item at the bottom of the chest. That Kevlar vest would not only add a layer of warmth, but it would also protect her back against the cold, hard ground. I felt a flicker of hope. I couldn't carry this woman to safety, but with these items, I could pull her.

I grabbed my found treasures and hurried back to the policewoman. When the SUV had rolled, it compressed the snow outside the passenger door, so I was able to spread the blanket out flat. I placed the Kevlar vest in the middle of it, right where her back would go. And then I reached into the SUV to collect her.

The cold metal cuffs bit into my wrists as I slid them across her lap to unclip her seat belt. As my fingers groped the mechanism, they stumbled across something hard and smooth and the size of a bottle cap. I took it between my thumb and forefinger. It was a key ring. On it was one key, small like the one for my childhood jewelry box. And my heart did a little backflip as I realized what it was for.

I raised the key to my mouth, pinched it between my front teeth, then brought my right wrist to meet it. It took a few seconds of hunting and pecking, but I finally got the shaft of the key inserted in the keyhole. I turned my wrists clockwise and my head counterclockwise and—

Pop! My hands were free.

I shook the cuffs off into the snow. Now that I could use my hands, unclipping the policewoman's seat belt was a snap. I wedged my shoulder under her midriff and—click! She fell right onto it. She was petite—at least ten kilos lighter than me—but I was so amped I could have pulled a rhinoceros out of that car. With her limp body draped over my shoulder, I eased out backward, careful not to bump her head on the running boards. I laid her diagonally on the blanket, centered above the Kevlar, then swaddled her in the blanket like a newborn baby. The jumper cables went under her shoulders. Once I'd clipped them together, her pinned arms held them firm.

The wapiti reserve was between ten and twelve kilometers from Banff. The highway arced north, away from town. If I followed the river, I could shave three kilometers off the route. It was risky in these conditions. I didn't know what I would find out there—uneven ground, fallen trees, wild animals. We had more dangerous animals than elk in these parts, and if they wanted to attack, I had no way to fend them off. In these conditions, walking a kilometer could take ten minutes or more.

I looked at the policewoman. Her lips were blue. Her skin was alabaster white. That extra thirty minutes could be the difference between life and death.

So I turned toward the river, then set out into the storm.

CHAPTER 43
Remy

"They're going to think I did it," Mackenzie Rousseau said when I reached him to tell him about the death of his wife. He already knew, of course. The chief of police called him right after I'd identified her. So I was spared having to pretend how shocked and sorry we all were.

"They have someone in custody," I told him. But that didn't make him feel any better.

"They had to arrest someone. Banff is a tourist town. They can't let people think there's a murderer wandering around."

"I think the evidence against her is pretty compelling." Julie's fingerprints were all over this crime. They had her at the scene, they had the murder weapon, they had motive. But Mac wasn't convinced.

"So they'll think it was a hit. We were going through a heated divorce. I stood to lose millions when it was all said and done." That may have been true. *But also . . .*

"She had no shortage of enemies, Mac." I personally could think of at least a dozen—front desk staff she complained to about noise or other nonsense, waitresses she snapped at about drinks being too weak or too strong, valets she accused of scuffing her luggage or nicking the paint on her car.

"What Ceci knew about Quantum Solar would have brought us to our knees," Mac reminded me. He had called me on the Signal app, like he always did, so didn't hold back. "It's my fault. I should have been more discreet."

There was a time when Ceci had stuck her nose into all of Mac's investments. Knowing them both, I'd often wondered if she was the engine of his success, because she certainly was the more ruthless of the two.

"She had nothing to gain by telling anyone," I said.

"If it would hurt me, that was reason enough."

"Yes, but your money was her money." *And my money,* I thought, but didn't say out loud. "She wouldn't have risked it just to hurt you."

We were almost at the end of the road. Mac had lined up a buyer—a Fortune 500 utility company with the means to bring Jeff's invention to market. As soon as the deal closed, my $300,000 investment would turn into $3 million. Yes, I had wanted to share this moment with Julie, but that was before I knew what she was. What a horrific disappointment she had turned out to be. But my life would go on, and—for the first time in my life—with real money in my pocket.

"I don't know, Remy. These things have a way of coming to the surface, especially when there's a murder investigation."

The mention of an investigation made my heart fill with dread. I reminded myself that the evidence all pointed to Julie. Ceci had been killed with her gun, they'd been seen arguing by my entire front desk staff, and the security footage clearly showed her in the room right before the discovery of the body.

Mac was right. She was not the only one with a motive. Right now, Mac's secret was buried. Most people wouldn't know where to look.

But most people weren't Julie Weston Adler.

CHAPTER 44
Julie

The Bow River cut a direct line from the crash site to downtown Banff. It was too early in the season for it to be frozen over—being able to skate would have made things a lot easier. But at least the route along the banks would be flat. The trick would be not falling into the icy water—easy to do in near whiteout conditions.

The SUV had rolled us into the gully. There were no streetlights out here, and the night air was thick as ash. I couldn't use my eyes to find the river, so I closed them and listened. Beneath the howling wind, the steady roar of rushing water revealed itself like an old friend. It was close. I tucked my chin and turned toward the sound.

I knew the river flowed south toward Calgary, so upriver I went. As I trudged through thigh-high snow, jumper cables digging into my waist, it seemed impossible that, just a few short hours ago, I'd been on my way to dinner with friends who still loved me.

I told myself eight kilometers was nothing for me. And on a clear day, with no sled to haul, it was. Tonight was a different story. The air was so thick with snow, I felt like I was wading through cotton candy, and walking into the wind was like trying to run up the down escalator—twice the effort got you half as far. My skin burned, my muscles screamed with pain, and the only thing I had to look forward to was jail. But I kept going for the simple reason that I'd never learned how to quit.

I found a pair of fallen branches and swung them like ski poles to help propel me forward. Just like when I was training, I focused on my breath. Deep inhales, all the breath out. It was easily ten below, but I was working too hard to feel the cold. It was the cop I was worried about. She had the Kevlar, the blanket, and a down jacket between her and the elements, but she was still at risk for freezing to death. If I was going to set a new time record for the human-sled race, today would be a good day to do it.

Ceci's leather pants turned out to be an effective barrier against the wind and snow. *Ceci.* One cop was dead, and one was fighting for her life because of her. If she had been murdered—which I was still struggling to believe—the person wearing her clothes was the obvious suspect. All I could think of was that someone had set me up. But the only person I could think of who would do that was Lady Ceci herself. That's a pretty radical thing to do to get revenge, even for her.

I didn't imagine anyone was crying over Ceci Rousseau's death. That woman was a monster. Surely there was someone who detested her more than I did. Even so, if I died out here, the investigation would die with me. And so I pushed ahead—to save my accuser, but also myself. The only thing that could clear my name was a not-guilty verdict, and my ego would fight for one like a hungry dog for a bone.

The river took a sharp turn due west, and I knew I was nearing the outskirts of town. If I continued at this pace, I would be at the hospital in about forty minutes. I didn't know how much longer my cargo could survive, so I picked up the pace. *Left, right, left, right.* As I settled into a rhythm, my mind wandered from my current predicament to the event that had started this all: Jeff's suicide.

Our relationship had been strained, but it's not like things were hopeless. And that wouldn't explain the money. *What happened to the money?* All I could think of was that the company had run out and he'd dipped into our savings, trusting he would get whole when the next round of funding came through. I knew he'd gotten an offer from a big energy company. Had it fallen through, leaving him too ashamed to face his employees, investors, and me?

The horror of the crash had pushed Izzy's near confession to the background, but now that I was alone with my thoughts, it was pummeling my brain like a drum solo. I understood why Jeff had turned to her. He was in crisis, and my soldier-on sensibility didn't exactly make it easy to confide in me. But it takes two to tango. Just because Jeff had needed a shoulder to cry on didn't mean she had to answer the call. I wanted to hate her. But how do you hate the one person who stood by you when everyone else fell away?

The river dipped south at the base of Tunnel Mountain, but I continued due west. The snow was swirling like a waterspout, spray-painting me from all directions. I put my head down, fired up my core, and churned my legs beneath me as hard and fast as they would go. The cop was the sled, and I was the wheel dog. I would get this woman to the hospital or die trying.

I was less than a kilometer from the edge of town now. Normally I would see city lights from here. The fact that I couldn't told me the power was still out. We humans think we have free will to do whatever we wish—drive to Calgary, go on a gondola ride, build a modern city nestled in the mountains—but if Mother Nature doesn't like your plans, she wins every time.

A Canadian flag fluttered over my head, and I knew I'd reached the campground just outside downtown Banff. I felt a pang of relief. Help for my wounded passenger was near. Then a rush of dread. Did the police know I was missing yet? Was the whole town on alert? What would I do if someone recognized me?

I pushed the thoughts away and kept moving forward. I could see the road now. I dropped my walking sticks and broke into a jog, and then a full-out run. I had reached the city limits. *Almost there.*

Tunnel Mountain Road had been plowed, but there were no cars. At least none in motion. The ones on the side of the road looked like giant frosted car cupcakes, fluffy and white and pretty enough to eat. The street was like a ghost town: empty, dark, not a soul in sight. I was running too fast to peer in any windows, but if I'd stopped and looked, I imagined I'd see the flickering lights of fireplaces, the bouncing orbs of torches, the hazy glow of candles burning on tables and hearths. Mountain people knew how to take care of themselves.

I made the final turn, and the hospital came into view. Unlike the rest of the town, it was lit up. The emergency entrance was in the front, beside a helicopter pad built to receive skiers who dared to go head to head with the elements . . . and lost.

When I reached the circular drive, I lifted the policewoman off the ground, then fireman carried her through double doors that opened automatically as I approached.

"Help," I shouted, as I charged into the dimly lit reception area with my foil-wrapped patient. The jumper cables dangled from her inert body, dragging behind me like a tail. The woman behind the plexiglass barrier looked up in surprise. I was caked with snow from my neck to my boots, my pink-hot face poking out from my tightly cinched hood.

The admitting nurse rounded the plexiglass, her eyes as wide as her open mouth.

"What happened?"

"There was a car accident. She may have internal injuries."

The nurse pressed a button, and the doors to the inner sanctum wafted open. I spied a gurney in the hall and beelined for it. Then set my cargo on it and left.

CHAPTER 45
Julie

"How much for a bed?" I asked the bleary-eyed attendant at the youth hostel. It was nearly midnight. I was exhausted and soaked to the bone. The cozy bunkhouse was four blocks from the hospital, and the only place I could think of to find shelter. Some of my teammates had stayed here when we were all young and poor, and I knew the place to be clean and safe and not somewhere anyone was likely to ask many questions.

"Thirty bucks," the shaggy-haired twentysomething said. "But we don't have power," he added, in case I didn't know he didn't normally work by candlelight. "And I can only take cash."

The hostel had a little kitchen and lobby downstairs, and bunk-style accommodations on the second floor. It was no frills, but I didn't care. All I wanted was a hot shower and a good, long sleep.

"That's fine," I said, pulling two twenties from the wallet I had lifted off the lady cop. Yes, I took her wallet. But in my defense, she took mine first.

"I can't give change," the attendant said, not reaching for the money. "Register won't open."

"I haven't got anything smaller."

The attendant considered our predicament. "I'll give you a discount," he finally said, plucking a twenty from my outstretched hand. "Given the lack of amenities this evening."

"Can I just take any bed?" My muscles throbbed, and my feet were killing me. I was desperate to get warm and horizontal.

"Yeah, we're not very full. I'll just need a driver's license or other photo ID."

I didn't look anything like Monique Ariel Montpelier, but it was either hand over her license or risk getting turned away. It wasn't likely my Gen Z host would have been friendly with the local cop, so I rolled the dice and handed him the Alberta license with her name on it. He either didn't look at the photo or couldn't see it in the dim light, because he handed it right back after scribbling down not-my-name.

"The sleeping area is coed."

"Right."

"Turn left at the top of the stairs. Washrooms are at the end of the hall."

And that was it. I was in. If he noticed I didn't have any personal items like a backpack or suitcase, he didn't seem to care.

I took the stairs two at a time, then made a beeline for the bathroom, which was (barely) lit with a lone camping lantern. There was a stack of towels next to the showers, so I threw one over the stall door as I slipped inside. I hung my jacket on the hook and kicked off my boots. Ceci's leather pants made a slurping sound as I peeled them off legs as pink as a beesting. The pits of her angora sweater were ringed with sweat, and my socks were soaked through. As for my body, it was tired, but had survived the crash virtually unscathed. I had my training to thank for that, and I felt a little vindicated that those hours in the gym weren't all in vain.

I took as hot a shower as I could stand, letting the water wash away the stiffness in my neck and shoulders. Running through thigh-high snow was not a workout I would have chosen, but it was neither the hardest, nor the most unpleasant, I'd ever done. I'd run marathons in the pouring rain, biked a century ride in one-hundred-degree heat. You don't know how hard your body can be pushed until you push it till it breaks. And, yes, I'd done that too.

I rinsed my socks and underwear, then wrapped myself in the towel. The beds were made with white sheets and army blankets. The one closest to the bathroom was unoccupied, so I laid my damp clothes out to dry on the upper bunk, then crawled into the lower and stuffed my boots underneath it. Finally, I closed the privacy curtain and burrowed under the blanket. I knew once the power came back on, or the officers' families reported their loved ones missing, or they found the car with me not in it, my face would be splattered on the walls of every police precinct in the province. Like bloodhounds on a scent, the RCMP wouldn't quit until they found me. My behavior tonight erased any doubt that I was guilty. Innocent people stay and defend themselves. Guilty people run and hide. Or so said conventional wisdom.

I can't really tell you why I was running. Maybe it was instinct. Or maybe escaping arrest was some bizarre game to me, and—as always—I had to win. I was gambling that the Banff police would not want the public to know there was a murderer on the loose and release my photo to the press, at least not yet. My indictment, on the other hand, would be broadcast far and wide. My mug shot would hit the internet like a storm. I knew there was a process, and I would eventually get a chance to prove my innocence in a court of law. My jail stint would be temporary, but the hit on my reputation would be forever. Unless they had another suspect, I was going down for this. Which meant I needed to find them one.

Miraculously, I fell asleep as soon as I closed my eyes. Visions of cops hauling me off to jail haunted my dreams as if it were the worst thing that could happen . . . because I didn't know there was somebody hunting me who I should have feared a whole lot more.

CHAPTER 46
Remy

The police showed up at the hotel at seven a.m. It had stopped snowing and was promising to be a beautiful bluebird day. The mountain had gotten sixty-six centimeters of fresh powder, and once the sun came out, the ski conditions would be epic. The crowds would be epic, too, but that never deterred me, given that I skied off-piste. Once I got up the lift, I could go into the trees and not see a soul the entire way down.

I was getting dressed for skiing when I got the call from my concierge that a policeman was in the lobby asking to talk to me.

"*Merde!*" I cursed as I swapped my snow pants for suit pants. *So much for getting first tracks.*

"Good morning, Officer Purdy," I said to the uniformed cop I'd met the night before. "How may I help you this morning?"

"Is there someplace private we can talk?"

"Of course."

I led him through the back-of-house to my cluttered office.

"Sorry for the mess." I cleared the chair so he could sit, but he remained standing, so I did too.

"We have some . . . unfortunate news."

He paused, like he didn't know how to tell me. My mind raced through the possibilities. Was I going to have to tell the guests about the murder? Post Julie's mug shot in the lobby? Close the hotel?

"The car taking our murder suspect to Calgary rolled on Highway 1 last night."

At first I didn't know how this concerned me, so I just said, "How frightening."

"An officer died. Another is in the hospital." I still didn't know how this concerned me. But I did my best to be polite.

"My condolences."

"The suspect . . . ," he started.

"Julie?" My heart quickened in my chest. "What about her?"

"We . . . don't know where she is."

"I'm sorry. I . . . don't understand." They had arrested and handcuffed her. How could they not know where she was?

"When the car rolled, she escaped. Because of the poor road conditions, she couldn't have gotten very far. We set up roadblocks outside Calgary and Lake Louise."

At first I thought it impossible that Julie had walked away from a deadly car wreck. But then I remembered: it's Julie Weston Adler.

"We're not telling the public about the murder, not while she's at large. People have enough to deal with after the storm." *In other words, keep your mouth shut.*

"How can I help?"

"We need to search the hotel, starting with her room."

"You don't think she came back here?" I asked, trying not to sound hopeful.

"Probably not. But we wouldn't be doing our jobs if we didn't look."

When one door closes, another one opens. When I'd failed to make the ski team, I joined the elite mountain-rescue team in Chamonix, France. When the PGHM let me go because I was the only one up on that mountain who had the guts to shoot a man who couldn't be saved,

I came back to Canada. When Julie told me she didn't love me and never would, I framed her for murder.

It was not premeditated. It was more like . . . serendipity. I was curious why Julie had gone up to the penthouse after her outing with friends—in her uniform, when she was off duty—so I monitored the security feed in my office, and when she returned to her room, I went to ask her. I expected her to look pretty when she opened the door all dressed for dinner, but her beauty was heart stopping.

"Remy!" she'd said when she saw me standing there with my jaw at my knees. "Is everything all right?"

Everything was *not* all right. Desire thundered through my body. I knew the clothes she was wearing were not hers—I had seen Ceci's bony ass parked on a barstool in those red leather pants many a time. I wasn't upset Julie had "borrowed" them, quite the opposite. They were made to be on a body like hers.

"What's going on?" she asked.

If there were words to describe what I was feeling, I might have used them. But I was moved to action, not words.

I was drawn to Julie the moment I'd met her. Her eyes danced with mischief, like she always had a secret that only a lucky few would ever know. Her laugh was liquid sunshine, to go with a smile as warm as a summer breeze. She had the kind of body you had to work for—strong and lean, with curves as smooth as polished stone.

My memories of making love to her were vivid and ever present. Merging with her body was like skiing fresh powder—she made me feel weightless, like I could go forever. It had been five years since we'd been intimate, but my longing had only grown more urgent. And I couldn't wait a moment more.

My hand reached for the small of her back as my lips devoured hers. She tasted earthy rich and vanilla sweet. I wanted to breathe in her warmth, drink from her skin, ride her body like an ocean wave. Like I had once before. Like I was destined to do again.

Slap!

The sting of her hand hitting my face was like falling off a cliff.

"How dare you!" Her eyes were fire.

"I'm sorry," I told her. "I thought that's why you came to Banff. For me. For *us*."

"My husband's been dead for two weeks."

"It's too soon, I understand." But I didn't understand.

"I came here because I needed a friend. I don't have those kinds of feelings for you, Remy. And I never will." And then she pushed past me to go meet her friends, literally slamming the door in my face.

I was shattered. I was humiliated. And then I was furious. She had shown up on my doorstep, offered me a beautifully wrapped gift, then slapped my hand when I tried to take it.

I choked back the memory as I escorted Officer Purdy through the back-of-house to Julie's room. Julie had never been wholly mine, but losing her was still devastating. She had let me believe she loved me—driving all the way here to see me, staying under my roof, accepting my help, my food, my comfort. I was crushed that she didn't want me. But nobody would want her now either. Even if she was acquitted, the accusation would stick to her like soot. I imagined the newspaper headline: "Olympian. Widow. Wanted for Murder." I wanted her to suffer, just as I had suffered because of her.

"Unlock the door, please."

I swiped my key card, then stepped aside so the policeman could enter. As I waited for him in the hall, I felt a twinge of satisfaction. I had put all this in motion. And it was proceeding just as I'd hoped.

Ceci Rousseau had been a scourge on this hotel. She made everyone miserable. The world was a better place without her. But that's not why I killed her. It was more personal than that. She knew what Mac had done to pave the way for the sale of Quantum Solar and was using it to blackmail him for a more favorable divorce settlement. If he didn't pay her what she wanted, she would squeal. And she wanted a lot. The more he gave in to her demands, the more she demanded. She was insatiable. And he was wavering. I didn't know if he would have blown the Quantum Solar deal to keep her from getting a generous settlement, but I didn't want to find out the hard way. I'd invested every penny I had in that deal. I couldn't afford to let her blow it up.

After Julie left for dinner, I helped myself to her rifle, which was just slim enough to fit under my blazer, then rode the elevator upstairs and entered Ceci's suite. She was standing in front of her bedroom fireplace, with her back to me. She hadn't heard me come in, so didn't turn around. I knew it was cowardly to shoot her in the back, but it was the quickest way and spared me having to hear her beg for her life. I thought the gasp she let out as she crumpled to the carpet would be the last sound she would ever make. So I left. Went back to my office to reset the security cameras I had paused to keep my movements unseen.

When she called me twenty minutes later, I thought I was hearing a voice from the dead. The sight of her bloody handprints all over the room made me dizzy from shock. I hadn't intended for her to die slowly, but perhaps the universe gave her what she deserved, just as it gave me a power outage to cover my tracks. Luck? Or a sign that it was all meant to be?

Framing Julie for Ceci's murder was a stroke of genius. Inciting Ceci's wrath, then sneaking up to her room to steal her clothes. I mean, she practically begged to be set up. Yes, my actions were vicious, but no more vicious than what either of those women had done to me. Ceci needed to die, and Julie needed to be punished. The two had dovetailed perfectly.

But now what? As I stood there in the wreckage of my broken future, I realized Julie's escape might be an opportunity too. Mac was right. A murder investigation had a way of unearthing things. I thought about what would happen if Julie got a fancy lawyer who started piecing it together. I couldn't afford to have Julie digging through Quantum Solar's confidential records. Which meant I would have to find a way to silence her too.

PART 4
Last to Die

CHAPTER 47
Julie

I woke to the sound of the TV. Someone must have forgotten to turn it off when the power went out, because it was blaring in the lobby downstairs.

Every muscle in my body hurt. It hurt to sit up. It hurt to turn my head. It hurt to breathe. I could barely lift my torso off the bed. I had no idea how long I'd slept, only that it wasn't enough.

My shoulder screamed with pain as I raised my arm and cracked open my privacy curtain. The bunk room was dark, but light was leaking out from under the bathroom door. Once my eyes adjusted, I could make out the objects in the room. Besides the bunk I'd slept in, there were a half dozen others pushed against the walls. Three of them had their curtains closed, so I presumed they were occupied. The other three were empty.

Across from the beds was a row of desks with nothing on them, and just beyond those, in the far corner of the room, was a row of metal lockers like they have at the gym. I eased my aching arms into my bra and stiff-as-cardboard legs into my underwear, then stood up. I had not pushed my muscles this hard for a long time, and they let me know they were not happy. I pivoted on my quivering legs to grab Ceci's clothes off the upper bunk, then tucked them under my arm and started toward the bathroom. My toes cramped with my first step, so I took ten seconds to stretch out my calves and feet. *C'mon, legs. Don't fail me now.*

It was ten agonizing steps to the lockers. One of them had a lock on it. The next one was empty, as was the one after that. But the fourth one had a backpack in it. I glanced over my shoulder. No one was watching. So I slid it out and took it into the bathroom with me.

I set the backpack on the counter. The upper compartment was stuffed with toiletries. I found a ponytail holder. I didn't want to leave hair in the hairbrush, so I finger-combed my tangled mane into a low braid. My face was tight and red with windburn, so I stole a pea-size amount of cleanser, and a dime-size dollop of moisturizer to ease the sting. There was a full-size tube of Colgate, so I put a dab on my index finger and rubbed it over my teeth. But my greatest find by far was the bottle of Advil. I opened it and took four, then prayed for it to work fast.

The main compartment of the backpack was a jumble of long johns and fleece. I didn't want to get greedy, so I just took a base layer and a pair of snowboarding pants. She had two pairs, it's not like I was leaving her with nothing to ride in. Plus the leather pants she was getting in exchange were worth five times as much. Hopefully she would appreciate that.

I got dressed as quickly as my stiff back and legs would let me, returned the backpack to the locker, then collected my boots from under my bed. The snow pants were belled out at the bottoms and white to match Ceci's angora sweater, which fit snugly over the stolen base layer. I imagined I looked hipster chic in my monotone outfit with mismatched textures, not that I cared how I looked. All that was important was that I was warm, dry, and inconspicuous: *mission accomplished.*

I slipped on my shell and the hat and gloves I'd stolen from the police car, and crept down the stairs. The TV was playing the news. I saw from the ribbon across the bottom that it was 7:26 a.m. A reporter was standing outside in the dark, talking about the power outage as she pointed to the building behind her. *"Banff was plunged into darkness when a tree fell on this transformer station . . ."*

"There's coffee if you want some," a voice said, and I looked over my shoulder to see a girl with tattoos down her neck sitting at the desk. "Pods are in the cupboard."

"Thanks, I'm good." I would have loved a cup of coffee. But I didn't want to get caught stealing someone else's clothes. *Again.* So I continued toward the door as the TV reporter signed off.

"This is Jenny Savage, reporting live. Back to you in the studio."

"Thanks, Jenny," the anchorwoman monotoned. *"In other news, a woman was found dead in her Banff Springs Hotel room last night."*

As I turned to look at the TV screen, I flashed back to the last time I'd seen Ceci. I was in her second bedroom, shopping for an outfit to borrow. The leather pants and angora sweater were still in plastic, fresh from the dry cleaner's. I figured I could take them, get them cleaned, then bring them back before she noticed they were gone. I had just put them in my laundry cart when the door to the suite swung open.

I'd watched through the crack in the door as Ceci kicked off her shoes, pulled a bottle of wine from the fridge, and poured herself a glass. When she set the glass down and turned on her computer, I got nervous she was about to start a marathon game of bridge, and I'd be stuck there all night. But instead of sitting down, she left the room. I didn't know where she went until I heard the tinkle of pee. I seized my chance and got myself and my cart out of there quick as a jackrabbit. Next thing I knew I was being arrested for her murder. Had they caught me on camera leaving her room? And if so, why hadn't they caught the person who'd come in after me and actually murdered her? Because if she had been found dead in her hotel room, the murderer had to be the person who came in after me.

I glanced over at the girl with the tattoos. She had headphones on and her nose in a book. I stared at the TV as a photo of Ceci in her signature red lipstick filled the screen. *"The deceased has been identified as Cecile Rousseau, wife of energy titan Mackenzie Rousseau . . . ,"* the anchorwoman said. The name Mackenzie Rousseau didn't mean anything to me . . . until the anchor's next sentence. *"After facing criticism for overdrilling in Western Canada, the oilman from Calgary expanded his empire into green tech, with big investments in California companies developing wind and solar."*

And then it clicked.

Mackenzie Rousseau was Megabucks Mackenzie, Jeff's lead investor.

Yes, it could be a coincidence that Mackenzie's wife died two weeks after Jeff, but what if it wasn't? Jeff had killed himself for a reason. Could it have had something to do with what was going on with the business? Something Mackenzie's wife was entangled in too?

My heart sped up in my chest. The police were either missing something or being misled. Someone went into Ceci's room after me. But who? And why were they looking for me and not them?

I couldn't solve the mystery locked up in jail. If there was evidence that would exonerate me, I had to find it before the police found me.

CHAPTER 48
Monique

When I was a kid growing up in North Vancouver, we used to hang out at a place in Lynn Valley called the Thirty-Foot Pool. The swimming hole was surrounded by cliffs on three sides. If you climbed to the top, it was a twenty-five-foot drop into the water. I jumped. But only once.

It wasn't the falling through the air that had spooked me. It was what happened after my body hit the water. When you jump from high, you go deep. It's dark down in the Thirty-Foot Pool. Scary dark. After I plunged into the water, I got turned around and didn't know which way was up. I panicked and swam into the rock face. I still have a scar in the middle of my forehead to remind me.

I sometimes had nightmares about being lost in that inky water—swimming in circles, my hands tearing at the limestone, frantic to find the way up and out. Over and over, I turned and flipped. The more I struggled, the more disoriented I got. My lungs burned, I couldn't breathe . . .

"Detective?"

My eyes flew open, and I gasped for air. Simon Stafford was sitting at my bedside, holding my arm. I must have looked terrified, because he said:

"I think you were dreaming."

I looked down at his hand. He let go of my arm.

"Where am I?"

"Banff Springs Hospital. You were in a car accident."

I gazed down at the front of my body. I was wearing a blue-and-white-checkered hospital gown. An IV line was taped to my hand.

I saw my parka draped on a chair. My gloves on the windowsill. And then I remembered. *The murder. The arrest. Driving on Highway 1 in a blizzard . . .*

"The car flipped," I said.

Stafford nodded. "More like rolled, but yes."

"We hit something. An animal."

"Bull elk."

"Where's Jarvis?" I asked.

The muscles in Stafford's jaw tightened.

"Simon?" I braced myself for bad news, but nothing could have prepared me for what he said next.

"He didn't make it, Monique."

Tears erupted from my eye sockets as a sob exploded from my chest. I shook my head, trying to make it not true.

"He died on impact," Stafford said. "There was nothing to be done."

I knew it was unprofessional to cry in front of my recruit, but I couldn't stop. Jarvis meant so much to so many people. He had a wife, kids, grandkids. This was far and away the worst thing to ever happen to the Banff police force, and it happened on my watch.

"Sorry," I squeaked.

"Don't apologize. I know how close you were to him." He reached over and grabbed a box of tissues from the tray. I took a handful and pressed them to my face.

"Poor Marlene." J. J.'s wife knew police work was dangerous, but her husband had served thirty years without incident. The news must have gutted her.

"Chief's been to see her," Stafford said, and I felt a rush of guilt. We should have gone together. I was the last one to see him alive. I didn't blame myself—it was not my decision to venture out in the storm. But he was still my man and my friend and such a deeply good guy.

I wanted to know how I'd gotten here, who pulled me out of the wreckage. But there was something else I needed to know first.

"What about the suspect?"

Stafford pulled out his phone and showed me security cam footage of a body wrapped in what looked like aluminum foil being fireman carried into the hospital.

"Who's that?"

"You." I leaned in for a closer look. At first I didn't know which one was me. Then I realized the answer to *How did I get here?* and *What happened to the suspect?* was one and the same.

"Oh my God. Did Julie Adler . . . ?"

"Save your life? Probably." Then he upgraded his answer. "Yes."

"Where is she now?"

"We don't know."

"So . . . what? She just dropped me off and left?"

He let the video run a little longer. I saw the nurse press the button to open the double doors to the emergency ward. I saw Adler, my apparent rescuer, walk through them and set me on a gurney, then walk right out the front door.

"Most of the cameras in town were out because of the blizzard," Stafford said. "She could have gone anywhere." Banff had a smattering of cameras—on buses, street corners, in front of ATMs and hotels. But the buses weren't running. And most of the establishments in town didn't have backup generators.

"What time did the power come back online?"

"Not until after seven this morning."

"So she had all night to move around without detection."

"Unfortunately, yes."

My body ached, and my head was as heavy as a block of concrete. But I couldn't stay in bed while a murder suspect was on the loose in my town.

"I have to get to work."

I tried to push myself out of bed. Pain shot through my right arm.

"Careful," Simon said, catching me as I nearly fell out of the bed. "I think your arm is broken."

I looked down at my arm. It was splinted with an Ace bandage around it.

"You took a pretty bad tumble. I think you should stay put for a while, boss."

Julie Adler saved my life, but she was still a killer. And I wanted her in custody.

"Go find her."

CHAPTER 49
Izzy

I don't know about the other girls, but I didn't sleep a wink. We didn't have to leave for the airport until ten thirty, but I still got up at the crack of dawn to pack. After the horrific events of the last twelve hours, *immediately* was not soon enough to, as they say, get outta Dodge.

The girls and I had gotten ready for bed in silence. I think we were in shock. It was inconceivable that Julie had murdered someone. She was our friend. Our brunch buddy. My emergency babysitter. Plus we were with her almost the entire day. Yes, she was grieving and under stress, but she could handle stress better than anyone I knew. So she didn't want us to know she was working as a maid? That's hardly a crime.

I took a shower, towel dried my hair, then got dressed in my "plane outfit": sweatpants and a matching hoodie. I never understood people who got gussied up to fly. Airplanes are wall-to-wall germs. First thing I want to do when I get home is throw my clothes in the wash. Why on earth would anyone want to wear dry-clean-only on a plane?

I was slipping into my UGGS to go downstairs and grab coffee when—

Bam-bam-bam!

"RCMP!" An aggressive visitor pounded on the door. My heart sped up without a caffeine boost.

"One sec!" I called out, pulling on my other boot. Christa and Suki were dead to the world in their earplugs and eye masks, so I went over and shook them.

"Guys, the police are here. Get up!"

The dead bolt thunked. I hurried over to the opening door.

"Hey! We're not decent in here!" I said, grabbing the door handle. And that's when I saw him: Julie's French Canadian boyfriend. Standing there holding the key to our room.

"What are you doing here?" I asked. My eyes floated down to the brass nameplate on his lapel. *Why does he have a name tag on?* And then it hit me. "Wait, do you work at the hotel?"

"I'm the manager," he said, tucking his key back into his breast pocket.

Behind me, Christa and Suki were scrambling to get dressed. I stepped out into the hall and closed the door behind me.

"You can't just come into somebody's room," I informed them. "What if we were naked?"

The skinny cop standing next to Julie's dreamboat boyfriend pulled a piece of paper out of his pocket.

"We have a search warrant," he said, holding it up for me to see. He had a nameplate pinned over his left pec too: Kyle Purdy.

"To look for what?" I asked. "Stolen minis of gin?"

"They're looking for Julie," Remy said. And everything about that confused me.

"What do you mean?" I turned to the cop. "You arrested her—she's in jail."

He looked at me blankly. So I looked at Remy. He raised an eyebrow.

"I'm going to have to take a quick look around, ma'am," the officer said. What the cop was saying made no sense, but I could tell from the look in his eye that he wasn't going away.

"My friends need to get dressed. Just . . . give us a minute."

I didn't have my key, so I signaled to Remy to unlock the door. He pressed his card to the keypad. Thunk!

"One minute," I repeated, then went back inside. Christa was on the toilet and Suki was riffling through her suitcase looking for clean underwear.

"What the hell, Izzy?" Christa said, pulling up her pants.

"Guys, you're not going to believe this," I said, not sure I believed it myself. "But I think Julie escaped from jail."

"What?!"

"They can't find her."

"Do they think she came here?" Suki asked.

"I don't know. But they have a warrant to search our room."

The girls threw on bras and T-shirts, and I let the policeman into the room. Remy stood in the doorway while the cop looked in the closet, the shower, under the beds, even out the window to see if Julie had jumped four stories into the snow.

"If she gets in touch with you, you need to let us know," Officer Kyle Purdy said, handing me his business card.

"If she's running, it's because she's innocent," Suki interjected. Christa put a hand on her to stop her from saying anything more.

"If we hear from her, we'll let you know," Christa promised.

I nodded in agreement. None of us believed Julie was capable of murder. But turns out we didn't know her as well as we thought.

CHAPTER 50
Julie

I left the hostel in my stolen ski pants with thirty-five dollars in my pocket. The sun was rising, but the temperature was dropping. I didn't need to see the weather forecast to know a cold front was rolling in. I could feel it.

The streets were coming to life. People were digging out their cars, walking their dogs, loading their skis in their Thules. Here in a ski town, a day with fresh powder and sunshine was called a *unicorn* because of how rare and magical it was. The ski hill would be a zoo: the perfect place to hide in plain sight.

The bus stop was two blocks from the hostel. There were a half dozen snowboarders already waiting there, so I got in line behind them.

"Ah, shoot, I forgot my GoPro," one said.

"You can take a run with mine," another replied.

I tried not to think about the cameras. They would be everywhere, including on the bus. And no doubt the police had eyes on as many feeds as humanly possible.

The bus pulled up, and we all got on. I tightened my hood and tucked my chin inside my coat. There was barely room to stand. Normally, I'd be annoyed to have the sharp edges of someone's skis pressing into my back. But I was grateful for the crowds today.

As the bus pulled out into traffic, I kept my gaze down and my ears open. The sound of boots thumping and ski pants crinkling brought me back to simpler days, when all I'd had to worry about was skiing fast and, shooting straight. Training was intense, but I loved it. I never felt more like myself than when I was on the snow. I would never call following Jeff to California a mistake—I loved him and would be forever grateful for how deeply he loved me. But if losing him meant starting over, where would I go from here? My friendships with Izzy and the girls were complicated—even more so now. Over the years, Izzy had given me way more than she had taken. But her betrayal stung. And it was hard for me to imagine going back to California without Jeff.

The road to Norquay was a steep swirl of switchbacks. The road had been plowed, but it was still slow going. As the bus chugged and swayed, I went over what I knew.

Jeff had been working with Mackenzie since before we were married, so for over three years. He'd called the $3 million he got from Mac and his investor group "seed money." That seed money was meant to be used to develop a prototype that demonstrated how his quantum dot technology worked. Once they had a prototype of the solar panel they were building, they would start shopping it to companies who could take the concept to market.

Jeff and Mackenzie had been practicing their sales pitch for months. Jeff was extremely stressed out. A multibillion-dollar energy company was on the verge of buying them, and Jeff was desperate to impress them. He and his lead electrochemist, a former MIT classmate named Fang Li, sometimes worked well into the night. Those late nights were not good for his health, or our marriage. But he promised it would soon be over. And I left him alone, misunderstanding the meaning of *over*.

My thoughts turned to the missing money. What had happened to it? If Jeff needed more, why didn't Mackenzie pony up? Did Mac not know they had burned through their cash? Was Jeff afraid to tell him? Had he mismanaged it? Is that why he did what he did?

And how did Ceci tie in to this? Her death two short weeks after Jeff's couldn't be a coincidence, could it? And why was I a suspect? Had someone framed me? Who would do that?

There was a piece missing. And somehow, on the run from the RCMP, with a cold front rolling in and thirty-five dollars to my name, I would have to find it.

CHAPTER 51
Monique

I was stuck at the hospital waiting for the guy from orthopedics to set my broken arm, but that didn't mean I wasn't working.

The Telus store didn't open until ten, so I used the landline in my room to make calls. The first one was to the Ventura County Sheriff's Office to request the police report from Jeff Adler's suicide. If that's really what it was. If Julie Adler had killed once, it wasn't far-fetched to think she'd played a role in her husband's death too. If there was anything suspicious about that incident, I wanted to know.

"Can I ask why you're requesting that report?" the deputy asked after I told her who I was.

"His wife is a suspect in a murder case here in Alberta," I replied. And there was an incredulous pause.

"You don't mean Julie?"

"Julie Weston Adler, yes," I said.

"Julie wouldn't hurt a fly. Did you know she volunteers at the animal shelter every other Saturday? And helps out the fire department from time to time. We have a very dedicated core of volunteer firefighters, and let me tell you, that woman can handle a hose. She puts those men to shame. Did you know fifty feet of fire hose can weigh up to nine hundred pounds?"

"I did not."

"Julie and her husband, rest his soul, started an annual 5K road race to fight child hunger. The whole town comes out. We get food trucks from all over the county."

"That does sound nice," I said. "But I'd still like to see a copy of the report, if you don't mind."

I gave her the police department's email, and she promised she'd get it to me "right quick."

While I waited for the police report, I called Purdy to see how his search of the hotel was coming.

"The friends' room was clear," he said. "Do you want to detain the three of them for questioning? They're scheduled to fly back to the States this afternoon."

"No, they can go home. Just get their contact information in case we have questions."

"Copy that."

As I hung up the phone, Officer Stafford walked in with my laptop, a new cell phone to replace the one I'd lost in the accident, and a cup of coffee.

"Oh, God bless you, Stafford."

"I have an update," he said.

"Go ahead."

"Teresa back at the station has been calling all the local hotels," he said as he pulled up a chair. I had asked our secretary to call around and find out if anyone had tried to get a room while I'd been a frozen burrito awaiting unwrapping.

"And?" Given the weather, I figured there were only two varieties of people who might have checked in to a Banff-area hotel last night—a local with frozen pipes in search of a shower, and a suspect evading arrest.

"While she was doing that, she got an incoming call from the hostel in town. Apparently someone stole some long johns and a pair of ski pants from a locker."

The hostel was a breeding ground for petty thieves. A missing pair of underwear was hardly cause for concern.

"I imagine that happens all the time," I said.

"Yes, it does. But Teresa still asked them to check the registry of guests." He had my interest now.

"And?" I brought the coffee to my lips with my good arm.

"Your name is on it." I lowered the cup.

"*My* name?"

"Your driver's license number too. Someone showed your ID to get a bunk."

I put the cup down and swung my legs over the side of the bed.

"Hand me my jacket."

Stafford passed me my coat. I patted down the pockets.

"You've got to be kidding."

"What?"

"She stole my wallet."

"Bold."

I pulled the coat on over the splint. "Help me get my boots on, would you?"

Stafford drove us the four blocks to the hostel on freshly plowed streets. My head was pounding, and my heart was shattered. I couldn't breathe this air without thinking of J. J. As the pain of losing him rose up in my throat, I clamped my lips together and hoped Stafford would think the sheen in my eyes was because of the cold.

The snowbanks on Banff Avenue were six feet high. We couldn't pull over, so we left the squad car in the middle of the road with the hazards on. Not ideal, but everyone was skiing anyway.

The bell on the front door jingled when I opened it, and I shook my head at the low-tech security. A dark-eyed girl with a tattooed neck looked up from the book she was reading as we approached the desk.

"Hello, Officers," she said as she snapped her gum.

"Someone reported a theft?" Stafford asked. An armed response for a petty theft was probably a first, but the girl didn't ask questions she knew we wouldn't answer.

"She's upstairs."

"Can you take us?" I asked.

The tattooed girl got up from behind her plexiglass enclosure and started up the stairs. I followed her, and Stafford followed me.

"Mia, right?" the staffer said to a tall girl sitting on a bottom bunk. "Cops want to talk to you."

"Is this about my stuff?" Her voice was hopeful, like she thought we were there to help her get it back.

"When did you notice your things were stolen?" I asked.

"About an hour ago, when I was getting dressed."

Stafford made a note on his trusty pad.

"How long have you been staying here?" I asked.

"Five days, including today."

Stafford's eyes flicked up from his notebook. We both knew that just because Mia had noticed her pants and long underwear were gone this morning, it didn't mean that's when they'd been stolen.

"There was something weird, though," Mia said.

"Go on."

"Whoever took them left these."

She held up a pair of red leather pants. That told us not only when her stuff had been stolen, but also who'd taken it.

CHAPTER 52
Julie

The sun was a fuzzy, yellow flare on the horizon as I exited the bus at the base of the ski hill. The cold front that had pushed the clouds away was plunging the temperature into the negative teens. It would likely get to −20°C by nightfall, even colder after that.

Despite the frigid temperatures, the resort was insanely crowded. The lines to get on the lifts fanned out in all directions. For someone who wanted to ski, it was a nightmare. For someone who wanted to disappear, it was ideal.

A ski resort is a terrible place to buy food. Everything is twice as expensive. But the last thing I'd eaten was a McDonald's hamburger, and that was before I'd hauled 120 pounds of human cargo ten kilometers in a blizzard. So, as my fellow bus passengers hurried to get in the lift line, I veered off toward the lodge.

The cheapest, most caloric option was the chili. It came with a roll, but I took two, and six pats of butter to go with.

"Can I sit here?" I asked a group of teenagers at a large table. They responded by moving their gear to make room for my tray. As I was eating and thinking about how I could do research up here without a laptop or a phone, one of my tablemates gave me an idea.

"Why are the lines *so* freakin' long?" a boy in a bright-orange jacket whined.

"Dude, half the mountain is closed," his friend responded. "You can see the ski patrol up top doing avalanche control."

After a big storm, it's the ski patrol's job to make sure it's safe to open the trails. Sometimes that means preempting avalanches by setting off explosions to cause them on purpose. Given how much snow had fallen overnight, it had to have been all hands on deck up on the mountain. Which meant their office would be empty.

The ski patrol holed up in a dumpy one-story building behind the lodge—really more like a hut than a building. I wolfed down my last bite of chili, then wound around the back of the lodge and knocked on the door.

"Hello?"

No answer.

I turned the knob and peeked inside. The place was cluttered but organized. There was a lumpy couch, a tower of folded blankets, a tackle-box-style first aid kit, a pile of helmets, a jumble of climbing skins, a plant stand with a bowl of fun-size Aero bars where the plant should be. Skis and poles were lined up two by two against the windows, obscuring the view of the mountain just beyond. An assortment of boots stood in front of them like soldiers in mismatched uniforms. I clocked a pair of Nordica SpeedMachines—same brand as my downhill boots—as if I knew I was going to need them.

I went inside and closed the door behind me. My boots were wet, but I kept them on as I helped myself to a candy bar, then sat down at the wooden desk by the windows. The password to the desktop computer was on a Post-it on the monitor. Ski bums weren't known for their abundance of caution.

But my husband, Jeff, was.

While Jeff and I had an online vault for our personal files, his sensitive business records were on an encrypted server that required dual authentication to access. If I tried to log on, a password would be sent to his email or one of our phones. Without his laptop or either of our phones, I couldn't access data about his company. And even if I could, I didn't know what I was looking for—at least not yet.

Besides Megabucks Mackenzie, who I obviously couldn't call, given that he'd probably been told I murdered his wife, there was only one other person who might know what was going on with Jeff's company. I didn't know Fang Li very well. We had had him over for dinner a few times, but other than that, I never spoke to him. I had no idea if he'd open up to me, but it was a place to start.

I opened Google, and after a few clicks, found his résumé on LinkedIn. It had a phone number on it. So I picked up the handset and dialed.

"Hello?" a male voice said after one ring.

"Is this Fang?"

Pause.

"Who's calling?"

"It's Julie Adler."

"Julie. Hi. I . . . uh . . . I'm sorry for your loss."

"Thanks, Fang." I didn't recall seeing Fang at Jeff's funeral. Which I might have thought was odd, if not for what he said next.

"Listen, Fang, I'm sorry to bother you," I said, "but I had some questions about the last few weeks at Quantum Solar."

"OK, but if it's about something that happened after I was fired, I won't be able to help."

"Jeff fired you?"

"Yes. Back in September."

"Why?"

Pause.

"Fang, are you still there?"

"Jeff was a really good guy," he said, and I knew he was bracing me for something uncomfortable.

"Thanks for saying that, Fang."

"The thing is, his process . . ."

"What about his process?"

"It didn't work."

CHAPTER 53
Monique

My arm was throbbing when I got to the station, and my fingers were ice cold. I couldn't get a glove over that bulky splint, and the temperatures were plunging into the negative teens.

"We should get you back to the hospital," Stafford said as he followed me into my office.

"Later. I want to hear the interview with the friends."

As Stafford pulled out his phone and opened the voice memo, I got on my computer to google *Julie Weston Adler*, awkwardly mousing with my left hand. I wanted to know everything about her—her favorite color, how she wore her hair, what she ate for breakfast, anything that might give me a clue about where she might have gone.

"Here we go," Stafford said, then pressed play.

"*What brought you all to Banff?*" his recorded voice said. I scrolled through pictures of Julie Adler as I listened. Most of the photos were of her skiing or shooting. She was an excellent shooter. In her sport, she had to hit targets less than two inches in diameter from fifty meters away. Her hit rate was 95 percent—among the best in her field.

"*And how do you all know Ms. Adler?*"

I changed my Google search to *Julie Adler + husband*, pecking awkwardly at the keys with my left index finger. I wanted to see personal photos. Get some insights on what made her tick.

"We're friends from back home."

Photos of Julie and her dead husband, Jeff, filled my screen—holding hands at a charity event, carrying surfboards at the beach . . .

"I think she has a boyfriend here. That's why she came. His name is Remy," one of Julie's friends said. And I recalled how the uppity hotel manager had resisted telling us anything about his newest employee.

"Is that true?" I asked Stafford.

"Not sure."

"Anyone else see them together?"

"I'll find out."

I scrolled through more photos: Julie and Jeff standing at the altar, she in Chantilly lace, he in a tux. They got married here in Banff. *Interesting.*

"Has your friend Julie Adler ever mentioned a woman named Cecile Rousseau? Or Ceci Rousseau?" Stafford asked the friends.

"Yes! That's her fake name!" one of the friends answered. I glanced up at Stafford.

"Bold," I said.

"Maybe her plan was to kill Mrs. Rousseau and steal her identity?" Stafford said.

"And maybe you watch too much Acorn TV." But I couldn't help but wonder why Julie would tell her friends she was using the name Ceci Rousseau, especially if she planned to kill her.

As the interview droned on, I clicked on more wedding photos. There was one of the newlyweds eating wedding cake. I stopped scrolling.

"Did we get the police report from Jeff Adler's suicide yet?"

"I'll check."

Stafford popped out of his chair. As I waited for him, I opened a new window and googled *Jeff Adler*. Photos of the tech genius filled my screen. Lots of shots of him on the golf course.

"Here you go," Stafford said, handing me the copy Teresa had printed.

I flipped through the report. *Self-inflicted gunshot to the right temple.*

I looked back up at my screen, at a golf photo of Jeff Adler in mid-swing. If I hadn't been struggling to type with my left hand, I might not have noticed that he was wearing a glove on his right . . . or remembered that right-handed golfers typically wore their glove on their left.

I went back to the photo of him eating cake, holding his fork *with his left hand.*

I went to YouTube. Found a video of Jeff Adler doing a PowerPoint presentation about quantum dot technology . . . whatever that was. I wasn't interested in *what* he was doing, but rather *how* he was doing it.

"Stafford . . . ," I said, pausing the video as Jeff Adler wrote on a whiteboard . . .

"What?"

I pointed to the image on my screen. Of Jeff holding a dry-erase marker . . . *in his left hand.*

"Jeff Adler was left handed."

"So?"

I pointed to the photo of dead Jeff in the police report, the fingers of his right hand wrapped around the grip of the gun.

"So I don't think he killed himself."

CHAPTER 54
Julie

"What do you mean the process didn't work?" I asked Fang. Jeff had been working on his quantum dot solar panel for five years. Rousseau had put up millions to fund production of the prototype. And now Fang was saying it didn't work?

"It's not that it *never* worked. We just couldn't get it to work consistently. Nanotech is like that. There are countless variables."

"So you're saying it sometimes worked?"

"Yes, and we didn't know why. We made a stupid mistake."

"What mistake?"

"We had a successful demo with an early prototype, and we told our investor."

"Mackenzie Rousseau?"

"Mac and his wife, Ceci." The mention of Ceci's name sent a prickle down my arms.

"Ceci Rousseau was involved with the company?"

"Not officially. But she was always lurking. I think she liked to know what her husband was up to."

I didn't tell him she'd been murdered—didn't want him to stop talking.

"Tell me more about Mackenzie Rousseau."

"Mac is a brilliant guy. He has a degree in chemical engineering from Waterloo. We told him we were having trouble repeating the successful demo, but he went ahead and told our suitors we had a viable product."

"But you didn't?"

"It was too soon to claim it was working. We didn't have the formula mastered. Nanotech is a precise science. You have to have your formulas calculated down to the molecule."

"Is that why Jeff fired you? Because you couldn't figure out how to fix it?"

"Things were getting tense between Jeff and Mac. Mac had an offer from a Fortune 500 company. He wouldn't say, but I knew it was someone who could pay big and make them all a lot of money. Mac needed us to demo the project for their VP of product development."

"And you wouldn't do it?"

"I *couldn't* do it. The current formula wasn't working. Jeff wanted to keep me on—it was Mac who wanted me gone."

"So they brought in someone who they thought could figure it out?"

"Oh yeah, a whole new team. They must have cracked it because they got their offer. It's not public knowledge yet. I guess these deals take time to close. Jeff was on his way to being the 'it' guy in green tech."

It's not that I didn't believe Fang, but ending it all was hardly what a future "it" guy would do.

"Did Jeff ever tell you what the fix was?"

And Fang didn't answer.

"Fang? Are you there?"

"That's the thing, Julie. I know he fired me, but we were friends. We were in the trenches together day and night for years. We coauthored six patents. My fingerprints are all over that product. No one would have been happier for him than me."

"But he didn't tell you what the new team did to make it work?"

"No. He never did."

"Why do you think that is, Fang?"

Another beat of silence. I didn't want to push, because I had a feeling I knew what he wanted to tell me, and if I pressured him he might not say it.

"I can't prove it . . ."

"Go on," I coaxed.

"I don't think there's an electrochemist on the planet who could have solved the riddle in the two short months between when I left and when they closed the deal. There's a scientific method. It would have taken huge amounts of time and money for a new team to complete the process."

Time *and money.*

"How much money?"

"Tens, maybe even hundreds, of thousands. We needed equipment and manpower to run experiments. Mac wasn't going to pay for that, not when he already had a buyer."

I couldn't help but wonder. Was that where our money had gone? To pay for the experiments Mac wouldn't?

Fang continued, "Right before I was fired, I would overhear Mac say things like, 'You can figure it out once we get the money—just show them the outputs from the early prototype.'"

"But Jeff wouldn't do it?"

"You know Jeff. He was nothing if not honest."

And I knew that was mostly true.

"The only way they could have closed the deal that fast is if Mac fudged the data," Fang said. "I think they wanted Jeff to vouch for it and he wouldn't. That's why he did what he did. They drove him to it."

"Fang, that's a bold accusation. Can we prove it?"

"I was gone by the time it all went down. Plus I signed an NDA, Julie. I shouldn't be talking about any of this, not even to you."

"So why are you?"

"Because he was your husband. You deserve to know what he was going through. That he acted with integrity even under the worst kind of pressure. And that what he did had nothing to do with you."

I didn't realize I was crying until a tear fell onto the desk in front of me.

"Thank you for that, Fang."

"I hope it helps." It did. It helped *a lot*.

"Just one more question, Fang. If you don't mind?" I had an ominous thought, so I had to ask.

"Of course."

"What would have happened if Jeff spoke up about the faked test results?"

"You mean if the buyer found out?"

"Yes."

"The deal would have fallen apart. And Rousseau and his investor group would have had to start over with someone else."

That ominous thought bloomed into suspicion. Jeff had put his heart and soul into that company. No one wanted it to succeed more than he did. But like Fang said, he wasn't going to lie.

"Do you think Jeff was going to tell the buyer?" I asked. But Fang wouldn't opine.

"I don't know, Julie. You knew him best."

And he was right about that. Some days I thought I knew my husband better than I knew myself. I knew he was brilliant. I knew he wasn't a quitter. We had that in common.

As I thought about the perseverance and intelligence that defined Jeff, I knew something else. The police had gotten it wrong. Jeff would never have taken his own life. Which meant that somebody else had.

CHAPTER 55
Izzy

We got to the airport three hours before our scheduled departure. We didn't want to risk the police telling us we weren't allowed to leave, so we split right after the cavity search. Not our body cavities, that would have been inappropriate. But the cops looked just about everywhere else—under the bed, under the sink, even in my suitcase, as if Julie could have squeezed in there!

There was a bar near our gate in the terminal, so we pulled up stools and ordered lunch. On TV, the Dallas Cowboys were playing some team with cats on their helmets. And then, instead of commercials, there was a news break, with a reporter standing next to an overturned police car with the hindquarters of a big-ass mammal sticking out of it.

"Oh my God, you guys, look!"

The girls looked up from their club sodas.

"Can you turn it up, please?!" I asked the bartender. As he raised the volume, a few other patrons turned to look too.

"*. . . fatal car crash that left one officer dead and another in the hospital. It's unclear where the police vehicle was headed in the middle of a snowstorm, and the RCMP won't say.*"

I looked at Christa, who looked at Suki, who looked at me.

"You don't think . . . ," Suki said.

"Shhh!" Christa shushed.

"The police aren't confirming, but it appears that a passerby or second passenger may have assisted in the rescue of the injured police officer"—the reporter pointed toward town—*"because Detective Monique Montpelier was admitted to Banff Springs Hospital shortly before midnight, and she didn't get there on her own."*

An anchorman popped on the screen to thank the reporter, and then the Cowboys were back.

"Whoa." I exhaled.

"It's gotta be Julie," Suki whispered. "Who else could have dragged that detective all the way back to Banff in the snow?"

"Not many people," I agreed.

"I hope she's OK," Suki said.

"She's Julie," Christa said. And we all breathed a little sigh of relief.

Our hamburgers arrived (well, Suki got a salad), and we stopped talking to eat. As I took a big bite and pickle juice ran down my arm, my phone rang in my purse. I figured it was the hub asking what time to expect me, so I wiped my hands and answered it.

"Hello?"

"Izzy?" a voice whispered. I peeked at the caller ID. *An Alberta number.*

"Who is this?"

"It's me."

"Julie?"

Christa and Suki looked at me like I was levitating above my chair.

"It's noisy in here," I said, covering my free ear with my finger. "Hold on, let me step outside."

I hopped off my barstool and made for the exit. Christa and Suki followed on my heels.

"Where is she?" Christa asked.

"Why is she calling you?" Suki echoed.

I held up a hand to shush them.

"Jules?" I said as I stepped over the threshold of the bar.

"I'm here."

"Are you OK?"

"Yes, I'm fine."

I gave Christa and Suki the thumbs-up.

"We just saw the police car crash on TV. Was that you?" I asked. She didn't answer.

"Was it her?" Christa asked, and I quieted her with my hand.

"We're just relieved you're OK," I said, not wanting to push.

"Thanks, listen. I need you to do something for me when you get back to LA."

"Of course. Anything."

"Go to my house and get Jeff's laptop. It's in his office. I'll call you tonight. What time do you land?"

"Five o'clock."

"I'll call you after that. I gotta go."

And the line went dead.

"Well?" Christa said. "What's going on? Where is she?"

"I don't know where she is—she didn't say."

"So the police haven't found her yet?" Suki asked, a little too loud.

"Shh! Suki!" Christa admonished.

"Sorry."

"What did she want?" Christa asked.

"She asked me to get Jeff's laptop."

"Get it and do what with it?"

"I'm not sure," I replied. "Maybe she's trying to solve that woman's murder?"

Because wasn't that just like her.

235

CHAPTER 56
Monique

"So what are you saying?" Stafford asked. "That Julie Adler killed both Ceci Rousseau and her husband?"

"I don't know," I said. *It's always the spouse* was true so often it had become a cliché. But I wasn't ready to apply it to Julie Adler just yet.

"What do we know about the alleged boyfriend?" I asked Stafford. Even if she was involved with another man, it was still a questionable motive to commit murder. Framing her husband's death as a suicide meant she wouldn't get a penny of life insurance, and a man as successful as Jeff Adler would have had a sizable policy, likely in the millions. If she was in love with another man, she could have just divorced him. And possibly gotten alimony too.

Stafford was typing on his computer. "Remy Claude Delatour," he read. "French Canadian dual citizen, born to a French mother and Canadian father. No criminal record. Home address is listed as the Banff Springs Hotel."

Julie had a good job in California. So why had she left to work as a hotel maid? And what kind of boyfriend would import his girlfriend to scrub toilets? Something wasn't clicking.

"What about travel to the United States?" I asked. "If they were a couple, presumably they saw each other periodically. Which would mean one or both of them were crossing the border, at least once in a while."

"I'll call immigration."

"Check exit and entry records for both of them."

"Copy that."

Stafford picked up the phone. While he was dialing the number, he asked, "You think that's why Delatour was cagey with us? Because he was covering for her?"

"Well, he certainly seemed to be covering something."

While Stafford waited on hold with immigration, I opened the file to look at the pictures of the crime scene. And something odd struck me.

"Do you remember what you said to me when I asked you your first impression of the scene?"

"Something about it being really bloody, I think?"

"You said, 'It wasn't quick and painless.'"

"That sounds right."

"I think that was an important observation. Look at all that blood." I pointed. "It's on the curtains, the rug, the coffee table, even all the way in the kitchen."

"Yes, I remember. And?"

"A .22-caliber bullet to the heart would have killed her instantly. But it didn't. Why?"

"It missed her heart."

"Exactly."

"I'm not sure I'm following, Detective."

"Julie Weston Adler is an Olympic-biathlon champion." I turned my screen to face him, so he could see the video I'd found of her hitting a 1.8-inch target from fifty meters away . . . *five times in a row*.

"So?"

"Julie Weston Adler doesn't miss."

CHAPTER 57
Julie

The ski patrol hut was drafty, and my nose was cold and running. There was a space heater next to the desk, but I didn't dare turn it on. Instead I grabbed two blankets from the pile—one for my shoulders, one for my lap. And another candy bar, which I ate in one swallow.

My conversation with Fang had rattled me. Jeff hadn't mentioned that there'd been upheaval at the company. Was he embarrassed? Trying to protect me from something? Or maybe he'd tried to tell me, and I'd said something glib, like *You got this*. I could be insensitive like that. Acknowledging that people sometimes needed a shoulder to lean on scared me, because what if I did too?

I logged on to our bank accounts. The flow of money told a story, and I wanted to know when ours had turned tragic.

I started with Jeff's business account. I scrolled through his bank statements to see it was flush with cash at the beginning of the year—close to a million dollars. Quantum Solar didn't have any revenue yet, so as expected, the balance declined every month. By July, the bank balance was down to half a million dollars. Then, in September—the same month he'd fired Fang—Jeff made three chunk withdrawals that completely wiped it out.

I looked at our joint account. Jeff didn't want to take a big salary at the expense of the company being able to grow, so for the first nine months of the year, the balance steadily declined. But come October, the account fell off a cliff. In the span of three weeks, he'd withdrawn all the money, again in big chunks.

The last remaining account was our brokerage account. We had vowed not to touch that one. Thanks to some smart investments, it had been growing steadily since January. But, like he'd done with the others, Jeff made a handful of chunk withdrawals toward the end of the year, plunging the balance into single digits.

I thought about what Fang had said, about the process not working and how Jeff was desperate to fix it. I looked at the recipients of all that money he'd spent: consultants, machine shops, industrial-metal supply stores. Jeff's sudden spending suggested that he threw money at the problem to try to get it fixed.

But then what?

Fang had said that Mackenzie was pressuring Jeff to "fudge the data." The only way to prove this was to see his correspondence. I needed Jeff's laptop. And for that I needed Izzy.

I looked at the clock. Izzy wouldn't be getting to my house in Dos Vientos for several hours. I didn't want to risk someone from the ski patrol catching me in their office, so I logged off the computer, folded the blankets and put them back on the pile, then slipped back outside.

In the three hours since I'd snuck into the hut, the temperature had dropped precipitously. The thermometer on the side of the building read $-14°C$ . . . but the biting wind told me the cold front wasn't done with us yet.

I still had twenty dollars, so I decided to spend half of it on a slice of pizza and a hot chocolate. I wasn't worried about running out of money. It was time that I needed. But I wouldn't be getting any more of that.

The lodge was a zoo. Rosy-cheeked skiers and riders swarmed the cafeteria, loading their trays with hot food and drinks. I didn't mind waiting in line. I had the whole afternoon to kill. My head was heavy with exhaustion. The ski patrol hut was cold, but it was nice and toasty in here. I knew it was risky, but that chair by the fire was too tempting. So after I ate, as the throngs of people headed back out into the cold, I curled up on it and gave in to sleep.

CHAPTER 58
Remy

Julie's friends had left for the airport, but Officer Purdy was still milling around the hotel interviewing employees, hoping one of them had information about where Julie might have gone.

The sun was out and the powder was fresh, so I left Purdy to do his work and went to get my fix. I didn't want to wait half an hour for the bus—it was noon, the day was already half over—so I grabbed my skis from the storage room and threw them in my truck.

Banff was the most beautiful place on earth after a snowstorm. The sun was a lemon yellow orb against a Côte d'Azur sky. As I drove down streets painted with glistening snow, I got a buoyant feeling in my chest. Money may not buy happiness, but it does buy the next best thing: freedom. And I was about to be as free as the wind.

My Chevy Blazer crunched up the mountain road, which was well traveled and heavy with salt. I passed a few cars on their way down—locals who'd come for first tracks and had to get back to their families or work. Thanks to those departing early birds, I got a parking spot right next to the lodge. It was cold, so I decided to put my ski boots on inside.

I found a bench near the door. As I sat down to take off my shoes, my phone buzzed in my pocket.

"This is Remy."

Susan Walter

"Holy hell, what a mess," Mackenzie Rousseau huffed into the phone.

"Mac! Where are you?" All around me, people were shuffling about, talking, taking off their coats. I would have stepped outside, but I only had one boot on. So I put a finger to my free ear to block out the noise.

"I'm in California, trying to find a new CEO. They don't exactly grow on trees." With Jeff gone, Quantum Solar needed new management. It's not that I hadn't thought of that, I'd just assumed it wouldn't be an insurmountable problem.

"But the deal's still going to close, right?" I felt a flicker of nervousness that maybe I'd miscalculated.

"Buying a company is not like buying a sandwich, Remy. It's not just the *thing* they're interested in. It's the team of people who made the thing."

"Jeff was not a team player," I reminded him. "You said so yourself." I hadn't realized I was shouting until two snowboarders turned to look at me.

"Calm down, they still want the tech. We're too far along for them to back out. They've seen all our trade secrets—we could sue them if they renege."

"You'll find someone," I said, lowering my voice. "Someone who can figure out what he couldn't." I finished putting on my boots and stood up. I was just about to head for the door when I did a double take. Not ten meters away from me, curled up on a chair by the fireplace, was a woman with honey-colored hair—*just like Julie's.*

"What a waste of a life," Mac said. He sounded tired. Sad, even.

"It wasn't your fault, Mac." And that I knew for a fact.

A woman with a baby in a front carrier passed in front of me, blocking my view of Julie's doppelgänger. I thought I saw Julie everywhere—on the street, on the slopes, in the hallways of the hotel . . .

"I shouldn't have pressured him to lie," Mac said. "Our buyer wasn't going anywhere. I just didn't feel like ponying up more cash. Not while I was telling Ceci's lawyers I was broke."

242

"You did what you thought was best for the company." The young mother moved off, and I once again had a clear view of the woman I wanted to be Julie. Of course it wasn't. Why would she come here? It annoyed me that I couldn't get her out of my mind.

"I'm flying in tomorrow to collect Ceci's things," Mac said. "We can talk more then."

"I'll have a suite ready for you," I said, zipping up my coat. That powder was calling my name. Time to stop chasing ghosts and get out on the slopes.

There was a pause in the conversation. For a second I thought Rousseau had hung up.

"Mac?"

He let out a sigh. "She was a piece of work, but I still can't believe someone murdered her."

"Yes, it is shocking."

"Who am I going to fight with now?"

"Your new CEO?"

"Not a chance. Once the deal closes, I'm out. That CEO is going to be someone else's problem. You and I are going to collect our money and never look back, you hear me?"

His pronouncement was music to my ears.

"Loud and clear."

"See you tomorrow," he said, then hung up.

I stepped out into the sunshine, and that buoyant feeling returned. My future was as bright as the bluebird day. Julie would fight her murder charge, there was no doubt about that. It only took one drop of reasonable doubt for Mac—and me by association—to wind up in the crosshairs.

But if that case never went to trial, the secret of what we'd done would be buried forever. All I had to do was keep the fighter from fighting.

CHAPTER 59
Julie

The heat from the fire lulled me into a light but peaceful sleep. As I snoozed, voices of strangers swirled with memories of the voices of people close to me. I heard Jeff's voice singing in the shower. I heard Izzy, Christa, and Suki telling me how proud they were to call me friend. I heard Remy expressing desire . . . and then, disappointment. His voice seemed to flutter both in the foreground and the background. At one point in my half sleep, I imagined he was sitting just a few feet from me, putting on his boots to get a fix of fresh powder. Guilt bubbled up and swirled around my heart. I'd been unkind to my old friend. He was inappropriate, but I could have been more forgiving, given our history. I told myself I would apologize the next time we spoke, not knowing what he'd done to me was a thousand times worse than what I'd done to him.

The thunk-thunk of ski boots clunking across the hard floor roused me from my nap. I sat up and glanced at the wall clock. It was just after five. People were heading home. I took a gamble that no one would check the kitchen after it closed for the night, so as the staff wiped down the lunch tables, I slipped into the food pantry to hide behind a pallet of kidney beans. Over the next hour, one by one, the lights went off. And then, silence.

I waited for another twenty minutes, then crept out from my hiding spot. I didn't think the door was alarmed, but there was nothing I could do about it if it was, so I just pushed it open and hoped for the best.

As I stepped out onto the wraparound deck, the cold seized my body. The moon was a dinner plate in the clear, black sky, and the air was deathly still. I could feel my eyelashes grow heavy with frost. The entrance to the ski patrol hut was twenty meters in front of me. So I snugged my shell around my body and beelined for it.

The door to the hut was locked, but my axe kick was up to the task. If I didn't find anything in the next few hours that could exonerate me, I would turn myself in and let the legal process play itself out. I was fairly confident prosecutors wouldn't be able to convict me of murder. Any "evidence" they'd found had to be circumstantial, given that I didn't do it. My name would be dragged through the mud, and I might face charges for evading arrest. But I couldn't keep running. If I didn't learn anything from the files on that encrypted server that would implicate someone else, it was game over.

I sat down at the desk and fired up the computer. It was nearly seven. Izzy should have had time to go to my house and grab Jeff's laptop. So I picked up the handset and dialed her number, thankful that it was one of the few I knew by heart.

"Julie!" she said after one ring. "How are you?"

"Ready for this to be over."

"I'm sure."

Her betrayal pulled at my heart. If she was two-faced for sleeping with my husband, I was equally two-faced for not calling her on it. But now was not the time for confessions.

"Did you go to my house?" I asked.

"Yes. But I don't have good news."

"You couldn't find the laptop?" I didn't mean to sound incredulous, but when I'd left, it was right there on his desk.

"I couldn't get in the house, Jules. It was swarming with police. There were four cars out front when I got there. I tried to tell them I was your Realtor and had your permission to enter, but they wouldn't let me in."

I tried to process what Izzy was saying. Why would police be at my house? Were they looking for evidence to connect me to Ceci's murder? Or did they suspect, as I did, that Jeff's death was not a suicide?

To get answers, I needed access to Jeff's confidential correspondence. Without that laptop, I had no way to log in. I'd hit a wall. I took a deep breath before speaking to keep my voice from cracking.

"OK, thanks for trying."

"What's going on, Julie? Why are there police at your house?"

"I'm not sure. It's possible they think the murder in Banff and Jeff's death are connected."

"Is that what you think?"

"I don't know, maybe. Without Jeff's laptop, I have no way of knowing."

"I'm so sorry. I wish there was something more I could do," she said.

"You've done enough already." Maybe it was frustration. Or fear. But I couldn't keep the anger out of my voice.

There was a beat of silence. For a second I thought she'd hung up.

"How long have you known?" she asked. And I had to hand it to her for not playing dumb.

"Since the gondola ride. But I suspected before that. I knew there was someone. I just didn't know it was you." And there it was. Out in the open.

"I was going to tell you. But then he died, and it felt cruel. Julie, I'm so sorry." I had thought this confrontation would hurt like hell. But I felt strangely . . . relieved.

I wanted to own my part in it—tell her I'd been a shitty wife and had brought it upon myself. But I knew she'd push back. So I just said, "I know you are."

"I love you, Julie," she said. "The last thing I ever wanted to do was hurt you." And I believed her. Because people hurt the ones they love. I'd learned that at sixteen.

"I lied to you too," I said. "About why I came to Banff. We were broke, Izzy. I took a job as a maid."

"I know," Izzy said. "The police told us. But that's hardly in the same league as what I did." Someday I would tell her I understood that she didn't do it *to* me . . . that it wasn't really about *me* at all. She had a moment of weakness. She made mistakes. Like we all do.

"Can we just put it behind us?" I asked. And I heard her exhale with relief. I'd had a lot of practice moving on from things that hurt. A bad lap, a bad race, a bad childhood.

"If we could, I'd be so grateful."

I told her I loved her, too, and we said our goodbyes. There might be more to say, but now wasn't the time. If the police were monitoring Izzy's phone, they would find me, and soon. I had to figure out how to get on that server. I put my head in my hands and pressed my palms into my forehead. *Think, Julie, think!*

I couldn't access any of Jeff's devices, that was clear. But what about mine? Jeff had set up the dual authentication three ways: an email to an account with a password I didn't know, a text to his phone, or a text to mine. I didn't have my phone with me when I got arrested. If it was still in my room, I could have the passcode sent to my number, then use it to access the encrypted files.

I couldn't risk going back to the hotel. But there was someone I could ask to look for it. Our last encounter was unpleasant, but our history was long. If I could forgive Izzy, he could forgive me. He might have been upset, but I was certain he didn't think I was a murderer.

So I picked up the handset to call him.

CHAPTER 60
Remy

There was only one spot left in the staff parking lot when I got back from skiing, at the end farthest from the hotel. Traffic coming down from the mountain had been insane. The ride back to the hotel had taken three times what it normally does. I was hungry and wanted to go straight to the restaurant, so I left my skis and boots in the car.

I jogged toward the front entrance. It was cruelly cold and getting colder. The valets were huddled together by the heat lamp, their breath forming steamy clouds above their heads.

"Look alert, team," I warned as I walked by. I would be giving notice any day now, but I still felt a sense of pride about the hotel I'd called home for the last eight years. Just because it was fifteen below didn't mean we could be unprofessional.

I waved to my front desk staff as I made my way through the lobby and up the stairs. The restaurant was busy, as it usually was at dinnertime, but there was an open stool at the bar.

"What'll you have, boss?" Johnny said, putting a cocktail napkin in front of me.

"Cabernet. And the porterhouse."

Johnny poured my wine. As I swirled it in my glass, I looked around the restaurant, at all the rich people enjoying their vacations.

I'd worked harder than all of them put together, yet they had lives of luxury while I worked my tail off to meet their every need. *Well, not anymore.* That $300,000 I'd invested in Quantum Solar was about to turn into $3 million, and I didn't feel the least bit guilty about what I'd done to protect my investment. Giving Rousseau all my money wasn't the biggest risk I'd ever taken in my life—I'd skied the most dangerous terrain in the world, guided lost skiers through blizzards, pulled bodies from icy crevasses—but this was the one that was going to pay off.

I took a sip of my wine. Johnny had poured me the good stuff—a Staglin cab from Napa Valley. Why did California get the best of everything? The best wine, the best weather, the best people? *Maybe I should go to California now?* The sky was the limit. With the money I was getting, I could go wherever I wanted. *No, not California. Paris.* I had wanted to take Julie there, shop for art at the Bourse de Commerce, drink wine by the Seine. But she chose that fat-cat American. *Her loss.* As I choked back my broken fantasies—

"Sorry to bother you, boss," Johnny said, holding the telephone, "but you have a call." He offered me the handset. "Detective Montpelier."

I'd given the detective my cell phone, so I was confused why she'd called the hotel.

"This is Remy."

"Remy, it's me. Julie." I nearly dropped my wineglass.

"Hold on, Detective," I said, feeling Johnny's eyes on me. "Let me step away to someplace quiet."

I set down my glass and hopped off my stool.

"Where are you?" I asked as I ducked into an alcove. There was no caller ID, because the call had been transferred from the call center off-site.

"I owe you an apology," she said. And I knew, once again, she needed something from me. I don't know what made me angrier—that she had used me? Or that I had let her.

"No. I was the one who overstepped," I said. Since taking a service job, I'd become a master of apologizing without being sorry.

"I hope we can still be friends."

"Of course," I said through clenched teeth. "Now how can I help you, my friend?"

"You've done so much for me already . . . ," she started.

"That's what friends do," I said, ignoring her fake gratitude. I figured she needed money or a place to stay. So her request caught me off guard.

"I need my phone. I'm hoping it's still in my room."

"What for?"

"I want to log on to Jeff's encrypted server, but it's protected by dual authentication, so I can't do it without my phone."

I felt my jaw tighten. She knew something. But not everything— otherwise, she wouldn't need that phone.

"Julie, we should focus on proving your innocence," I started, but she interrupted me.

"There was something going on with Jeff's company, Remy. I know it sounds crazy, but I think his and Ceci's deaths might be connected."

A bead of sweat formed on my hairline. "Why would you think that?"

"Her husband was an investor in his company."

"Ceci's husband?" I tried to sound surprised. "How do you know?"

"I made the connection after seeing the news on TV. I think Ceci may have known her husband had done something illegal—that's why she was killed. Maybe he had something to do with it."

"That's quite an accusation." Mac would have an alibi. It was almost certain. Investigators would start looking under rocks. Rocks that would lead them to me.

"Maybe. But I'd like to do some digging. While I still can." The last thing I wanted was for her to start digging.

"OK, I'll go check your room," I lied. "Give me a number where I can call you back."

"I'll call you. How much time do you need?"

"Ten minutes. Call my cell. The portable won't reach all the way to that part of the hotel," I said, even though I wasn't going to her room.

I gave her my cell number. She thanked me and hung up. I walked back to my stool, returned the handset to Johnny just as he was putting my steak down on the bar top.

"Everything OK, boss?"

"Yes, fine."

I sat down and took a bite of my steak. The Calgary beef was buttery smooth with hints of peppercorn and rosemary. This should have been a meal to savor, but I ate quickly. Julie was getting dangerously close. She had to be silenced . . . *and soon.*

I ran through what I could say to get her to tell me where she was. If I pressed her, she might get suspicious. Plus she wouldn't want to make me an accomplice by asking me to keep her whereabouts to myself. I could tell her I had her phone, but she might ask me to relay information from an incoming text or call, not bring it to her, and then I'd be caught in a lie.

As I was agonizing over how to play this, my mobile phone rang. The caller ID said Banff-Norquay. And I almost laughed at how easy this would be. I imagined her huddled in an office, clutching the phone to her ear, praying I would save her like I always did.

"This is Remy."

"Did you find it?" Julie asked without saying hello.

"No, sorry. I think someone might have taken it." I didn't say the word *police*, but she knew that was the unspoken word.

"I was afraid of that. Thanks for looking."

"Are you OK? Can I bring you anything?" I asked because that's what a friend would do.

"No, I'm fine. I'm stowed away . . . well, you probably know where I am." *Yup.*

"What's your plan?" I asked. And there was something in her voice I had never heard before: defeat.

"I don't have one."

And I smiled to myself. Because I did.

CHAPTER 61
Monique

"Julie Adler's and Remy Delatour's immigration records came in," Stafford said. "And you're not going to believe what they show."

He set two printouts down on the desk in front of me. I'd just gotten off the phone with J. J.'s wife. She couldn't have been more gracious, comforting me more than I comforted her. The conversation made me more determined than ever to bring Adler in. Officer Jason Jarvis deserved to be remembered for a successful investigation, not a botched one.

"Julie Adler's is one page," Stafford said, pointing to the sheet on top. "She left Canada three and a half years ago. She came back for one week, looks like for her wedding, then didn't return until nine days ago, when she crossed the border at Sweetgrass–Coutts."

"She entered Coutts by car."

"That's right."

"So if they saw each other, Delatour would have had to have traveled to the US."

"That's right. Except he didn't. Not until very recently." Stafford laid Delatour's record on top of Julie's. "This is Delatour's travel history. In the last three years, he crossed the border into the US twice. Once on December 6th of this year, by plane—"

"He went through customs in Calgary."

"That's right. Returned the next morning."

"He went for one day?"

Stafford pulled up an article from the local newspaper on his laptop.

"Jeff Adler's funeral was on the 6th," I said, skimming the obituary.

"Yup."

"So Delatour flew to LA for the funeral."

"Makes you wonder how he knew about it," Stafford said. "A suicide of a random tech inventor is not exactly international news."

"Maybe they stayed in touch. He admitted they were friendly when she lived here."

"Or maybe there's another reason."

He put a second sheet of paper down on the desk in front of me.

"Delatour crossed the border one other time in the last three years, five days earlier, on Friday, December 1st," Stafford said, pointing to the date.

"What happened on December 1st?" I asked.

"Nothing. But look what happened on December 2nd."

He opened another window on his laptop. Another article from the local newspaper . . . announcing Jeff Adler's apparent suicide.

"Jeff Adler died on the 2nd," Stafford said. "One day after Delatour arrived in the US."

"When did he fly back to Calgary?"

"Same day Adler killed himself. But he didn't fly."

He pointed to the record.

"He crossed the border into Montana by car on Friday, December 1st," Stafford said. "Then crossed back into Alberta on the night of Saturday, December 2nd."

"He crossed the border both times by car?"

"Yup."

"It's a four-hour drive from Banff to Coutts, why not just fly from Calgary?" I asked.

And this time it was Stafford who got it.

"Because when you fly internationally, you can't bring a gun."

I thought about the possibility of Delatour driving four hours, then taking a two-and-a-half-hour flight from Montana to LA, only to do the same thing in reverse the next day. Was it to see his girlfriend? Or something else?

"He was in the US at the time of Jeff Adler's so-called suicide," Stafford said.

"Which is now under investigation," I reminded him.

"The gun wasn't registered to Adler. The police don't know who it belonged to."

"If we're going to allege Delatour murdered Jeff Adler," I said, "we need a motive."

"Love?" Stafford guessed. And I shook my head.

"He and Julie Adler hadn't seen each other for over three years, remember?"

"You think the friend was lying about them being a couple?"

"Not necessarily. The friends didn't even know she was working there—they thought she was a guest. They could have seen Delatour and jumped to the wrong conclusion."

"OK, so why did Delatour go to the US on the weekend of December 2nd if not to see her?" Stafford asked.

And I wondered that myself.

CHAPTER 62
Izzy

I was in my bedroom, surrounded by all those books meant to help me be a better person, when Julie called me. The hub was putting the boys to sleep. I had offered to do it, but he could tell I was exhausted and sent me to go lie down. These two days had been eye-opening for him. When forced to do everything—mealtime, bath time, story time, bedtime—he discovered he was not only good at it, but he also enjoyed it. Had I insisted on doing everything because I was trying to manufacture reasons to resent him? Because it was becoming pretty obvious that the problem wasn't him, it was me.

As I hung up the phone, I reflected back on how easy Julie had made it to confess. Perhaps I'd watched too many episodes of *Real Housewives*, because I was expecting her to be out of her mind with rage. But she was calm. Forgiving. As if she knew not everyone was as perfect as she was.

Now that Julie knew, I had to figure out what to say to my husband. I hated having a lie between us, but I also knew some things were better left unsaid. If he'd had a one-night stand, would I want to know? Was it better to be honest about the past or focus on a more honest future? Telling him wouldn't take back what I'd done. It would only hurt him.

Our relationship wasn't broken. I was. And it was time to figure out how to fix that.

I picked up a book of inspirational quotes and opened to one by the poet Anaïs Nin: "We see things not as they are. But as *we* are." Did I see my husband as a disappointment because I was disappointed in myself? I blamed him for our financial struggles, but I had a real estate license—if I had time to run off to Banff, I had time to grow my business. He wasn't the one slacking off, *I* was. It was just easier to blame him than to blame myself.

My thoughts turned to Julie. I had assumed when I saw her handsome French Canadian friend at the hotel that they were a couple—that she had been cheating on her husband just as I had cheated on mine. I chided myself for my rash assumption. Of course Remy was at that hotel—he worked there! I looked back down at Anaïs Nin's words: "We see things not as they are . . ."

I opened my suitcase to unpack my clothes. Jeff's things were on top. The sight of them filled me with shame. Julie saw me as a kind and generous friend. Because that's what *she* was to me.

I separated out Jeff's things. I would put them back. It was for Julie to decide what to do with them. The tote I'd borrowed was in the closet. As I took it off the hanger, I saw something at the bottom. It was flat, rectangular, and inky black . . .

I'd forgotten that I'd taken Jeff's phone. I'd done it for selfish reasons, so Julie wouldn't find out about Jeff and me. But she already knew. And I was done being selfish. I needed to admit I'd taken it, even if it threw salt on the wound I was desperate to heal. There might be something on that phone that could help her, and I needed to stop worrying about what was good for me and do what was good for her.

Because that's the kind of friend she'd always been to me.

CHAPTER 63
Julie

I logged off the computer and sat back in the chair. I was out of time and ideas. I didn't know if my outgoing calls to Remy and Izzy had tipped the RCMP off to my whereabouts, but I also didn't care. I had a hypothesis but no proof, and with no way to access that encrypted server to look for it, it was over. I was going to jail.

I reached for the pull chain and clicked off the desk lamp. Moonlight poured in through the blinds, creating vertical stripes across the desk that looked eerily like prison bars. I almost laughed at the blatant foreshadowing. There was no way I'd make bail. Every morning after tonight, I would be waking up in a room with no windows, shut off from nature and the sport that gave me joy. My name would be dragged through the mud. Even if I was exonerated, I would forever be known as that Olympian who got arrested for murder. All because I was ashamed to tell my friends that my perfect life was a lie. I didn't know what was more embarrassing—that Jeff had spent all our money or that he'd done it without telling me. Withdrawing all our money behind my back was wrong, but so was treating him like he wasn't allowed to fail. I'd held us both to an impossible standard. And we both had paid the price.

I didn't want the RCMP to spend any more time and resources looking for me. It was time to call and give myself up. As I reached for the phone to call 911, it rang. I recognized the number immediately.

"Izzy?" I had no reason to think she had good news, but I still felt a surge of hope.

"I don't know if this will help, and maybe it's too late . . ."

"What is it, Izzy?"

"I have Jeff's phone. I took it when I stopped by your house right after you left. I know I had no right—"

"Is it charged?" I interrupted. I knew why she'd taken it. I didn't need her to explain.

"I just plugged it in," she said. "There! Yes, it's working now."

I sat down at the computer and logged in to Jeff's encrypted server. The dual-authentication program asked where to send the passcode. I clicked the option to send it to Jeff's phone. Then I prayed.

"OK, you should get a six-digit code."

I heard Jeff's phone ding!

"Got it! You ready?"

"Ready."

Izzy read me the passcode, which I typed into the browser with eager fingers. A second later, the screen came alive with all things Quantum Solar.

"Izzy, you're a lifesaver!"

"I hope it helps."

"I don't know where I'd be without you," I said, because it was true. "You've always been there for me when it counted the most."

"Good luck, Julie. I'm here if you need anything else."

We hung up, and I logged on to Jeff's email server. It took only a few clicks to confirm Fang had been right about the prototype not working. Two days before Jeff died, he wrote this in an email to Mackenzie Rousseau: I can't represent that the solar cell is viable. And I don't have any more personal funds to put toward the effort. If they believe in the product now, they will believe in it in two months when we identify the critical variable.

Rousseau's reply was curt and decisive: I need this to close by end of year. Investors are counting on it. I already submitted the successful trial. Congratulations.

Once again, Fang was right. Mackenzie Rousseau had forged ahead despite Jeff's objections. Jeff's response left zero room for interpretation.

Mac, that's fraud.

To which Mackenzie replied, It's only fraud if you contradict me.

Blood rushed into my cheeks. Was that a threat? That Jeff better not tell, or else? I took a screen grab of the email chain and saved it to the desktop.

I scrolled past some housekeeping emails: all-hands meeting . . . policy change . . . revised schedule . . . I was about to close the window when an unopened email from the day after Jeff died caught my eye. It was addressed to Mackenzie Rousseau. Jeff was cc'd. The subject line read: Confidential Investor Identity Disclosure. He'd never clicked on it, so I did.

Per regulatory requirements of an acquisition by a public company, someone with an @fortiselectric email address wrote, Fortis Electric requires that the identities of all partners and investors be disclosed prior to funding. Please provide the name and contact information for the "Undisclosed Investor" listed in the private placement memorandum so that we may be in compliance.

It wasn't the request that sent a chill down my spine. It was the response from Mackenzie Rousseau: The undisclosed investor in the private placement memorandum is Remy Claude Delatour, of Banff, Alberta.

Remy Delatour?

Ten minutes ago, when I'd told Remy that Ceci's husband had invested in Jeff's company, he acted surprised. But he was an investor too. So he had to have known.

I flashed back to Jeff's funeral, how shocked I'd been to see Remy there. Jeff's death had gotten a mention in the local paper, but it was hardly national news, never mind international news. I didn't post on social media or tell any of the friends we had in common. So how had he known?

I thought about the evidence that might have led them to arrest me. If they'd interviewed the staff, they would have known Ceci and I had sparred. But Mrs. Rousseau sparred with a lot of people. Unless the police had inventoried Ceci's closet, they had no way of knowing I was wearing her clothes. And even if they knew those leather pants were hers, that was not enough for them to accuse me of murder. For all they knew, she had loaned them to me.

I'd watched enough crime procedurals to know that the key to nailing someone for murder was to either have an eyewitness or connect the accused to the murder weapon. I didn't do it, so there could be no eyewitnesses. But I did have a weapon. It was in my room, under my bed. Only one person knew it was there: the person who'd let himself in to leave a note on my desk.

Remy.

He had access to my weapon. He had a key to Ceci's room. He had a motive to kill anyone who threatened to sour the deal (Jeff) or could reveal his identity as the undisclosed investor (Ceci). I had just told him that I had connected the two deaths. And, by calling him on his cell phone, I had also revealed where I was.

My hands shook as I reached for the mouse. If I didn't make it through the night, I wanted the police to have the evidence I'd just found. I clicked forward on the email disclosing Remy's status as the "undisclosed investor," attached the screen grab of Jeff's emails to Rousseau, and wrote one short sentence.

It was Remy.

I found the general email for the Banff police department online and put Detective Monique Montpelier's name in the subject line.

Then I sent it.

CHAPTER 64
Monique

Officer Purdy had just left the Banff Springs Hotel when I called him, so I had him turn around to meet Stafford and me in the lobby. I needed to know why Remy Delatour had driven to Montana on December 1st only to return the next day. We weren't going to arrest him—there could be a very simple explanation for the trip. Maybe a cousin had gotten married or he wanted something from Trader Joe's. We didn't assume he had anything to do with Jeff Adler's death, but we wouldn't be doing our job if we didn't investigate the coincidence of him being in the US when he died.

"Front desk says they think he's at the bar," Purdy said when Stafford and I walked through the front entrance.

"Let's go."

As for whether Montana had been Delatour's final destination, that would take more digging to ascertain. If he had boarded a US airline, we would need help from the FBI to get those flight manifests. But we were hoping he would just tell us himself.

"You learn anything from the hotel employees you talked to today?" I asked Purdy as we walked up the stairs toward the bar. Purdy had spent the day talking to staffers who knew Julie, and I was hoping one of them had told him something that could help us track her down.

"Not much," Purdy said. "It appears Ms. Adler largely kept to herself. Seems she wasn't too interested in making friends."

"Well in this weather, she's not out wandering the streets. She had to go somewhere to keep warm. We'll find her," I said. We had roadblocks up on Highway 1, but I had a sneaking suspicion she was still somewhere in town. At this point I had more questions than answers. It wasn't logical that she and Delatour would commit unrelated murders, but I had no way to connect them, at least not yet. The fact that the bullet that had killed Ceci Rousseau was off target was also troubling me. Julie Weston Adler was too good a shot to miss. And then there were those twenty-seven minutes when the cameras were off. The door to my open-and-shut case suddenly had a big crack in it—one I was hoping Remy Delatour could help me close.

We reached the entrance to the bar. It had been an epic ski day: the mood was buoyant, and the place was packed. There was a tiny opening at the bar, so I squeezed into it.

"Hello, Johnny," I said to my bartender friend. He eyeballed Stafford, Purdy, and me with apprehension.

"I take it you're not here for a drink."

"We're looking for Mr. Delatour. Front desk said he might be here."

"He just left."

"What do you mean *just?*"

"Like, five minutes after he hung up with you." *Hung up with* me? I hadn't spoken to Delatour all day.

"What makes you think he was talking to me?"

"I answered the phone. You told me it was you."

I thought back to the hostel, how my name was in the manifest.

"Can I see the handset?"

He reached for the phone. But as he handed it to me, he warned, "It was transferred from the call center—there's no caller ID."

"On it," Purdy said, taking off for the lobby.

"Did you overhear any of the conversation between Delatour and this person who claimed to be me?"

"Nah. He walked away to talk somewhere quiet."

"Then what did he do?"

"Came back and finished his dinner."

Stafford's cell phone buzzed in his pocket.

"Stafford," he said into the phone. Then to me, "It's Teresa back at the station. She says to check your email—she just forwarded you something."

I took out my phone and opened my email. Our secretary had forwarded a message from info@norquayski.com. One sentence—It was Remy.—above a forwarded email, with one attachment.

I opened the attachment: a screen grab of an email chain between Julie Adler's dead husband and Mackenzie Rousseau.

"What was Ceci's husband's name?" I asked Stafford. He typed on his phone.

"Mackenzie."

My skin tingled. *So there was a connection between Jeff Adler and the Rousseaus.*

I skimmed the screenshotted email chain . . . some disagreement between Jeff and Mackenzie. I didn't know the significance, so I read through the forwarded email. It was a confidential investor identity disclosure request.

"Holy shit."

I held up the screen so Stafford could see. "Delatour was an investor in Jeff Adler's company," I said.

"So?"

I went back to the screenshotted email from Mackenzie to Jeff. "I need this to close by end of year. *Investors* are counting on it," I read aloud, leaning into the word *investors*.

"The investors wanted Jeff Adler to do something he refused to do," Stafford guessed.

"Investors that included Remy Delatour."

"If it's not love, it's money," Stafford said.

The coincidences were piling up. Delatour was in the US the day Jeff Adler died . . . after investing in his company . . . when a disagreement was brewing . . .

"Detective!" Purdy said, jogging up to us. "That call that came in for Delatour originated at Norquay Ski Resort."

Same as Adler's email.

Dread washed over me. We were wrong about Julie Weston Adler. Delatour wasn't trying to protect her. He was trying to protect himself.

My officers were looking at me, waiting for my command. So I gave it.

"Bundle up. We're going up the mountain."

CHAPTER 65
Julie

Walking down the windy road to town would be slow going in the dark. The snow was deep, and it was bitter cold. But I didn't have to walk.

Those Nordica SpeedMachine boots were a size too big, but the Black Pearls they paired with were a good length for me, and I didn't have time to reset bindings.

I riffled through the desk. The top two drawers were full of office supplies, but I found what I was looking for in the bottom drawer. The headlamp was old and scuffed, but it worked. The moon would provide some light, but it wouldn't be much help if I had to cut into the trees. And this was not a night you wanted to get lost in the woods.

I pulled on my hat and gloves, helped myself to those Black Pearls and a pair of poles, then stepped out into the dark night.

The temperature gauge on the wall read -23°C. I was obscenely underdressed in my thin base layer, sweater, and shell, but I didn't plan on taking a leisurely run. I'd trained in colder weather than this. The trick was to keep moving. As long as my muscles were working, I would be fine.

As I clicked into the skis, I took some deep belly breaths and imagined my blood pulsing through my body, flooding my extremities with warmth. I pulled the headlamp over my hat, then pushed off toward the parking lot. The road was not only the easiest way down, but it was also the most direct. But my plan to ski it into town was immediately thwarted by the sight of headlights turning toward me. If the SUV hadn't had a Thule on top, I would have thought it was the police and waved them over. My heartbeat quickened. There was no reason for anyone to come up here . . . unless they were coming for me.

I did an about-face and shot off in the opposite direction. The ski patrol hut butted up against the woods, but I could see the head of a narrow snowmobiling trail just beyond it. I had no idea where that trail went, but tonight was the night I was going to find out.

The trail was as wide as a bus, with towering pines on both sides. A sliver of moonlight snuck in between the treetops, making the snow glow indigo blue. The first stretch was flat, and I skied skate-style, making tracks that looked like the letter *V*. I'd been skate skiing since I was five years old, and the motion was as natural to me as walking a straight line.

The path narrowed. Tree branches crowded the moon now, so I switched on my headlamp to light the way. It didn't occur to me that I had just revealed my location to the one person who could not only catch me, but also had no intention of letting me leave this mountain alive.

The town was behind me, to the south. To avoid getting lost in the wilderness forever, I would have to turn around. That's the thing about Canada. Once you leave the corridor of towns at the southern border, there's nothing to the north but icy wilderness. Just because there were trails didn't mean they led somewhere. Many of them were long, arcing paths to nowhere—gifts to cold-weather explorers in search of adventure and themselves. But I wasn't here to explore. Which meant I was going to have to find a place to turn off. There would be nothing to follow except my instincts. All I could hope was that they were up to the task.

I estimated that I was about a kilometer from the resort—time to start heading down. The snow would be thick and uneven in the trees, and the terrain would be steep. I hadn't known it until right then, but I had been training my whole life for this moment. As I turned off the trail and ventured into the woods, I prayed that my training would be enough.

CHAPTER 66
Remy

It's illegal to buy a handgun in Canada. The black market is not as robust as it is in America, but I've always been resourceful. I got mine right after I returned from military service in France. I didn't think I would need more than one bullet, but I didn't want to make the same mistake I'd made with Ceci. I'd gotten away with a poor shot the last time, but Ceci was no Julie Weston Adler.

I took the gun out of my safe, put ten bullets in the magazine, then slipped it in the inside pocket of my parka. The Sig 9 mm weighed less than a pound and was slim enough to be concealed by the quilt lines in the down. Julie wasn't expecting me, but she wouldn't run away. Unless she saw the gun.

I rehearsed my lie. *I have a friend with an empty cabin,* I would say, then offer to drive her there. It was credible. I'd lived in Banff for eight years and knew just about everyone. Once I lured her outside, the rest would be easy. Glaciers stay frozen forever, that's what makes them glaciers. She'd be just like all the other animals that met their demise at the bottom of a crevasse, except for the bullet between her eyes.

I tucked a balaclava in my outer pocket, along with a wool hat. I went with mittens instead of gloves. I might only have a split second to pull that trigger. I didn't want to have to wrestle with a tight-fitting glove.

I exited the hotel through the side door by the loading dock, where nobody would see me. Yes, there was a camera, but no one would be watching it. The police had concluded their search of the hotel. Plus I knew how to delete security footage. I'd already done it once—right before the power outage that served to explain why the footage was gone. It was almost as if the universe wanted me to finally get what I deserved, and I said a silent thank-you for how it had lined everything up so nicely.

On the drive up the mountain, I thought about Jeff—how surprised he'd been to see me when I dropped in on him. I'd told him I was in town for a corporate retreat in Santa Barbara, that I would love to stop by and say hi on my way. Julie had just left for the gym and then lunch with her friends, he'd apologized, as if I hadn't just watched her drive away. He was too polite to say no when I asked him for a tour of the house. I had a good twenty pounds on Jeff, but that gun was all I needed to force him into the bathroom. He thought I was going to rob him. What a fucking insult. I'd locked the door behind me when I left to sell the suicide, grateful for the window that opened to the backyard and the forgiving grass below.

The parking lot at Norquay was predictably empty. I drove all the way to the end and parked by the lodge. I didn't know what building Julie was in—lodge, day care, ski school, administrative offices—so where to start?

I scanned the buildings for signs of life. I didn't think she would turn on the lights, but I also had a hard time imagining her just sitting there in the dark. I was about to start peeking in windows when I saw it. A flicker of light between the trees. It looked like a firefly, dancing and weaving between the trunks. Not a firefly. A headlamp. Skating away from the resort. She was a fugitive. It made sense that she would want to keep moving. But I also had to consider the possibility that she had pieced it all together and was running from me.

She was heading north on the snowmobiling path. It didn't lead anywhere but into the wilderness, but surely she knew that. She wouldn't try to camp in this weather—no one would. Eventually she would have to cut back through the woods to seek shelter in town. The terrain through the woods was steep, and the snow was deep. That's where I'd catch her. She was faster on the flats, but no one beats me in the verticals. Not even Julie the Great.

My skis were still in my Thule from my afternoon run. I had my boots, too—they were in the back seat. So I put on my gear, grabbed a headlamp from my glove box, and went to finish this once and for all.

CHAPTER 67
Julie

Here in the trees, the untracked snow was knee deep. I wasn't an experienced powder skier, but I knew if I went too slow, I could sink and get stuck. Falling into a tree well was harrowing under any circumstances. I didn't want to do it in this cold with my husband's killer on my tail.

As long as I was going down, I knew I was headed in the right direction. Mountains are kind in that respect. Gravity always shows you the way. I might have to traverse across a frozen field at the bottom, but traversing was my specialty, and I'd have the moon to light my way.

My plan was to ski to the bottom, go to the first open restaurant or bar I stumbled upon, then call the police and turn myself in. I might spend a night or two in jail, but I believed my evidence would raise reasonable doubt about my guilt, and once they saw it, I would be set free. In any case, it was the right thing to do. The police had more important things to do than spend their days and nights hunting a fugitive, and I didn't want to be the reason a real emergency went unanswered.

My headlamp lit up the snow like a spotlight as I carved crescent-shaped troughs between the trees. The upside of skiing fresh powder was that it was forgiving. If I cut a turn too tight or not tight enough, the snow would absorb my mistake and give me time to regain my balance. Sliding out of a turn too quickly on ice can send you tumbling over your skis. But these conditions were soft and slow. A little too slow, as it turned out.

The woods opened up, and I found myself in a wide-open bowl. The hill spread out in front of me like a fuzzy blanket. The terrain was steep, but with no trees to force tight turns, I could take them wider, give my tired legs a rest.

Unlike skiing ice or hardpack, skiing powder is eerily quiet. The skis don't chatter. There is no scraping sound when your edges grab, because you're not skiing your edges. The silence allows you to feel like you're all alone on the mountain. Even when you're not.

Thanks to that sweet silence, I didn't hear my predator approaching. But the snow revealed him in a different way. We think of avalanches as these big, scary tsunamis that destroy everything in their paths. But they can also be gentle, like tumbleweeds in a summer breeze.

My body was pointed straight down when I noticed the pebbles of snow bouncing by and around me. I glanced over my shoulder to see what had triggered them.

My first reaction to seeing Remy at the top of the bowl was surprise. How had he gotten here so fast? And how had he found me? There was no path through the woods—I'd made my own. And then I realized that while the fresh powder may have muffled the sound, it also left tracks as easy to follow as a trail of wet paint.

He was less than a hundred meters above me and gaining fast. My surprise turned to terror. He'd murdered Jeff. He'd murdered Ceci. And now he was coming for me. I couldn't outski him on the vertical. He was a downhiller and an expert in these conditions. The only way I could put distance between us was to make him traverse. I had a decisive edge on the straightaways. And as luck would have it, the terrain was about to flatten out.

I chose a line that would take me into the trees. It was dangerous to enter the forest at this high speed, but if I veered off too soon, he could ski the hypotenuse of the triangle and cut me off. So I crouched into a bent-over squat, tucked my head, and beelined for the woods.

The canopy of trees blocked the moonlight, and it took several seconds for my eyes to adjust. But that's not the reason I didn't see the creek. The day's deep freeze had left a thin layer of ice on the surface, hiding the churning water underneath. There was no way to jump it, even if I had seen it in time. Plus I came in at the worst possible angle—more diagonal than perpendicular. As soon as my skis pierced the icy surface, I knew I was going down.

Ski bindings are designed to release your boot when you fall, to reduce the chance of serious injury—it's much easier to tear an ACL or break a bone if you fall with your boots clipped in. You can adjust the binding to respond to little, medium, or maximum force. Your setting, or DIN, is determined by your ability and your weight. A one-hundred-pound beginner would have a low DIN setting and pop out of her skis with a mild jolt. A two-hundred-pound expert would set her DIN much higher, so that she would only pop out in a fall involving a great deal of force. Advanced skiers don't want their skis popping off when they ski hard. A too-low setting can be just as dangerous as a too-high one, depending on who's wearing them.

I didn't know what kind of skier my borrowed Black Pearls belonged to. Until I needed that binding to free my leg, and it didn't.

CHAPTER 68
Remy

Once a year, locals flock to Lake Louise to participate in the annual New Year's Eve torch ski. If you're invited to do it, which only a select few are, you report to the Glacier Express chairlift at eleven p.m. Once you get off at the top, you are handed a lit torch not unlike the ones they carry at the Olympic games. On the ringleader's command, the skiers start down the hill in a single file line. Spectators at the bottom are treated to a magical light show, compliments of the brave souls who dared to risk their hair catching fire to make the descent. It's the one time all year they open the mountain at night. It's also the only time I ever skied in the dark. Until tonight.

Tonight's torch was a headlamp, but the effect was the same—dim, uneven light that illuminated the ground in front of me, and not much else. I got a little help from the moon, which glowed creamy white in the indigo sky.

It was easy to find the path Julie had taken out of the resort. Her tracks were fresh and exactly what you'd expect from a skate skier—wide and diagonal like the two sides of a V. Despite my being taller, my strides were not as wide as hers. Skating was not my forte. Luckily, the only way off the top of a mountain is down, so I took heart that I'd have the opportunity to do what I did best soon enough.

Julie's tracks turned off the trail about a kilometer out from the resort. I followed them into the woods. It was pitch black in between the trees—I couldn't see the trunks until I was nearly upon them. That Julie had navigated the darkness with no tracks to follow was mind boggling. But then again, Julie always was able to do things no one else could.

Julie had a sizable head start, so I skied as fast as the conditions would allow, occasionally grazing the edge of a tree well in my attempt to keep my turns tight. I didn't know where she was going, just that I had to get to her before the police did. She might not call me from her next hiding place. And she was too close to the truth to let her keep digging.

The trees thinned, and I found myself atop a wide-open expanse of white. After the blackness of the woods, the moonlit bowl felt like a miracle. And even more miraculously, there, near the bottom of it, was Julie.

I thought about calling out. I was behind her, she couldn't see me there at the top of the bowl. I clung to the possibility that she didn't know I was a threat. If she did, I reasoned, she wouldn't have phoned me. Then again, she was Julie Weston Adler. Just because I hadn't helped her access Jeff's encrypted files didn't mean she hadn't. And of course there was the fact that I was following her. Would she wonder why? Or know immediately?

My Sig was heavy in my pocket as I pointed my skis down the steep incline. In my eagerness to catch her, I pushed off a little too aggressively, triggering a mini avalanche right below me. I'd ridden sliding snow before. The trick was not to stop, but to ride it like a surfer on a wave. This was a relatively small surge. More like riding the foam than the wave itself.

The loosened top layer of snow tumbled past Julie, and I saw her head turn up the mountain in my direction. When her wide arcing turns abruptly became a beeline for the woods, my question was answered. She wasn't running from the police, she was running from me. She'd pieced it together. She knew what I'd done.

"Merde!"

She disappeared into the trees. I couldn't cut her off, because I didn't know which way she had veered. She would be fast in the flats—way faster than me. If I turned left but she had veered right, I would never catch up. So I maintained my course, riding the loose top layer of snow to the bottom, then shooting straight ahead into the woods. I picked up her trail as it banked to the right, back toward civilization. And I smiled to myself. Because I knew something about this terrain that she didn't.

I had never skied this stretch of mountain, but I'd hiked here many times in the summer. These woods backed up to the campground. And that campground was surrounded by a creek that ran nearly all year round.

I found Julie, as expected, face down in the creek bed. Her left ski was jammed between two rocks and sticking straight up. Her right was turned on its side. Her lower leg had turned with it. Her upper leg had not.

The bulge in her pant leg indicated that she had broken her tibia. A circle of blood around the bulge suggested the break had pierced the skin. She wouldn't bleed out, but I knew from my time in the PGHM that without prompt medical attention, she was at risk of infection. And also that infection was the least of her worries. Because she'd have to survive the night for the infection to take her, and in these temperatures, that was impossible.

"Could it be? The great Julie Weston has fallen?"

She turned her head to look at me, eyes frantic with fear. She wasn't afraid of freezing to death. No, she was afraid of me.

"Remy," she said through purple lips. "Help."

It was minus twenty degrees. Icy water bubbled up from all around her, soaking her hair and clothes. The average person would go into cold shock in five to ten minutes. She was Julie the Great, so I gave her fifteen.

It was sad to see her like this, all tangled limbs and terror. Not the way I wanted to remember her.

"My leg is broken," she gasped. "I can't get up. Please . . . help me."

"Help me, help me, help me," I mocked. "It's all I've heard from you since the day we met." And she knew it was true. I'd fed her when she was hungry. Put her up when she had nowhere to stay. I invited her into my bed when she was lonely. Then stood by in silence while she'd married someone else.

"Yes, it's true," she conceded. "You've been way more generous with me than I've ever been with you. Please, forgive me."

"Stop it!" I snapped. It made me sick to hear her begging. I was kind to her because I loved her. I wanted her devotion. Not her fake gratitude.

"You thought I would never give you the life you wanted, so you left me for someone who could."

"What? No!" She tried to deny it, but I knew the truth.

"I was never good enough for Olympic-gold-medalist Julie Weston."

"That's not true—" she started. But I didn't want to hear another word.

"What goes around, comes around," I said.

I was relieved that I wouldn't have to shoot her. Mother Nature would claim her quickly and cleanly. I wouldn't have to do a thing.

"How did you figure it out?" I asked. And she had the audacity to pretend she didn't know what I was talking about.

"Figure what out?"

My breath was a plume of white smoke as I sighed in disgust.

"And now you're treating me like I'm stupid."

"Remy, please," she begged. "Help me out of here and we'll talk it through." We both knew there was nothing to talk about. She was not going to jail for me. And she was too proud to let the world keep believing Jeff's death was a suicide.

"I'm sorry, Julie. But my help just ran out," I said. And then I turned my back on her for the first, and last, time.

CHAPTER 69
Julie

I felt no pain. Maybe it was shock that numbed me. Or cold. Or despair. My left leg was sandwiched between two rocks, my right was broken, and half my body was submerged in a river of ice. I yanked and twisted and flexed and howled, but the rocks held that left leg like a vise. I cried out in anguish as I realized I was going to have to do something I had never done: *Give up.*

I rolled onto my hip and turned my face toward the sky. I didn't know I was panting until I saw the rapid-fire puffs of steam coming out of my mouth. Shallow breathing is the first symptom of hypothermia. I tried to slow my inhales, but my lungs refused to expand. I tried to tuck my chin and look down at my legs, but my neck muscles wouldn't let me. All I could do was stare up into the darkness and wait for death to take me.

The outline of the moon was fuzzy. When a shadow moved across it, I thought I was hallucinating. But then something rustled above my head. I shifted my focus to a tree branch hanging over the creek. Whatever had smudged across the moon was perched on it. A raven? A vulture? Had it smelled death and come to pick my carcass clean?

The creature's tail feathers caught a glimmer of moonlight. They were pearl white, to match her head. Not a vulture. A bald eagle.

For as long as I could remember, eagles had appeared at the most important moments of my life. The day I qualified for the Olympic team, one swooped in front of the windshield of my truck outside the arena and followed me all the way home. They seemed to visit me at inflection points. The beginnings of things. The ends of things.

Eagles sleep at night and hunt during the day. I assumed this one was about to tuck her beak under her wing and peace out. But instead, the majestic raptor stretched her neck, opened her mouth, and let out a shrill, high-pitched whistle. *Get up*, she seemed to shout. *GET UP!*

Her claws dug into the branch as she spread her wings out wide, like a rosebud blooming.

GET UP NOW!

Snow wafted down on me as the bird shook the branch with an angry flap of her wings.

"I can't," I whispered. She shrieked again.

YES, YOU CAN!

Maybe that eagle couldn't care less if I lived or died. Maybe she was just mad I was mucking up her creek. But her intensity stirred something in me. Her strength became my strength. I hugged my arms to my body and pushed myself up on my elbows.

My wet skin screamed as it was slapped by the frigid night air, but I ignored it. If I was going to get out of this creek, I had to get those skis off. *But how?*

My left leg wasn't injured, but the ski was holding it hostage between the rocks. I couldn't reach the binding with my hand to release it. I needed something long, like a stick. *Or a pole.*

I turned my head to look for my ski poles. One of them had flown ten feet in front of me and was leaning up against a tree. But where was the other one?

I looked to my left, then to my right. Could it be somewhere in the water? I extended my left arm to grope beneath the surface. But my hand found nothing.

I went to raise my right arm, but I couldn't. At first I thought it was frozen. Or broken. I gritted my teeth and pulled with all my might. I felt a stabbing sensation in my belly. That's when I realized I couldn't move my right arm because it was tethered to something underneath my body . . . *my ski pole.*

I inchwormed my butt in the air and pulled at that pole with all my might. My shoulder burned from the effort, but on the third tug I wrenched it free. I wrapped my fingers around the pole handle. Then I maneuvered the tip into the divot in the binding, and I pushed.

What was bad news—my ski would not move—became good news, because when I pushed, it resisted. I repositioned my fingers so that I could push with the heel of my hand and—

Click!

My boot popped free.

The eagle whistled and fluffed her wings. But it was too soon to celebrate. I still had to get out of that creek and to safety, in temperatures that would flash freeze meat. But I had one thing I hadn't had two minutes ago: *hope.*

I bent my freed leg and rocked back onto my knee, raising my torso out of the water. Icicles hung from my hair and chin. My teeth were chattering like a jackhammer. I estimated I was about midway down the mountain. Still a long way to go. All I could do was take one step at a time. But I couldn't go anywhere until I'd gotten my broken leg out of that ski.

The bottom of my boot was flat and hard. I could use it to karate chop the binding of the ski clipped to my bum leg. For the mechanism to release, I'd have to hit it hard and dead center. And that would hurt.

I gritted my teeth for the pain I knew was coming, then pulled my knee to my chest and released it like a slingshot. Pain shot up my broken leg as I made contact. But the binding didn't release. So I did it again. And then a third time.

"C'mon!"

My head was spinning. My vision was starting to blur. I had to get out of this creek. I closed my eyes and visualized the heel of my boot connecting with the sweet spot of the binding. And then I kicked as hard as I could.

"Ahhhh!"

Pop!

Success! My broken leg was free. It was also useless. But no matter. I still had my arms and one good leg. The creek bed was too uneven to try to stand, but I could crawl. I spun around and pulled myself hand-hand-knee-knee out of the creek and into the snow.

Now what?

I had one pole, still around my wrist, one good leg, and a mission that could only be completed by me. If I died, the truth of what happened to Jeff would die with me. So I planted that pole in the snow, grabbed it with both hands, and pulled myself up.

Cold coiled around me like a snake, pressing against every square inch of my body. *Breathe, Julie, breathe.* I closed my eyes and pictured my heart as a raging campfire, pushing heat through my veins. *Mind over matter.* My chest filled with warmth. My breathing slowed. I blinked back eyelids heavy with frost and looked around.

I knew the snowmobile path wrapped around the bowl I'd skied down, and that it was the most direct route down the mountain. I had no idea how I'd get down it, but that was a problem for later. First I had to find it.

My broken leg was beyond hurting. If I tried to put even an ounce of weight on it, it would buckle. So I locked my right elbow and leaned on the pole, and took a step. Then another. One uneven step at a time, I retraced my tracks out toward the bowl.

The woods opened up into a field of white diamonds. The beauty took my breath away. As my eyes swept across the blanket of white, I was humbled by the vastness. I was a star in an endless sky. A pebble on a white sand beach. A buoy bobbing in a bottomless ocean. I was lost. But I was also home.

Home.

I finally knew what the word meant. Home isn't a place. It's a purpose. Being great is not about breaking records, it's about moving powerfully into your purpose. My achievements inspired others to skate faster, shoot straighter, reach their personal best in sports and in life. My purpose—my *home*—was on the mountain.

But my revelation came too late. As eager as my heart was to reclaim its raison d'être, my body had already given up. My brain was telling my legs to move, but they weren't listening. The campfire in my chest had burned through its fuel. I had nothing left but a few smoldering embers.

I didn't know I had collapsed until I looked down to see why I couldn't take a step. The snow was chest high and sucking every last bit of warmth out of my body. I didn't feel scared. I felt betrayed. I thought I knew cold. It had been my loyal companion. It was the dance floor. I was the dance. I gave it a purpose as it gave me mine.

But just as the extremes of love and hate are so close they sometimes switch places, my lifelong friend had just become my worst enemy. Every other time cold had invited me out to play, it let me go home when I'd had enough. This cold was different. It was tenacious. It was greedy. It loved me so much, it refused to let me go.

I tilted my chin and looked up at the stars. The glacier blurred into the sky, as if to say there was no beginning and no end, just a continuation. Cold burns like fire. Love turns to hate. Death gives life meaning as life gives death power. In their extremes, opposites merge, as if their differences are merely imagined.

As my thirty years of life fanned out in front of me and my mistakes turned into milestones and my struggles to triumphs, I moved into a profound sense of peace.

I closed my eyes, and for the first time, but also the last time, I let go.

CHAPTER 70
Monique

Our search for Julie Weston Adler was all hands on deck. She was no longer a suspect. She was a witness. And if we didn't find her, Remy Delatour's probable next victim.

My team spread out along the base of the mountain. There were a half dozen places where you could enter town from Norquay, and I had an officer at every one of them.

Purdy rode with me up the zigzagging switchbacks to the top. The parking lot should have been empty. I got a prickly feeling down my neck when I saw that it wasn't.

"Whose car is that?" I asked as we pulled up behind the black Chevy Blazer. I had reworked my Ace bandage so I could get a mitten over my hand, but it was still largely useless.

"I'll find out."

Purdy pulled out his piece and circled the vehicle, peering in the windows as he rounded the front.

"Clear!" he shouted. "But come look at this."

I joined Purdy by the driver's side door. He pointed to the windshield, where a Banff Springs Hotel employee parking permit dangled from the rearview.

"Delatour," I intuited.

"Think he came to get her?" Purdy asked. I touched the hood. It was cold.

"If he came to get her, they'd be gone by now."

"Then why is he here?"

I hadn't told Purdy about the email, so he didn't know.

"To kill her."

"Then I guess we'd better hurry up and find them. Where do we start?"

"Those buildings are the offices, day care, and ski school," I said, pointing to the twin buildings butting up against the side of the mountain. "You start there. I'll check the lodge."

"Copy that." His eyes floated down to my holstered gun. "Can you fire that thing?"

"Probably not." I took off my mitten and tried to grip the handle, but I couldn't hold it steady. "Definitely not."

"Take the rifle," Purdy said, rounding the back of the squad car and pulling it from the trunk. "It's still a good weapon, even if you can't pull the trigger." He made a swinging motion, like I was meant to use it as a baseball bat.

"All right," I said, holstering my pistol and taking the rifle from him. "Let's move out."

We split off, him toward the admin buildings, me toward the lodge. I crept up the deck stairs, then peered in the windows by the front entrance. It was too dark to see inside.

I tried the door.

Locked.

I circled the building. Side doors: locked. Rear doors: locked.

I made my way toward the loading entrance. As I approached the heavy double doors to the kitchen, I saw something in the snow. Footprints. They were fresher than the others and headed for the ski patrol hut just beyond.

I raised the rifle and approached the hut. I didn't have to peer inside to see that it was empty, the fresh tracks leading out gave it away. Unlike the rounded tracks going in, these tracks were narrow and rectangular: ski boot tracks . . . leading away from the resort.

The boot tracks led to ski tracks. I followed them toward the snowmobile trail . . . where they were joined by another set of tracks.

"Ah, hell."

I jogged back toward the hut. There was a snowmobile parked right outside. I took out my phone and called Teresa back at the station.

"Call Jed and ask where the keys to the ski patrol snowmobile are, stat."

"Will do. Stand by."

Jed Frakes was the GM of Norquay, and a friend. While I waited for Teresa to connect with him, I examined the door to the hut. The wood was split where someone had kicked it open.

I pushed on the door with the tip of my rifle. The desktop computer monitor was on, bathing the room in cool-blue light. I walked up to the desk. The email application was open. I clicked on the sent folder. And there was that email to me.

I made a silent promise: *I'm going to find you, Julie.*

My phone rang.

"Teresa?"

"Keys are on top of the high file cabinet, on a rabbit-foot key chain." I turned my head and saw them poking out from behind a mug of pencils.

"Got 'em," I said as I scooped them up. "Call Purdy and tell him I'm taking the snowmobile trail and to meet me at the bottom."

"Copy that."

I wouldn't say I was an expert snowmobiler, but I knew how to ride. My dad used to take me for all-day tours through the backcountry in Whistler, on the glaciers behind the resort. When I was little, I sat in the back and held on to his waist. But when I turned fourteen, he started letting me drive. I learned the key to a smooth ride was maintaining constant speed. Don't accelerate too quickly. Don't slow down in the turns. Work your edges in the steeps.

I secured the rifle under a bungee cord on the side of the seat, then put the key in the ignition and started up the engine. The snowmobile was equipped with a sled and a first aid kit. There was also a crate with blankets, mittens, a lantern, and a down jacket in a stuff sack. I didn't want to take the time to unload everything. Plus what if I needed it?

I put my hands on the handlebars, then pushed the throttle with my mittened right thumb. The engine roared to life. Pain shot up my arm as the vehicle lurched forward onto the trail. The vibrations rattled my broken bone under my skin, but I held on—for my team, for my town, for J. J., who gave his life in the pursuit of justice.

The dual headlights lit up the path, making the two sets of tracks easy to see. About a kilometer out, when the tracks veered into the woods, I opted to take the long way around and pick them up on the other side. There was no way I could navigate trees with a basket in tow. I had no idea how steep it was in there. Delatour and Adler were expert skiers, and neither my snowmobile nor I was equipped to do what they could do.

Two kilometers out, there was a fork in the path. The left fork continued out into the backcountry, so I took the right, which curved sharply, then headed down. The terrain was steep, but the treads on my snowmobile held the snow. I leaned into the turns like I'd been taught, sometimes lifting my butt off the seat to weight the downhill leg. My arm roared with pain as I pressed the nose into the snow—it was deep out here. If I weren't aggressive, I would grind to a stop.

The trail swirled through cascading switchbacks, then dumped me out at the bottom of a bowl. I looked up the hill. Two sets of tracks bisected the bowl, then disappeared into the trees. I was about to follow the tracks into the woods when my light picked up an oddly shaped lump about fifty meters in front of me. I might have dismissed it as a snow-covered rock or bush if it weren't for the thin rod sticking straight up in the air next to it. Not a rod, a ski pole, as impossible to miss as a flagpole on the moon.

I turned the throttle and accelerated toward it. As I approached, Julie Adler's motionless form came into view. She was on her knees. Her chin was slumped against her chest. Her right arm was raised above her head, hand still clutching the pole.

"Adler!" I called out, but she didn't move.

My heartbeat accelerated with the snowmobile. I drove up beside her and jumped out of my seat. Her skin was a ghoulish shade of blue, but when I put my fingers to her throat, I felt a pulse. She was cold, but she was alive.

"Hang in there—I'm going to get you out of here."

Adrenaline tamped the pain in my arm as I slipped my wrists under her shoulders and lifted her out of the snow. Her legs dragged behind her as I pulled her toward the sled. I lowered her butt onto the basket, then swung her legs out in front of her. I saw through her bloodstained pant leg that one of them was broken.

"I got you, we're good," I said to reassure us both.

Her jacket was covered with a thin sheet of ice, so I pulled it off and wrapped her in the spare. She groaned as I forced her arms in the sleeves.

"That's it, come back to me."

"Cold," she muttered.

"I know. We're going to warm you up right now."

I laid her down flat, then opened the first aid kit. In addition to hand warmers, there were two battery-operated heating pads the size of cloth diapers. I switched them on, put one on her upper back, and the other on her belly. I ripped a pair of hand warmers out of their package, shook them, then stuck them in the spare mitts and pulled them over her hands. I put a second pair of warmers on her forehead, a third under her chin. Her hair was tangled with icicles, so I took off my scarf and wrapped it around her head.

"Hurts!" she cried out as sensation flooded back into her body.

"That's good. Means that you're alive."

Her eyes were frozen shut, so I took the hand warmers off her forehead and set them on her eyelids.

"Give it a minute before you try to open them."

"Remy," she said. "He's getting away."

"Don't worry about him—we have units all around the base of the mountain to pick him up."

"He killed my husband," she said.

"I know."

She raised her arms and slid the hand warmers off her eyelids.

"You know?"

"Can you let me worry about the police work and focus on getting warm, please?" I said, but she ignored me.

"He killed Ceci too."

"Do you want my job?" I asked.

"I could never do your job." I could have corrected her. What she could do with a rifle would put even the most experienced sharpshooter to shame.

"And I could never do yours," I said. And that part was true.

"Thank you for saving my life," she said. And I had to smile.

"Just returning the favor," I said, not knowing one of us was going to have to do it again.

CHAPTER 71
Julie

Being dragged behind a snowmobile was not as fun as it sounds. Even in fresh powder, the ground was hard. I had to flex my neck muscles to keep my head up so it wouldn't bounce against the basket. I was lying sarcophagus-style on my back, my arms crossed in front of my chest. Kind of like a dead body in a coffin, which was what I would have been if Detective Montpelier hadn't found me when she did.

The trail curved back into the woods, and the branches overhead whirred by in a dull-gray blur. I flexed my fingers and toes, and a thousand tiny needles prickled my skin. I reminded myself that blood flowing back to my extremities was a good thing. Thanks to those heating pads, the only thing that was freezing was the tip of my nose.

The forest opened up, and we started the descent into the campground. We were almost at the bottom. Now that the path had straightened out, I anticipated the detective would accelerate. But instead, she let off the throttle and we came to an abrupt stop.

"Don't move. Don't make a sound," she whispered. I tilted my head back to look at her, and saw her arms raised above her head.

"Don't come any closer!" a male voice shouted. *Remy?*

"What's happening?" I whispered.

"Shhh!"

"Toss your gun into the snow!" the voice commanded. "Now!" *Yes, definitely Remy.*

I heard the click-clack of her holster releasing. Then the thump of the gun landing in the snow.

"Stand up slowly," Remy said. "Try anything funny and I'll shoot him. Don't test me."

Shoot who?

The snowmobile rocked as Monique stood up, straddling the vehicle. I was lying flat in the basket. If Remy was directly in front of us, he couldn't see me, just as I couldn't see him.

"Keep your hands up!"

I wanted to stay hidden, but I needed to see what was going on. I extended my elbow and undid the strap across my chest with my mittened hand. Then, slowly, silently, I rolled onto my side, then eased forward to look.

Remy was standing in the clearing, his gun drawn and pointed at a uniformed cop's head. Like Monique, the policeman had his hands raised toward the sky. They were about fifty meters away. The snowmobile's headlamps lit them up like a spotlight. As long as those lights were shining in his eyes, Remy couldn't see me. I had the advantage. What I didn't have was a weapon.

"Get off and walk toward that tree," Remy shouted.

Monique's leg passed over my head as she got out of the seat.

"Slowly!"

I heard a gunshot. Then a man cry out.

"Hey, hey," Monique said. "Take it easy!" I peeked around the side of the snowmobile to see the male cop had fallen to his knees. There was a crimson stain spreading across the snow. The memory of Jeff's blood on our bathroom floor hit me like a sucker punch. Rage pulsed through my body. It was everything I could do not to scream.

"I'm coming," Monique said. "No need to escalate this."

Monique stepped into the snow with one leg, then made a low, arcing donkey kick with the other. At first I was confused by the motion.

Susan Walter

But then I saw her .22-caliber rifle sliding along the side of the bench toward me.

"Shoot to kill," she whispered without looking at me. Then she brought her right leg to meet her left and stood with her back to me, knee deep in the snow.

I had been shooting since I was eight years old—cans and paper targets, mostly. The thought of shooting a person seemed positively insane. I was an athlete, not an assassin. Why on earth did she think I could do this?

"Walk to that tree," Remy said. I glanced at him. One arm was extended, pointing toward a tree. The other held a gun to Monique's partner's head. All these years, I'd thought he was my friend. But looking at him now, all I saw was a monster.

His eyes were on Monique. I had fifteen seconds before she got to the tree and he killed her and her partner both. Just ten minutes ago, I'd told Monique I could never do her job. But Remy had killed twice. I couldn't just lie here and watch him kill again.

I used my teeth to pull off my mitts. My hands were warm and supple. I flexed my trigger finger. It was ready.

Fifteen, fourteen, thirteen . . .

I rolled onto my stomach, then reached for the rifle and pulled it toward me. The bungee cord snapped as it let go of the barrel. I looked up at Remy. He didn't look back at me. I said a silent thank-you to the wind for camouflaging the sound.

My belly and elbows sank into the snow as I got into prone position. I had shot targets less than two inches in diameter from this distance as many times as I had brushed my teeth. But not with this kind of rifle. And the targets weren't moving.

Twelve, eleven, ten . . .

I looked for the safety. It wasn't beside the bolt. Or on the top of the grip. *Where are you, where are you . . . ? There!* Found it. It was on the tang. I flicked my thumb to release it.

I glanced at Monique. She was halfway to the tree. I shifted my eyes back to Remy. He was standing in profile. I couldn't aim for the heart. I'd have to choose another target.

Nine, eight, seven . . .

I steadied the rifle in the palm of my left hand and locked my elbow. I raised the barrel and pointed it at Remy's temple, using the center of his ear as my bull's-eye. My margin for error was less than an inch in any direction.

Six, five, four . . .

I closed my eyes to feel for wind. A light breeze tickled my cheek. It was blowing left to right. I made the micro adjustment, then curled my right index finger around the trigger.

Three, two, one . . .

If I missed, we were all dead.

I had one shot.

And I took it.

CHAPTER 72
Monique

Remy Delatour had killed twice. I had no doubt he would kill again. He had already put a bullet in Purdy's kneecap so he couldn't run. There was no way to escape. We were out of options. But we did have a secret weapon. I knew what Julie Weston could do with a rifle. So I gave her the chance to do it.

The .22 was strapped to the side of my seat with a bungee cord. If I hadn't almost tripped over it, I might have forgotten it was there. I didn't believe in higher powers, but if I did, I might've said the universe wanted us to have a fighting chance.

If Delatour had ordered me to turn off the headlights, he would have seen Julie. And she wouldn't have had a clear view of him. But his mistake was my opportunity.

The snow was knee deep, but if I slow-walked it, he might get suspicious and look around. So I waded through, hands in the air, toward my inevitable execution.

This was a shot Julie had made a thousand times. But this rifle was new to her, and the snow was up to her eyebrows. Plus she had been a human ice cube just ten minutes ago. I put the probability of her making the shot at less than one in ten. She was an Olympian, not a magician.

I glanced at Purdy, his head tilted toward the ground in defeat. He didn't know about Julie. Which was just as well, given how unlikely it was that she or anyone would save us.

I was three steps from the tree when I gave up hope. *Killed in the line of duty,* my obit would say, as if I were some sort of hero. But of course I wasn't. I'd gotten it wrong. Delatour had set Julie up, and I'd fallen for it. A man was already dead because of my mistake. And three more of us were about to die too.

I was two steps from the tree when I said a silent prayer for forgiveness—to Officer Jason Jarvis and his family; to Officer Kyle Purdy, who was about to die; to Julie Weston Adler, who I'd misjudged; to the citizens of Banff, who I'd failed in spectacular fashion. *I'm sorry,* I prayed. *Forgive me.*

I was one step away from the spot where Remy Delatour planned to kill me, when the crack of the rifle pierced the night air. Hope seized my despair. *She got the shot off!*

I gasped as Delatour's body corkscrewed backward into the snow. Julie Weston Adler had hit the bull's-eye. Right down the middle. As always.

Purdy reached for his weapon.

"Stand down, Purdy!"

He did as commanded. I looked over at Julie. She lowered the rifle and met my gaze. Something passed between us. A silent understanding.

I gave Julie the thumbs-up to ask if she was all right.

And she nodded as she gave it back.

EPILOGUE
Rebirth

Julie

Six months later

"OK, it's small but it has a great view," I said as my Subaru rounded the last turn up the mountain road.

"Wow, you're really up here!" Christa said.

"On top of the world," Suki added.

"Right where you belong," Izzy said, squeezing my arm. Izzy and I'd had several heart-to-hearts over the months. She'd worked hard to earn my forgiveness, and I gave it to her to heal the relationship and myself. We agreed that there was nothing to gain by telling anyone else. It didn't concern them, and not all friends have to know everything.

The road flattened out, then continued to the right, but I took the cul-de-sac to the left, which bordered the shore of a crystal-blue lake.

"Can we go swimming in the lake?" one of Izzy's boys asked from his seat in the back. And his twin brother chimed in.

"I want to swim!"

"That water is cold," I warned them. "But I'll go in with you." I didn't tell them I had been in water much colder. That memory I would always keep to myself.

I turned off the road into my gravel driveway. The house was a traditional A-frame log cabin with a double-wide chimney made of locally sourced limestone. The wraparound deck had views of Canmore's Three Sisters mountains in the distance and the golf course in the valley below. It was remote but not isolated, both a return to myself and the start of something new.

I'd bought the place three months ago, right after the money from Jeff's life insurance policy came in. Once the manner of his death was reclassified as a homicide, I was able to collect. I gave a big chunk to charity—our local food bank, our county animal shelter . . . I even set up a STEM scholarship for at-risk kids in his name. He may not have lived to see his dreams come true, but perhaps someone he helped with that scholarship fund would pick up where he'd left off.

The place needed work and I needed a project, so you might say we were a perfect fit. I had spent the last six weeks getting it ready for my invited guests—refinishing the kitchen cabinets, refreshing the bathrooms with new light fixtures and vanities, polishing the hardwood floors throughout. My friends had stood by me during the most difficult months of my life, and I wanted to thank them with a vacation they wouldn't forget.

"This place is insane!" Izzy said as she got out and breathed in the sweet mountain air. It was nearly the summer solstice, and the days were long. We'd get a spectacular sunset in a few hours, if everyone could stay awake for it.

"The boys are here," Christa said as the husbands pulled up in their rented Jeep. I had enticed them to Canada with the promise of a round of golf at the great white north's most scenic course, and was thrilled they'd agreed to come.

"Let's get your stuff inside," I said, grabbing a suitcase in each hand. My leg was healed, and I was feeling stronger than ever. "I have some treats for you on the kitchen island," I said, looking at the twins. I opened the front door, and they sprinted ahead to see what they were.

The main floor was an open-concept kitchen-living-dining area with floor-to-ceiling windows. I had three bedrooms, a den with a pull-out couch, plus a loft. Not as grand as the house I'd shared with Jeff, but there was a bed for everyone.

"Julie, this place is so . . . ," Christa started. And Izzy finished the sentence for her.

"You."

As the boys helped themselves to my homemade Nanaimo bars, I gathered the adults for news I couldn't keep to myself anymore.

"So I have an announcement," I said, opening the fridge and pulling out a bottle of champagne.

"You're pregnant!" Suki shouted.

"No." I laughed. "But interesting guess." Finding a new man had been the last thing on my mind. Besides being too busy, I was not remotely ready. In many ways, Jeff was still with me. If I hadn't let him show me a different way of life, I might not have realized my place was right here.

"OK, spill," Suki insisted as I set the champagne flutes I'd bought for the occasion on the counter. So with no more fanfare, I did.

"I'm back on the Olympic team," I announced. "I'm going for my third Olympics."

There were gasps and hugs and the pop! of champagne as Izzy opened the bottle right on cue.

"I'll drink to that!" Izzy said, filling the flutes.

"You'll drink to anything," Suki teased, just like old times.

"To Julie!" Christa said, raising her glass. Because turns out toasting to friends *is* something friends do.

"You sure you should be drinking that?" Izzy's husband said as I put the glass to my lips.

"Not pregnant," I reminded him.

"That would be me," Christa said, setting her glass down. And there were more gasps and hugs.

As the sweet tang of champagne touched my tongue, my heart grew buoyant with joy. Not two days after the news that I had rejoined the team had leaked, the sponsors started calling, and their offerings were even more generous than the last time around. Everyone loves a comeback. It's the place where quitting and starting meet. A convergence of opposites . . . like so many things in life.

The moment I decided to return to professional sports, I knew it was right. I also knew it wouldn't all be about winning this time.

Because, as the smiling faces of my friends reminded me, I had already won.

ACKNOWLEDGMENTS

The first time I visited Banff, I walked around with my jaw on the ground thinking, *This place can't be real.* It was wintertime. Chalk-white peaks as sharp as knives pierced a sky so blue it looked photo-shopped. As I strolled down streets named after the town's beloved year-round residents—Elk, Moose, Caribou, Grizzly, Muskrat, Otter, Lynx—redwood-and-river-rock storefronts beckoned me in out of cold so biting I could feel it in my bones.

While there were dozens of cozy-chic shops and eateries, the star of the show was the Banff Springs Hotel. Built in 1887, the medieval castle was straight out of a fairy tale, complete with stained glass accents and menacing gargoyles in the eaves. Wandering through the haphazard corridors and grand banquet halls, I heard whispers of the things that had happened between those walls: adventure, romance, betrayal, and yes—murder.

Some say the story of a murder-suicide in room 873 is a rumor churned up to add intrigue to the moody, old castle. Some tell it as an undeniable fact. Whatever the case, the hotel and its lore were too enticing. I had to set a murder mystery there—one that spilled out of the historic fortress into the snow-covered mountains that enshroud it.

What you can learn about a place as an outsider is limited. Lucky for me, longtime residents Steve and Jessica Orchin generously sat with me to share what it was like to grow up and live in this magical town, and I am so grateful for their frothy insights. Thank you to Tyler

Weltman for making the introduction, and inhaling the first draft when it was done.

I write alone, but that doesn't mean I do it by myself. Thank you, Debra Lewin, Miranda Parker Lewin, and Avital Ornovitz for reading my bumpy early drafts and helping me see the forest for the trees. My editor at Lake Union, Melissa Valentine, is nothing short of a miracle, and I feel insanely lucky to have her as my creative partner. Thank you to all the professionals at Lake Union who lent their talents to the book—editor Carissa Bluestone, developmental editor Jenna L. Free, production manager Jennifer Bentham, copyeditor Alicia Lea, proofreaders Stephanie Chou and Angela Vimuttinan, and Danielle Marshall for assembling the dream team.

Writing murder mysteries when you yourself are not a murderer requires research, and I have a secret weapon in the brilliant Dr. Judy Melinek, who so generously helps me find my way around a crime scene. Thank you to my fellow authors who always make themselves available when I need guidance and support—T.J. Mitchell, Alethea Black, Ken Pisani, Gary Goldstein, W. Bruce Cameron, and the incredible authors of Blue Sky Book Chat—Barbara Davis, Paulette Kennedy, Thelma Adams, Christine Nolfi, Marilyn Simon Rothstein, Patricia Sands, Joy Jordan Lake, and Kerry Schafer.

I would be adrift without the loving support of my family. Thank you, Uri, Sophie, and Taya for entertaining my countless what-ifs, and bringing me a cup of coffee or three when I'm struggling to get it all sorted. Victoria Sainsbury Carter, thank you for helping me when coffee is not enough.

My books would be dusty printouts on my coffee table if not for the wizardry of agent extraordinaire Laura Dail. Thank you to Katie Gisondi and all the talented professionals at the Laura Dail Literary Agency, you guys are the best of the best.

Dear readers, there's no point to any of this without you. I know you have a lot of books to choose from, thank you for choosing mine. Special shout-out to my beloved online communities—Thriller Book

Lovers, curated by Tonya the @blondethrillerbooklover, Dawn Angels and her wonderful group of authors and readers at Psychological Thriller Authors and Readers Unite, Suzanne Leopold and all the bloggers on Suzy Approved Book Tours, and everyone who hangs out with us on Blue Sky Book Chat. Your love of books is the engine that drives my creativity, and I'm so grateful to know you all!

ABOUT THE AUTHOR

Photo © 2020 Maria Berelc

Susan Walter is the author of *Lie by the Pool*, *Good as Dead*, and *Over Her Dead Body*. She was born in Cambridge, Massachusetts. After being given every opportunity—and failing—to become a concert violinist, Susan attended Harvard University. She had hoped to be a newscaster, but the local TV station had different ideas and hired her to write and produce promos instead. Seeking sunshine and a change of scenery, Walter moved to Los Angeles to work in film and television production. Upon realizing writers were having all the fun, Susan transitioned to screenwriting, then directing. She wrote and made her directorial debut with the 2017 film *All I Wish*, starring Sharon Stone.

For more information about the author, visit www.susanwalterwriter.com.